CW00468870

Four Sacred Treasures

(Matt Drake #22)

By

David Leadbeater

Copyright © 2019 by David Leadbeater

ISBN: 9781079874235

All rights reserved. No part of this publication may be reproduced, distributed, or transmitted in any form or by any means, including photocopying, recording, or other electronic or mechanical methods, without the prior written permission of the publisher/author except in the case of brief quotations embodied in critical reviews and certain other non-commercial uses permitted by copyright law.

All characters in this book are fictitious, and any resemblance to actual persons living or dead is purely coincidental.

Thriller, adventure, action, mystery, suspense, archaeological, military, historical, assassination, terrorism, assassin, spy

Other Books by David Leadbeater:

The Matt Drake Series
A constantly evolving, action-packed romp based in the
escapist action-adventure genre:

All genuine comments are very welcome at:

davidleadbeater2011@hotmail.co.uk

Twitter: @dleadbeater2011

Visit David's website for the latest news and information:
davidleadbeater.com

Four Sacred Treasures

FOUR SACRED TREASURES

CHAPTER ONE

When Zuki Chiyome first heard that an ancient ninja clan still operated in Japan, she was a young girl. The knowledge evoked fanciful notions and dreams of noble quests. She spent hours and days imagining herself a member of what her friends called the shinobi; conjuring up missions where her tight-knit group of fellow warriors were sent in to rescue one of the Japanese royal family's princesses or a kidnapped son. And then another mission where they embarked upon an epic journey to Mount Fuji and then on into China, to seek out lost relics.

But the purpose and deeds of the ninja class had long become tarnished. All but one—the Tsugarai Clan—had faded into history. And Zuki had lost her innocent childhood dreams as she grew older and learned the responsibilities of adulthood.

When she turned thirty-five—more than two decades after she forgot all about her childhood dreams—she overheard one of her bodyguards talking about the fabled Masamune—the greatest swordmaker that ever existed. His most famous sword, the Honjo Masamune, had a rich history—it was crafted in competition with his own master. But there was another sword—called Kusanagi—this one as infamous as any sword throughout history.

It included shavings from the first ever meteorite to strike the earth, a rock millions of years old. The sword became a national treasure and was then lost to Japan after the Second World War. It was considered the most principal of the Three Sacred Treasures of Japan.

1

But it wasn't this information that raised Zuki's attention. That was information she'd discarded long ago. It was what she heard after this, as her bodyguard continued casually: "It is said the Tsugarai know the whereabouts of that sword."

She'd frozen in shadow, in darkness, listening to their chatter with interest.

"The ninja clan?" another man asked. "I've heard they are the oldest clan of their kind."

"They know where one of the Sacred Treasures is. Finding that would lead to the others. The knowledge is a . . . campfire legend."

"So it may be untrue."

"The Tsugarai hail from ancient times. They are the oldest ninja clan, founded I believe around 1200, which was when these low-life mercenaries started emerging. It is possible that one of the treasures passed to them."

"Then what Three Sacred Treasures hang in the National Museum?"

"Fakes. All the Sacred Treasures are fakes."

"Don't be a fool. They would never deceive us that way."

"Are you joking? Everything is a fake. The Mona Lisa. The dinosaurs in London. Van Goghs. Diamonds. The real things are collecting dust in the basements."

Before their conversation strayed any further, Zuki stepped out, confronted the guard, ordered him stripped and chained, then dragged down to the dungeons of her royal abode. Down there, she tortured her loyal guard with needles and fire until she was confident that he'd told her everything he knew.

That was two weeks ago.

Since then, she'd reflected day and night on the information. If the Three Sacred Treasures were fakes and, privately, many knew about it, then *where were the real ones?*

Five years ago, she wouldn't have cared. Five years ago her royal family bloodline was prospering, probably the wealthiest noble clan in the world. Today, it was floundering, being overcome due to several rash decisions in the stock markets, scandals that crippled their influence and severe infighting.

The other two principal royal family bloodlines had now surpassed hers, gloating and chirping their derision almost daily in one way or another. Four others were chipping away at her heels, eager to become one of the top three— because the top three were the highest regarded, most powerful and ultimate ruling entities of all Japan.

She was losing everything she, her father, and their ancestors had ever worked for. But she would not let that happen. She would see all of Japan in flames before that ever happened. She would tear the royal blood lines apart with her own bare hands if she had to.

The information about the sword interested her because it intertwined with the history of the Tsugarai, an ancient warrior clan that, Zuki knew, now worked purely for money. They were the world's deadliest and most capable mercenaries. They recruited young boys and girls in their early years, often finding destitute families with too many children and offering to buy at least one. Frequently, they were successful. That new purchase was then trained in savage conditions until they attained the rank of shinobi. Any that did not achieve that rank were murdered, their bodies hung around the Tsugarai compound as examples and never taken down.

If the Tsugarai once held the sacred sword, Kusanagi, maybe they still knew where it had been taken. Maybe they had information about the other two Sacred Treasures.

It was impossible to underestimate the significance of these three imperial heirlooms. They were legendary, their locations always unconfirmed, but it hadn't occurred to Zuki before now that, on the odd occasion they were brought out—at a new Emperor's coronation for example— they were fakes. It hadn't occurred to her that the ones on display were fakes. It simply wasn't mentioned; no doubt those that spoke about them were forbidden to disparage them. Since the seventh century the presentation of the sword, the mirror and the jewel at enthronement ceremonies had been a central element. The treasures defined and fortified the royal family. They were so sacred, no known photographs or even drawings existed.

If Zuki was instrumental in finding the lost treasures, her power would be restored, her wealth would be limitless, and she and her family would rule Japan for a thousand years. The relics were that important.

And she would be able to continue to order the sniveling emperor and his puppet government what to do, working from behind the scenes as the most powerful shadow family in the world, as she had up to just a year ago.

That honor was now undertaken by the Sulaimans, the shadow family of Brunei. The sultans had always trodden close on the heels of the Chiyome family. Now, they were ahead and grinding out that knowledge every chance they got.

But she could handle it. Zuki had been the head of her household ever since her parents and younger brother died in a car accident almost fifteen years ago. She was also supposed to have been in that car but stayed at home after contracting a nasty bout of flu. It had never been proved that the crash was anything other than an accident in a tunnel but Zuki knew—she knew there were many powerful shadow elements at work in the world and one of them had killed the people closest to her in the entire world. Whether it be entities working for the sultans of Brunei, the Chakri family of Thailand or one of the upstart royal bloodlines, she had vowed to avenge her parents and her brother.

It had never happened. Now, she wondered if it had been the most vicious of the upstart families—the Shingen Clan of Tokyo. They were pure-bred samurai and eternally infuriated that they were not one of the top three royal bloodlines.

But Zuki had rallied her family, rallied it well. With the help of clever advisors, she had seen off the bloodbath that had ensued after her father died; eliminated all that sought to overthrow or depose her, and come out known as a shrewd and ruthless leader. It had never been an image she'd courted.

But it was an image she'd been forced to uphold ever since.

Her enemies, her advisors, her guards and even the odd friend she still had, lived in perpetual fear. Over the years, Zuki had lost most of her empathy; she had become the thing her enemies thought she was. And now, faced with her family's latest difficulties, she knew she was going to have to embrace that image.

She believed her family had the best claim to the shadow throne, the ultimate seat of power in all of Asia. She was a descendant of the legendry female ninja warrior that built her own clan—Mochizuki Chiyome—and even bore her name. Chiyome had become the first woman in history to head a warrior class, and the first female ninja. Zuki was proud to bear that name.

After two weeks of deliberations, Zuki had a plan. The

other two principal royal families and the upstarts never stopped hounding her, attacking her territories, her men, her business dealings and long-term agreements with many countries. The intrigue involved was wide and often several layers deep. She found that if she didn't follow it without rest, she couldn't keep up.

New gangs appeared in Tokyo; offshoots of the Yakuza sprang up, taking out those she controlled. Her warehouses and office buildings were torched; things the world at large blamed on bad workmanship or faulty cladding but was in fact part of a shadow-war that had existed for thousands of years and would never end.

Zuki made her plans then fine-tuned them. She told nobody. She locked herself away, researching the Sacred Treasures and the Tsugarai, devouring every morsel of information she could find. It was true, she learned, that the Tsugarai were the most ancient shinobi clan, hailing from around 1200. She sent men out to find a way of getting in touch with them. Those men turned up in boxes eight inches square until she finally found out the honorable way to contact them. She didn't like it, but there was no going forward without the Tsugarai.

A meeting had to be arranged.

A meeting where Zuki would fear for her life.

She balked. She knew she was safe in the large, modern, palace-like home where she lived, surrounded by guards and gang members, protected by paid policemen and politicians. She could live out the rest of her days—and so could any children she might one day have—in absolute luxury.

But second and third place wasn't in her. Zuki wanted to win, to be first, to look down on all that opposed her. It most likely derived from the day her family had been killed—or murdered—and she'd been forced to step up to the mantle, to lead her men into battle.

She would do it again. Against the royal family, the sultans or any horde the samurai could put on the field— she would do it again and she would be at the head of her men, fighting for the Chiyome dynasty. Her legacy.

Her family's legacy.

All she needed was the Tsugarai and the Three Sacred Treasures.

CHAPTER TWO

Zuki sat upright in the back seat of her blacked-out SUV limousine, studying her own pale reflection in the side window. Her long black hair fell below her shoulders and to the middle of her back, and always needed tying. She had wide, deep black eyes that she searched now for any outward signs of fear.

There were none.

Which belied everything she felt inside. In all her thirty-five years she couldn't recall feeling this nervous. She looked entirely normal: elegant, tall, wealthy. She carried what the guards called a "pocket pistol" in her handbag, a tiny Beretta that packed a punch despite its size. She carried the pistol everywhere, from bed to the shower to the boardroom it was never more than a foot from her right hand. She had a reputation for being po-faced, never betraying emotion, a quality that would serve her well now.

One of the three bodyguards that surrounded her put a finger to his ear. "Lead car says we're five minutes out."

She nodded without speaking. She'd long ago told her subjects to drop the boring honorifics every time they addressed her. A knot of tension roiled in her gut.

"Rear car reports all clear."

Again, she nodded. It wasn't the journey that was bothering her. It was the fact that the Tsugarai had insisted she meet them alone, in a most unsavory place, to discuss her requirements. Right now, they had no idea what she was going to ask them. They didn't know she knew they'd once owned a Sacred Treasure. She gripped her handbag, taking solace in the shape of the Beretta that nestled inside. *Against them, it will be useless.* Nevertheless.

Her driver slowed and pulled into the curb. Her bodyguard listened to chatter through his earpiece then nodded at her.

"It's all clear. We cannot go any further, but you must enter through that yellow door."

Zuki peered out of the window. The night was lashed by an almost horizontal rain and was barely lit. There were no streetlamps in this part of town.

"Are you sure we can't accompany you?" another bodyguard asked.

"No. The Tsugarai expressly forbid it. I must go alone. You will wait right here for me."

"Don't forget your pocket pistol," another guard said into the darkness inside the rapidly cooling car.

"I never do."

Zuki cracked open the door and felt the cold air rush in, biting at her face. She stepped out onto the sidewalk, drawing her thick black coat around her shoulders. Her handbag was slung over her shoulder, its zipped top within easy reach of her right hand. She rested that hand atop it now, peering left and right through the rain. Nothing moved. Lurid, dilapidated signs shone from the roofs of nearby establishments, bright yellows and reds, and deep blues. She'd never visited the more dangerous and run-down parts of Tokyo before. She knew they existed but seeing really was believing.

The yellow door stood in front of her. When she pushed, it opened easily. With a final glance back at the car and its cocoon of safety she braced herself, thought of her family's welfare and her plan to restore its glory, and moved on.

A narrow corridor opened out into a large room. It was dimly lit and extended to left and right and ahead far beyond what she could see. The stench hit her first. Human waste and body odor, blood and decay. Her eyes watered with the disgusting smell, and then were forced closed as a particularly acidic smell wafted past her. She heard many sounds—groaning and snoring; weeping and some subdued laughter, but most of all she heard the hysterical—those that were no longer a part of this world.

Needles littered the floor. As she froze, she saw at least two hands scrabbling among them, searching for a tube where liquid remained. As her eyes grew accustomed to the dim light, she made out irregular shapes pressed up against the wall—many people covered in blankets in varying stages of consciousness. They lined the floor too, rows deep. Zuki wondered if she should pick her way through them.

"Walk forward," a voice spoke up, "to the back of the room."

Hiding her fear, taking a deep breath, Zuki recalled the days when her father had made her train with swords, with shuriken, with fists, feet and hands. It was the time she had felt at her strongest, most confident. It was a time when she had been a warrior.

She picked her way steadily, stepping among bodies and on blankets. The heavy odor deepened. Her fists were clenched, her heart hammering. She took several minutes to make her way to the back of the room. A long white hand reached out for her right ankle, maybe asking for help, maybe trying to bring her down. Zuki kicked out at it, sending it back to where it came from. A second hand brushed her knee. She jumped aside, biting her lip against a scream. This was totally outside her experience.

Of course, the Tsugarai would know that.

Zuki was a great fighter. She'd clung to that knowledge for decades now, allowing it to boost her confidence, her motivation and increase focus. But her experience of life was shallow.

You are royal. You do not need to see this.

But now she did, and she wished she'd been prepared for it.

Eight figures stood at the back of the room. They wore traditional black robes covering their entire bodies, including cowls that hid their faces. As she approached, three figures stepped forward.

"Stop," the voice said.

Zuki paused and held her hands out. She couldn't really believe the Tsugarai regarded her as a threat in this moment.

"I'm here to talk."

The robed man in the middle drew back his cowl. She saw a hard, scarred face with a narrow, unsmiling mouth. The man's head was bald.

"I am Saizo, a Tsugarai captain. Talk to me."

She watched as the other two figures drew back their own cloaks. One man and one woman were revealed, their expressions equally as severe as Saizo's. Zuki wanted nothing more than to turn around and get the hell out of this dreadful place, away from these murderous people.

Get to the point then.

She drew a breath and spoke. "It has recently come to my attention that the Three Sacred Treasures, the imperial relics of Japan, are fakes. They have been for centuries, even though they are a major part of every emperor's enthronement ceremony. Of course, this is understandable. They are priceless. Any good ruler would follow that course of action."

Saizo narrowed his eyes. "What does this have to do with the Tsugarai?"

"They didn't make fakes to protect the treasures. They made them because they lost the treasures a long time ago."

Saizo betrayed no emotion. "Or maybe they never had them. But go on."

Zuki hesitated. She hadn't thought of that, but Saizo was right. Maybe the Sacred Treasures had been lost all along.

Not lost. Somebody knows where they are.

"This brings me to you," she said. "The Tsugarai. The last of the shinobi. I know your history goes back beyond the thirteenth century, before my own family starts. I am a direct descendant of Mochizuki Chiyome, the first woman to create a group of all-female ninja warriors which were called kunoichi."

"I know of Chiyome." Saizo bent his head ever so slightly.

"Thank you. Our histories are rich with intrigue and bloodshed, with warlords, seductresses and civil wars. They intertwine. They clash. It is ever the way. But, deep in your history, it is mentioned that the Tsugarai were once the sole protectors of the Three Sacred Treasures."

Saizo nodded. "That is true."

Zuki steadied herself by taking a deep breath and gradually exhaling. It wasn't just the surroundings now that made her nervous—the sounds and smells of the damned—it was the crucial point of why she was here.

"I need the treasures," she said. "The real ones. And I think, if anyone might have a clue as to their whereabouts, it is the Tsugarai Clan. I will pay you well to find them for me."

"You *need* them?" Saizo frowned. "What does that mean?"

Zuki quelled a flash of annoyance. She wasn't used to being questioned so directly. Usually, her first comment and will was obeyed.

But this is the real world. A place you do not know.

She blamed her parents, her mentors. She blamed the state in which she lived. She wasn't prepared.

"Okay," she said. "You know who I am and the power I wield. You know the *real* power that I wield. It is always behind the scenes and has been for a thousand years. I am of the principal royal bloodline. The emperor and his government are our puppets."

"I do know," Saizo said. "I know also that there are *three* principal royal bloodlines and that your family has been . . . losing ground of late. Others are seeking to usurp you."

"They have been seeking to usurp us for centuries," Zuki acknowledged. "It has never happened. It is true that a leader's back is always exposed. But between my family and those others is a separation between clouds and mud."

Saizo raised an eyebrow. "You quote proverbs at me? Well, here's another. You all have the relationship of dogs and monkeys. Why should we trust you?"

Zuki knew he was referring to a relationship between all the royal bloodlines—a relationship of mutual hatred that bred natural enemies in every generation. This next part was delicate.

"Through the years, the centuries, it has become known that the Tsugarai have . . . sought a more material source to maintain their standing, and their existence as the last ninja clan. I offer money. I want to hire you to work for me, to seek out the treasures. I also thought you would be best prepared since, once, you owned them. Perhaps some knowledge was passed down."

"You still haven't told me *why* you need the treasures."

"Yes, I know." It appeared he wanted it spoken out loud. "My family has been beset of late. Betrayed. Attacked. Framed. We have lost ground. I believe the revelation that Japan's imperial relics are fake and then the announcement that I have found the real ones, will secure my family's future for centuries to come. It will make us untouchable."

Saizo nodded, his eyes showing a little respect for the first time. "I understand. It is true that we once protected the treasures for the emperor. We are the oldest clan, the most respected. We can trace our early roots back to the sixth century, not the thirteenth as is commonly believed, seven hundred years before it is universally acknowledged the shinobi were even active. We led the great armies of the shoguns in many wars. We assisted in ten thousand campaigns without any kind of written history. But . . ." Saizo paused. "It is as the westerners say. Times change. We try to maintain our ways however we can. Remember . . . not succeeding is mostly the result of not trying. There can be no excuses. We will take your money, and we will find the treasures."

Zuki fought hard to maintain a stoic face. "Tell me what you know of them."

Saizo shifted his feet. "The treasures vanished long ago from the Tsugarai ranks amid much secrecy. I think . . . five hundred years? I am not sure. It is said the clan's innermost secrets are always passed down among the masters. One by one, with only the grand master truly informed. But now . . . we have no real master."

Zuki felt her new optimism quenched. "What . . . I don't understand."

"Our master's true name is usually a great secret, even inside the clan. Not many know who it is. The master is guarded this way, out of danger, away from harm. A sacred island to which we can turn in times of trouble and crisis. He is our greatest shrine, our deepest fountain of knowledge. Our last master was murdered quite recently, and quite unexpectedly, and has not yet been replaced."

Saizo turned away for a while, conversing with his companions and others that remained in secrecy at the back of the room. Zuki realized she was gripping the Beretta hard through her handbag and realized the Tsugarai must know that. She let it go now, looking left and right. It was only then that she noticed the four robed figures directly behind her.

Zuki's heart leapt. She flinched on the spot, almost crying out. The dark figures stood within a dagger's thrust of her and she hadn't even known they were there.

Saizo caught her attention once more. "Our last master was one called Gyuki. He led the clan, and trained the initiates for decades. A good master. A fair master. As I said, he was murdered unexpectedly, during a raid on our home, and had no time to impart his vast knowledge. Whatever he knew, was lost."

"That all seems . . . a little short-sighted," Zuki said.

"It is what it is," Saizo said. "But the masters always picked and started training their replacement as soon as they found the right candidate. It is known Gyuki trained his replacement for several years before she killed him. It is also known he left many papers behind."

"Wait, the person Gyuki picked as his successor *killed* him?"

"Yes, she lived among us for many years. Learning our ways and being trained to be the very best of us. But that is another story, not relevant. What *is* relevant is that Gyuki left a Haiku—a Japanese poem—that our elders always believed pointed to the hiding place of one of the Three Sacred Treasures."

"A poem?" Zuki was interested. It reminded her of an earlier, simpler life when she and her parents and brother had been happy, learning history and chasing after some of Japan's many rich, imaginary treasures.

"It is famous among the Tsugarai," Saizo said.

"Beneath Himiko's place,
"Yomi's Mirror will wait,
"For those who know me."

Zuki memorized it. "What does it mean?"

Saizo showed emotion for the first time, offering a wry smile. "We do not know."

"Then how can you help me?"

"Because that Haiku was written for a very special person. It was written for Gyuki's intended successor, the woman who killed him. Only she will know what it means."

"So I'm guessing that she is still alive? And that you know where she is?"

"She will not come willingly. We will have to take her by force. And we will put every effort into finding her because, without her, there will be no quest. The treasures will stay lost forever."

"Perhaps I can help," Zuki said. "I have a vast network of informants, from those that listen and whisper among the other families, to those that are embedded among the government and police. Nothing escapes me."

"That is good," Saizo said. "This woman is an ex-cop, ex-Special Forces and ex-shinobi. She will be hard to track. Her name is Mai Kitano and it will all start with her."

CHAPTER THREE

"Hard to believe," Matt Drake said, "that only two weeks ago we were chasing thieves out of Las Vegas."

Alicia, walking at his side, sighed. "I'd take a Hawaiian sunset any day."

Drake nodded. The whole team were here, spread out, walking across Waikiki Beach in front of the Outrigger Reef. A wooden jetty stood to their left. On the right were several small benches where couples sat and, beyond those, a small grassed area that led to an army museum.

Alicia tapped Drake's arm. "Hey, see there. That guy's proposing."

Drake looked over at the benches and saw a young man presenting his brown-haired girlfriend with a dainty box. He looked away, not wanting to intrude, concentrating on the thick sand beneath his feet, the vast stretch of ocean to his left and the blaze of red and orange that dominated the evening sky.

"No better place," Kinimaka said. "Didn't I tell you?"

"When you suggested a brief break in Hawaii," Hayden said. "I didn't think anyone was against it, Mano."

"I'd rather be breaking heads," Luther growled. "Just saying."

"Ooh," Alicia sent a roguish glance at Mai. "The new boyfriend's bored already."

Mai ignored her, the lithe Japanese woman staring out to sea. Drake wondered what she was thinking about. Once, they had shared everything. Known before speaking what the other was about to say. Now, they remained close, but the warm intimacy was gone.

"What I meant," Luther said quickly, "was that the Fabergé thing didn't last more than a few days and that was our first action in months. Yesterday, I found myself licking a donut."

Alicia chortled. Mai looked over, prepared for anything. But it was Drake that spoke up with a glum tone in his voice.

"Yesterday, I bought this shirt."

His friends laughed quietly. He knew the genuine Hawaiian shirt was loud but then, if you couldn't wear a Hawaiian shirt whilst walking in Waikiki then something was wrong. He'd bought Alicia an ornamental lei at the same time and was pleased to see that she wore it now.

The blonde was eyeing him. "Yep, you definitely fucked up with the shirt, Drakey."

"Why? What the hell's wrong with it?" he said defensively.

"It's so loud it has a personality all its bloody own. It's like a third person in the bedroom."

Mai leaped over a hole somebody had dug in the sand. "I remember a time when that didn't bother you."

"Fuck off, Sprite. That was weeks ago."

They laughed, even Drake. The one thing about this team, and his closest friends who'd been with him for decades, was that there were no secrets. No skeletons in the closet. He plucked at the shirt to make it hang looser and moved ahead to catch up with another old friend.

"How's it going, mate?"

Torsten Dahl had been walking alone. Now, he turned and nodded at Drake. "As well as can be expected, I guess."

It had only been two weeks since Dahl's wife, Johanna, had moved back early to Stockholm with their two children. Dahl had returned briefly to DC to say goodbye to his girls for a while before joining the team in Hawaii.

"You spoken to them?" Drake knew where the worst of Dahl's pain was sourced.

"Yeah. Johanna isn't making it hard. They're looking at schools already. It helps that they have friends there."

Drake looked around as footsteps thudded across the sand behind them. Kenzie and Dallas were approaching, the former looking fit and healthy, the latter still a little awestruck on his first visit to Hawaii.

"You learn anything earlier?" Kenzie asked Drake.

About an hour ago, in their hotel lobby, Drake, Hayden and Dahl had been checking the status of the Strike Force teams.

"SF Two is on mission in Syria," Drake said. "SF Five is helping out with some ISIS stragglers. That's it."

"Okay," Kenzie said dispiritedly.

"Hey, cheer up. It's a good thing that international special forces teams created to deal with the worst situations imaginable aren't always required."

"I guess. I didn't realize there'd be this much downtime."

Drake raised an eyebrow. "Yeah, me neither."

"The Blood King?" Kenzie prompted. "The Devil?"

"No luck there either. I want to take them down as much as you, Kenz, and we're first on the notification list for either of them. You really do have to see it as good news that nothing big is looming."

Inside, he knew the words he spoke were genuine. The world had faced some serious threats over the last few years and not all of them handled by the old SPEAR team. It needed a break. As for him and his friends, they were pretty much rested up.

"Here!" Kinimaka called.

They all turned to see the big Hawaiian kneeling, trying

to set alight a pile of wood that had been laid in a hole in the sand. Drake winced. "That could end badly."

By the time they reached it the fire was blazing. The team sat in a circle, several feet away from the flames, as the night sky turned black.

"Who brought the food?" Mano asked.

"Crap, I forgot the bag," Karin said with a straight face.

Kinimaka's face fell. "What?"

"Don't worry," Dino produced the bag from behind his back. "We got coconut shrimp tacos. Fiery shrimp tacos. And cheeseburgers for the wimps."

Drake waited for his burger, facing Waikiki and the hotels and restaurants that made up the beach's skyline. Though the sky was dark, hotels and high-rises rose above everything, throwing their lights down at the streets which, in turn, were illuminated by streetlamps and flickering torches. The sidewalks and streets he could see bustled with life. The noise of the city was dulled out on the beach, but he knew Waikiki thrived at night. He'd been thriving among the tourists for the last week or so.

He looked over toward the great crater of Diamond Head, the extinct volcano that looked across the ocean around Waikiki. "The Gates of Hell," he said, remembering. "You know, they're still exploring what's left of that site."

Those that had been a part of it nodded. The others dug into their food. A short time went by when the group was quiet, content in each other's company. Drake expected Alicia to break the comfortable silence in her typical manner and wasn't disappointed.

"I feel bloody naked."

All eyes went to her. Alicia gestured with her burger. "I mean without a gun. Not even a friggin' knife."

"I have to agree," Kenzie said. "Being unarmed worries me."

"Don't be afraid," Luther said expansively. "I'm here."

Mai gave him a sharp glance. "Don't be a meathead. I feel the same."

Molokai, the quietest of them all, unwrapped his robes then, careful to keep them away from the spitting flames. "I am never unarmed," he said, showing them some inside pockets. "Inside these I have two knives and a small Glock."

Drake shook his burger at the man. "How the hell did you get them? And why didn't you get us some?"

Molokai shrugged. "We've been here for two weeks. And you never asked."

Drake took the hint. If he'd been serious about acquiring weapons there were many ways to do so on the island. Including any of the local safe houses where their Strike Force team had priority status.

When they'd finished eating, the team packed away and headed back up the beach toward Kuhio and the iconic Cheeseburger in Paradise. They planned to continue the night there with a few drinks. Soon, they'd left the sand behind and were walking along Kalakaua Avenue, surrounded by tourists and locals out for the night. It was hard to talk as a group, so Drake dropped back to chat with Kinimaka and Hayden.

"I want to thank you for letting us into your Hawaiian home," Drake told Kinimaka. "I can see why you love it here."

Mano smiled. "My second favorite Hawaiian proverb states 'distance is ignored by love.' No matter where I go, this will always be my home."

"I wish I had something like that," Drake said. "I never grew roots. Always a wanderer. That's why Alicia and I get on, I guess."

"I knew there had to be a reason." Hayden grinned. "But

Mano, what's your *first* favorite proverb."

"Ah, I was hoping you would ask. It's simple. 'Dare to dance, leave shame at home.'"

Drake nodded in appreciation. They were walking down the wide, well-lit street with traffic to the right and people all around. He couldn't prevent his inner antennae from constantly assessing his surroundings and the sea of people passing him by. He knew the others would be monitoring it too. One of the consequences of being a soldier.

The team was twelve strong. Twelve of the best Special Forces soldiers on the planet. And still, when the attack happened, they never saw it coming.

CHAPTER FOUR

Drake approached the entrance to the restaurant, walking underneath its undulating white roof when Mai let out a yell. He never knew what alerted her, call it sixth sense, instinct or old training, but he was grateful for it.

It probably saved his life.

He turned to look past the restaurant, along Kalakaua. An incredible sight met his eyes. Several figures were running toward them, now only ten feet away. They all wore similar clothing—thick leather jackets almost medieval in appearance, a well-used mix of blacks and browns, and sturdy black boots. They wore steel masks and carried swords over their shoulders.

And they carried compact MAC-10 machine guns.

Drake struggled between disbelief and action for about two seconds. Impulses struck him, trying to force him into a decision. The torpor that inactivity brought refused to lift. Just a few feet away from the restaurant he grabbed the door handle and wrenched it open.

"Get in!"

Mai, Alicia and Dahl were already moving, slipping through the door. The others were falling back, separating. Drake had no choice. As the MAC-10s leveled, he dived through the door, hit the wooden floor and rolled. People looked up from their meals, staring in disbelief.

"Down, down!" he cried. "On the floor!"

Outside, there was gunfire. Drake saw his main group of friends start running east along Kealohilani Avenue, away from the restaurant, but he saw three others forced to go in the opposite direction, back toward Waikiki Beach.

Molokai, Hayden and Kinimaka.

Shit, this is bad.

Separated and unarmed, they stood little chance against the unknown enemy that had come to engage them. Drake ducked down low as the dark figures ran by the window, following Dahl among the tables.

Inside, the restaurant was well-lit, with an abundance of wooden fixtures and fittings. Dahl ran toward the bar, following Alicia, and vaulted over. Drake was a step behind, landing in a crouch and waiting for three seconds.

Silence reigned. He looked up over the lip of the bar just in time to see four men entering through the front door.

Alicia saw them too and ran, Mai at her heels. Dahl followed closely, searching along the bottom of the bar for a weapon.

"Not that kind of place," Drake said.

"Shame," Dahl replied.

Still, no shots were fired, but the men chasing them were fast. Drake saw that they were nimble, strong and determined. The part of their faces he could see bore swathes of black greasepaint to help conceal their identities.

Still, they look familiar, he thought.

Beyond the bar, a door gave on to the kitchen. Drake raced after his companions, but his enemies had already caught up to him, defying everything he knew about speed and training. Nobody was this fast.

A figure struck his back, sending him to the ground.

Kenzie knew she'd never reach the restaurant before their attackers. She was too far behind Drake and the others. Quickly, she searched left and right, decided the lengthy street of Kealohilani offered the best prospects for flight, and ran. Luther, Karin, Dino and Dallas were at her back, all without time to choose, and seeing hers as the only escape route. Kenzie had a figure count of more than twenty attackers splitting and pursuing the three Strike Force groups.

She barged her way through tourists, running into the road and toward the headlights of approaching cars before threading her way back to the sidewalk. A quick glance assured her the others were right behind. At least ten black-clad figures were giving chase, their machine pistols positioned downward, their swords untouched. She caught a very brief glance of hard, rugged faces, half-blacked out, of grim expressions and fluid, capable action and knew they were in trouble.

No weapons. No comms. No body armor. Ambushed in a busy street by skilled opponents.

"Where's the hotel?" She felt a little turned around.

"Three blocks left and closer to the beach," Dallas said.

Maybe they could make it. Everything they needed was in their rooms.

"Safe house?" Luther voiced the other option.

"Five blocks same direction," Dallas said. "Or there's a police station back on Kalakaua."

"No matter where we go," Karin yelled, "we're among civilians. On the plus side, that seems to be giving our enemies restraint."

"Who the hell are they?" Kenzie ran faster, expecting and receiving no answer to her question. They ran as a tight group, past well-lit grocery and clothes stores, expensive jewelers, watch shops and busy hotels. Their pursuers offered nothing except the chase. Ahead a commotion encircled them. People darted out of the way. A large parking area opened out to the right as they approached the intersection of Kealohilani and Kuhio.

Options hit Kenzie hard. She wasn't used to leading in this way.

Weapons, she thought.

As one, they raced left.

Hayden had been walking at the back of the group when Drake yelled out a warning. Her mind had been elsewhere, relaxed, her attention low. She'd looked up, taken the situation in, and acted within seconds. Knowing she couldn't reach the door, she turned and ran in the opposite direction.

Across the street. Toward the beach and more shadowy areas. Heading back to the hotel.

Eight assailants peeled off to give chase. Kinimaka was at her side and so was Molokai. They didn't have to talk to know they were in a bad situation with no weapons, no way to stay in touch and little protection.

Hayden ran between cars. One screeched to a halt at her right hip, so close it lifted her a few feet in the air. She slid along the hood and kept on running, straight into the other traffic stream.

Kinimaka was holding out both hands and gesticulating. It seemed to do the trick. Cars swerved across the road and into the curb. They managed to gain the far sidewalk.

But their pursuers were close.

Hayden turned and hesitated on the edge of the beach. Back at the restaurant, she saw other assailants entering in pursuit of Drake. She saw more giving chase along the street.

"Come on." Kinimaka grabbed her arm, still running.

But they weren't fast enough. Their attackers hit them hard, driving them onto the sand and among racks of surfboards, outriggers and open-air lockers. Hayden saw a blur, a man flying at her, and felt a kick to the chest that knocked all the breath out of her. She fell and rolled, tried to stand, but the man was already striking again. Punches rained down on her shoulders and neck, on her ears and throat, forcing her further down.

All she could see was sand. She was aware of many feet shuffling around her, of grunting and quiet words.

All of a sudden, the noise stopped.

A hand grabbed her under the chin, forcing her face up. Bruised and aching, she stared at a grease-covered face, a Japanese face that even under the paint she could see was scarred from brutal previous encounters.

"Is that her?" a man asked with a heavy accent.

Hayden was aware of men fighting left and right as she tried to recover. Kinimaka was borne to the ground by three opponents, struggling but gasping, his movements weak. Their attackers knew exactly which parts of the body to hit. Hayden saw their fluid, perfect moves, all done with an economy of movement and precise amounts of energy. They didn't rush, they didn't panic, just watched and hit harder than anything she'd witnessed before.

Except Mai. The thought flashed through her head as her opponent held a photo next to her face.

"No. Not her."

"Then she must be with the others," the man shouted in Japanese. Four men detached from the fight and ran back across the road.

"Wait," she gasped. "What do you want?"

"You will never know."

The hand gripping her face tightened. A fist was raised,

fingers extended. Hayden gathered all her energy, not willing to go out this easily, but then a mountain rushed past her, crashing into her opponent and two of the men fighting Kinimaka.

She'd lost track of Molokai. Now she saw his black robes undulating around him like a cape as he spun, kicked and punched. The dark figures hadn't been expecting his attack and fell back.

Kinimaka sat up. Hayden stuck her legs underneath her and pushed hard, rising to her feet. Her head spun, but she staggered to Molokai's side. Together, they were stronger. Kinimaka forced himself upright at her back.

Hayden watched five enemies set themselves around her. They crouched. They focused, preparing to attack. She hadn't seen this coming. Hadn't expected it all to happen so fast and with such finality. She'd always expected to go out fighting alongside her whole team.

And then death fell upon her.

Drake dashed through the restaurant's kitchen, scattering pots and pans and shelves full of ingredients in his wake. Ahead, Mai, Alicia and Dahl reached the far door, flinging it open and disappearing into a dark alleyway. Drake cast a quick glance back, saw his pursuers only ten feet away, and picked up speed.

The night air was soothing. Dahl raced up the alley, heading toward a road that Drake knew was Kuhio Avenue. They'd been here long enough to know their way around. Without thought the Yorkshireman tapped his ear to speak to the Swede before remembering they had no comms.

Dickhead.

Probably best not to mention that later, if there was a

later. His pursuers were already out of the restaurant door, probably twenty feet behind now. Drake put on a burst of speed. He could see as well as the figures behind that this alley was dark and deserted.

Perfect to start using their MAC 10s.

CHAPTER FIVE

Drake lost precious ground watching them. Two men raised their weapons but then lowered them. Drake wondered if they wanted him alive; him or one of the others.

We need to capture one of these medieval-looking fools.

Ahead, Dahl exited the alley and swung left. He was headed for the hotel, a good move. Drake poured on the speed until he came close to Alicia's heels, but their pursuers were still gaining.

"We're not gonna outdistance them," he shouted.

"They want us alive," Dahl cried back. "Which is good for us."

Drake grimaced. Good wasn't the term he'd use. "Well, whoever they are," he said, "we need to take them out."

"I know exactly who they are," Mai said as they ran into the road, a tight, four-strong knot. "They're Tsugarai."

Alicia's whole frame straightened in shock, which almost unbalanced her. Drake felt similar surprise.

"Ninjas? Fucking *ninjas*. Are you kidding me?"

Mai didn't answer, which was enough. Drake fought off a very dark feeling. Even fully armed they'd be hard pressed to defeat more than twenty of Mai's former comrades. The Tsugarai were the most skilful warriors in the world.

Ahead, the road was packed with cars, red taillights filling one side and bright front beams the other. Dahl weaved between them. Drake heard a thud and turned to see a dark-clad enemy leaping off the roof of a car straight at him.

Drake spun and shrugged the attack off. The man rolled

against the wheels of a slow-moving truck before jumping back to his feet.

He ran harder. The noise was tremendous, made up of car engines, vocal civilians and his own pounding heart. He sensed a presence at his back, darted left and managed to evade a strike. As he found the sidewalk, he saw familiar figures up ahead. Kenzie and her companions had reached the top of Kealohilani and were close to Dahl.

Together, nine members of the Strike Force team pounded along the streets of Waikiki, hard pursued by at least twenty expertly trained shinobi warriors. Drake found a moment to bemoan their new regime—all this relaxation and downtime bred complacency. During their years of non-stop fighting they'd never been caught out like this.

And there was no way he was going to be able to pry weapons from the cold, dead fingers of *this* enemy.

The hotel was two blocks away. Onlookers gawped from the side streets and through shop windows. Youths leaned out of car windows or swiveled on bike seats to take pictures and video. Drake's chest was burning, his legs aching. His mind dwelled on Hayden, Kinimaka and Molokai, but he forced the thoughts aside.

Just as Dahl swung right.

Drake saw a wide-open entryway into a shopping area called the International Market Place. They rushed under an "aloha" sign, now among an irregular array of small stalls selling many different goods. It was busy and it was disorderly, just the kind of place to lose someone.

Drake ran left, splitting from the others as they darted in different directions. Ultimately, they all knew where they were headed. He ran around a stall and swung right, then raced between two more, wondering if he might be able to double back. A quick glance told him no. Three Tsugarai were hard on his tail.

To the right he saw flashes of his colleagues. Dallas and Kenzie racing around a colorful book stall. Alicia heading up a flight of stairs. Mai turning and swinging, catching an opponent with a hard punch, sending him sprawling into a pop-up gin bar. Dahl became tangled with some tourists but managed to plow on.

Drake grabbed a large vase off a counter, turned and, without slowing his pace, hurled it at the closest man. The man threw up an arm, brushing the vase aside, but lost momentum. Drake gained several feet. Already, they were halfway through the market place, aiming for the rear entrance. Unfortunately, it was taking them away from their hotel.

But it was worth the risk. Ahead, Drake saw Dallas and Kenzie running without pursuers. Luther was alone, searching left and right and helping where he could. Karin and Dino were already approaching the back of the open-air mall.

Drake darted right, heading back to Mai. It was easy to believe the Tsugarai had come to kill her. The reason didn't matter. She was the most likely target. He saw the Japanese woman fighting off another attacker as two more converged. He hit them from behind, flooring one and dizzying another. He kicked out at a third and urged Mai to run.

"Go!"

They converged at the rear of the mall. It was darker back here, with less people. Kenzie and Dallas were there, waiting, clearly unwilling to leave anyone behind. Dahl had the door wedged open. Drake looked around, seeing that the Swede's mall ruse had worked to a degree. They had lost about half their pursuers, but that still left a good dozen.

Better odds. Should they stand and fight?

"Too many variables." Dahl read the thoughts in his expression.

He was right. Twelve opponents could become twenty in a matter of minutes.

"Go then," he shouted.

But then figures crashed among them, coming from left and right and even from the shadows above. Drake staggered under a heavy blow. This whole thing was rapidly going to hell. Sirens wailed in the distance. People were screaming.

And the shinobi drew their swords.

Drake acted instantly, knowing he needed to get close. He elbowed a man in the ribs, then jabbed him across the face. The man barely flinched. Drake grabbed the sword arm at the wrist and held tight. Around him Alicia was on her knees but managing to fend an attacker off. Mai had disarmed an enemy and was trying to grab his fallen sword. Dahl had charged back from the doorway, felling two Tsugarai. It was chaos. Splintered vision after vision; struggle, combat and yelling. A book stand to the right disintegrated as Luther and two opponents crashed into it. Tourists scattered. Kenzie engaged two Tsugarai in combat, frantically trying to get a sword of her own. Drake saw her go down on one knee; then blood exploded form a gash in her head.

Dallas leapt to her aid.

Drake knew desperation when he saw it. He twisted his opponent's wrist hard; heard a crunch but then spun away, knowing his friends needed his help more than he needed to pick up a sword. He vaulted over Dahl and used Karin's lowered back as a fulcrum, striking one of Kenzie's opponents hard in the face with his feet.

Blood flew, spraying the gaudy Hawaiian shirt he wore,

adding to the pattern. Kenzie looked up, her face crimson and bruised. A man had an arm around her throat, squeezing every last ounce of breath out of her. Dallas elbowed that man in the throat from a prone position.

When the blow had no effect, Drake jabbed Kenzie's attacker through the eyes of his steel mask, making him reel away. Then, he dragged Kenzie aside. No sooner had he done that than two more Tsugarai were upon him, punching and kicking, and then a third holding a sword at arm's length.

"Get her," the sword-wielder hissed at his men.

Thinking he meant Kenzie, Drake moved fast to cover her but both men peeled away to the right. They were headed for Mai.

"What do you want?" he asked.

"Stand down, walk away." The masked figure paused for a moment. "We are not here to kill you. We only want her."

"Who? Mai?" Drake hesitated, seeing his friends losing the battle to left and right. There were too many Tsugarai.

"You can't beat us," the man said.

"Give me even odds. Give me a Benelli M4 Tactical with even half a mag. Hell, give me a sharp fucking pencil and I'll take you bastards out."

The apparent leader of the Tsugarai regarded him for a long moment before reaching into his waistband, drawing out a six-inch dagger, and throwing it at Drake's feet.

In answer to Drake's question he said. "Our history shows and states that only the worthiest can possess the Three Sacred Treasures. Let's see how worthy you are."

Drake scooped up the dagger and attacked. He feinted right, threw the dagger to his left hand and thrust. The blade cut through his opponent's leather top and drew blood. The man swerved away, body language showing surprise.

Beyond them both the battle raged. Alicia and Dahl fought back to back, barely fending off four attackers. Mai had killed two and was dueling with two more. Luther, Karin and Dino had their backs to the wall but were protected on two sides by large concrete pillars, reducing the amount of opponents they faced. Even so, the Strike Force team was wearying, outnumbered, unable to thin the Tsugarai herd. The sirens were practically outside now. A whole knot of shinobi were converging on Mai.

Drake struggled, as close to his opponent as he dared. The man struck at him with sword, hands and feet, never stopping, never slowing. It was an art, deadly and savage. Drake had never fought against anything like it. Kenzie was on her feet at his back.

And it was Kenzie's scream that caught his attention.

"NO!"

To Drake's right, Dallas had gained his feet. As he did so a dark-robed shinobi fighter jumped in from behind and thrust his sword straight through Dallas's back, severing the spine. The point exploded from the front of Dallas' chest and stuck there as he fell face first to the ground.

Kenzie went crazy, darting around Drake and flinging herself at Dallas's killer. She rained down blow upon blow, breaking the man's cheekbones and eye sockets, destroying him. Drake backed away from the Tsugarai leader.

"You can't have Mai."

And then the police arrived, guns drawn, stentorian shouts to "stand down" being flung out like weapons. There were at least a dozen of them, and mixed among them he saw plain clothes officers. A shout went up from the Tsugarai; their leader making an instant decision. In seconds they melted away, fleeing for the back exit or jumping for the stairs. They left swords and guns behind if they had to; focusing on escape, showing no threat to the police.

"On your knees!" a man screamed at Drake.

Still standing, he indicated that he needed to reach inside his pocket. To left and right his team was on its knees, not because of the cops but due to battle weariness. Kenzie was lying across Dallas and Dahl was moving toward her.

Drake showed them his ID; which was verified before the guns were lowered. "We were ambushed," he told them. "About thirty men, all wearing similar clothing. Some kind of medieval-looking garb." He beckoned his team to him and walked over to stand beside Kenzie.

"I'm sorry," he said, "but we still have three friends missing. We have to go."

Kenzie looked up, dark hair matted with blood, her face a mask of crimson. Her eyes were wild. "I'm ready," she said.

Leaving Dallas's body for now, they moved out.

CHAPTER SIX

Hayden kept to the shadows cast by hotels across the beach. She hugged the areas that were infrequently lit. Kinimaka was at her side and Molokai a step behind. For a while, she thought they had escaped attention, but then she saw four dark figures tracking them at the shoreline. Her heart fell, but they came no closer.

Maybe they were in communication with someone else, taking orders. Maybe they were waiting for reinforcements. All Hayden knew was that every step brought them closer to their weapons.

"One more block," Kinimaka said. "I can see it now."

Their own hotel jutted out ahead, its upper floors hanging slightly over the beach. Their shadows kept pace as they closed in.

"I think the time for finesse has passed," Hayden said. "Once we reach the back doors we run like hell to our rooms."

"My kind of plan," Molokai said.

"You hear those sirens?" Kinimaka said. "I wonder how the others are getting on."

"Focus on your own situation for now," Molokai said. "There'll be time enough for wondering later."

Some time had passed since the skirmish on the beach. Hayden kept her eyes on the following figures, which drifted in and out of focus. They continued to keep their distance. Something didn't add up.

Hayden reached the hotel, found the rear doors and put a hand on one of the handles. "Ready?"

"Go for it." Molokai's face was set hard.

And then something came barreling out of the door, bursting it open and smashing it into Hayden's face. She saw stars, staggering back, struggling to stay upright. Her vision was full of figures, so many of them she couldn't count, all rushing out of the hotel's back door.

Robed figures. Reinforcements.

She struck out. The haft of a sword smashed her across the temple. She found herself face to face with the same man she'd confronted earlier.

"What . . ." she began.

He hit her again. To her left Kinimaka was swamped. The big Hawaiian had a man under each arm and was squeezing their necks. His own head was lowered so that the man in front of him couldn't smash him in the face, only the skull. To the right Molokai was in similar straits, wilting under the force of five attackers. Hayden leapt forward.

Two men came in from her blind sides, smashing her in the ribs. Hayden folded, hitting the sand hard. Her eyes clouded over, but then she forced the pain aside to rise again.

"You have spirit," the leader told her. "We will see how long it lasts."

His sword came down and she knew no more.

Drake's lungs were on fire as he rounded the far end of the chain of hotels that bordered Waikiki Beach. Ahead, the stretch of sand that led from the hotels to the Pacific Ocean sat in sporadic shadow. Where it was illuminated the pools of light were bright, further disrupting his vision.

"There!" Dahl shouted.

Drake saw figures struggling, some being dragged across

the beach. He recognized Kinimaka's bulk more than anything. The Hawaiian was unconscious; six men were half-carrying him between them. Molokai and Hayden appeared to be in similar states.

No words were needed. Drake and his companions set off at a rapid pace, searching the area for makeshift weapons as they tried to close the gap.

Out here they were exposed. Though they made little sound they were seen within ten seconds. The alarm was raised among the Tsugarai.

The leader turned to face them and held his sword high. Drake grimaced. Was that a salute? Or a goodbye? He'd find out soon enough. The gap was down to about one hundred yards. Dahl scooped up a beer bottle, smashing the neck. Alicia grabbed a steel pole that had been part of a table canopy. Images of Dallas dying and dead ran through Drake's head.

The Tsugarai fought to drag their three captives across the beach toward the pounding surf. Drake didn't have time to wonder why but then, suddenly, he found out. Several, small inflatable zodiacs, all black in color, skipped in along the waves. Men carrying machine guns leaned out over the sides, targeting Drake.

"Down!"

The entire team dived, scrambled and rolled, hitting sand and scrabbling for cover. Bullets flew across the tops of their heads, impacting with the sides of hotels and smashing windows. It was a constant stream, never letting up for a whole two minutes.

Drake and most of the others were sheltered by a delve in the ground; bullets skipped off the top of the sand inches above their heads. Kenzie was behind a low wall, screaming in frustration. Luther had dived through a window into a restaurant to find cover.

When the stream of bullets stopped, Drake raised his head.

The zodiacs were full. There was no sign of anyone on the beach. He made to move but more shots were fired, pinning him down. It was an impossible situation. All he could do was live today so that he could save his friends tomorrow.

Helpless, he watched Hayden, Kinimaka and Molokai being kidnapped by the Tsugarai. They had come for Mai, but had left only with those they could manage to take.

"What the fuck is going on?" Alicia cried out.

Drake wished he knew.

CHAPTER SEVEN

Hours later, the Strike Force team gathered in a CIA safe warehouse in downtown Honolulu. They were now fully armed, armored and ready for war.

Drake stood near the center of the large storeroom. A scarred wooden table and plastic chairs stood nearby, occupied by some of his friends for now. Nobody spoke. The atmosphere was tense, the air cold in the early morning. They barely moved. Drake's thoughts were of Dallas and the three who'd been captured.

Taken . . . taken to God only knew where.

Ironically, it seemed everyone was waiting for their leader to begin. But their leader was Hayden, and she was missing. Drake was about to step up when Luther rose from a seated position and placed both hands on the table before him.

"Vacation's over, boys," he said to the room. "Let's hear options."

Kenzie looked up, only her eyes moving. "Whatever it takes," she said. "Anything."

"Agreed," Dahl said. "But what do we know?"

"We know our enemy is the Tsugarai," Mai said. "The ninja clan I was bought and trained by. They are entirely mercenary these days, allowing their services to be bought by those that can afford them. But they still live by the old ways in Japan, following parameters laid down since 1200, when they were founded. They are the last clan of the shinobi and they are very deadly."

"So they took Hayden and the others for a reason. And they were hired," Karin said.

41

Drake spoke up. "I think they were after Mai," he said and explained what he'd seen and heard during the fight in the International Market Place. "They also mentioned the phrase: Three Sacred Treasures."

Mai frowned. "I've heard of that. They are the Imperial Regalia of Japan. They're legendary, priceless and irreplaceable. Their theft would start more than one war."

"Like stealing the Crown Jewels," Karin said. "I get it."

"No," Mai said. "More like stealing the Queen, her family and her palace."

"So just say we're at Keanu level," Alicia said. "That'll do."

Mai shook her head. "Keanu level?"

"America's greatest national treasure," Alicia spread her hands as if the answer were obvious.

"I thought that was David Boreanaz?"

"I'd take either," Alicia admitted. "Or both."

"Any clue as to why they would want you?" Luther asked Mai.

"I've been gone a long time. I killed Gozu, the assassin they sent after me. I killed Gyuki, their ultimate grand master. I took Grace from them. I guess they might want me dead, but the timing is odd."

"How so?"

"Like I said, I've been gone a long time. Their profession is covert assassination. They could have gotten to me any time during the last few years."

Drake ignored that sobering thought. "You think they'll make a demand? For Hayden and the others?"

"It's possible."

"What about the other angle?" Dahl asked. "That they may have been hired?"

Drake looked over at the Swede. He was seated close to

Kenzie, but not touching her. He was offering solace with his presence, his bulk, an unspoken support. Kenzie herself was staring into space, her eyes red-rimmed.

"That is more likely," Mai said. "The question is: How do we find out why?"

Drake nodded, feeling the aching in his neck where blows had landed. His ribs hurt. His thighs and knuckles hurt more. It had been a cruel and vicious battle and they were lucky more of them hadn't lost their lives.

"Going up against the Tsugarai," he said, "is gonna take everything we've got. We've never prepared for a war with the shinobi."

Mai shook her head. "You're damn right. From now on we sleep by rota. We investigate every shadow. We use state of the art surveillance equipment. And we need a plan."

"The plan is," Luther said, "to find out what the hell's going on. We're fighting in the dark already, people. We need help. And time is of the essence."

They turned to individual tasks. Luther called up friends in the military. Dahl called Interpol and other European agencies. It was Drake's job to take over Hayden's role and contact the US agencies that needed to know.

An hour later a global machine was asking questions, fishing in murky waters for a, so far, unfathomable answer.

Drake found a seat and sat back when the job was done. He hadn't known Dallas well, hadn't even found time to properly vet the man. They'd all relied on Kenzie's judgment which proved how deeply they'd accepted the Israeli into their inner circle. Drake felt wretched for Dallas but there was also a twisting knot in the middle of his stomach that worried for Hayden, Kinimaka and Molokai.

"We'll get them back." Alicia was at his side and ever upbeat.

"I know. I just hate not knowing what's going on."

"Trust Mano to get kidnapped with Hayden," Alicia said lightly. "Big guy never leaves her side."

"Yeah, he's always been the best of us," Drake said.

"I'm just thinking now that I don't know enough about Molokai."

"He's an ex-bomb tech. Fought in a few US wars, official and covert. Rotated back more times than he can remember, I think. He's a good fighter, good man."

"This extended break we've been taking." Alicia leaned into him. "You think it's made us rusty?"

"I feel better," Drake admitted. "My head's clearer. I think when you take a break it dulls your battle wits but sharpens other senses. And Alicia, don't beat yourself up about it. We needed a break. We still do."

"Any news on the other Strike Force teams?"

Drake kicked at a table leg. "Yeah, Two through Six are active. Trent came back to me, saying his Disavowed buddies want to help but are bogged down trying to sort out some Somalian pirate syndicate called the Sea Rats. Strike Force Five had a lead on the Blood King. The others are busy."

"The world's gone to shit again."

"Yeah, and just because we took a month off."

Alicia smiled again. Drake looked up as Mai came to stand before him.

"There's another possibility," the Japanese woman said.

Drake looked at her, seeing reluctance and anxiety. "What?"

"Over here." Mai walked away to a corner of the warehouse. Drake shrugged at Alicia. "Give me a minute."

"Am I not invited?"

"I doubt it. That's Mai over there."

"I thought we were past all that."

"We have history. She trusts me. You, not so much." Drake rose and walked toward Mai. As he approached, she turned.

"I don't like it," she said. "But I could ask Dai for help."

Drake pursed his lips, thinking it over. He saw her quandary. Dai was her oldest friend, now married to her sister, Chika. Dai and Chika looked after Grace, the young girl Mai had rescued from the Tsugarai years ago, the girl she thought of as a daughter.

But Dai was also an ex-cop. And a good one. His contacts were as good as anyone else's in Tokyo. Dai was the perfect person to find out what the Tsugarai were up to.

"Idea's a good one, love," he said gruffly. "Other times— I'd say no. It's too dangerous. But with Dallas dead and the others kidnapped . . ."

He let it hang, seeing the struggle in her face.

"If anything happened to Dai, Chika or Grace, it would end me."

"We can prevent that," he said. "We can go to Tokyo. That's where the Tsugarai are based anyway."

"Japan," Mai said. "But, yes. We could go."

Drake turned to evaluate the rest of the group. Alicia was staring at them both with narrowed eyes, clearly wondering what was going on and upset not to be a part of it. Alicia wasn't a worrier or a controlling person, but Mai had always presented a threat to her. Luther also had his head up, watching them. Dahl was talking quietly with Kenzie and most of the others were still on their phones.

"Are you and Luther a thing now?" he asked without thinking.

"I think so. It's early days."

"Good. Let's go to Tokyo. You can call Dai on the way."

45

Mai agreed with the briefest of nods and chewed her lip.

Drake called for attention. When everyone looked over, he said: "We have a plan. If we can board a CIA bird it would be better. That way we can take all these bloody weapons with us."

CHAPTER EIGHT

By the time they landed in Tokyo, nine hours later, Dai Hibiki had put in several hours of hard work. Alicia listened when Mai called him as they disembarked and walked toward the VIP lounge area, ready to bypass customs and climb into waiting, blacked-out SUVs.

"He doesn't have a lot yet," Mai informed everyone. "But he does have some background information. He wants to meet us at a Special Unit safe house."

Karin turned to her once they'd settled in the back seat of the car. "Special Unit?"

"They're the tactical unit of the police force. Their equivalent to SWAT, I guess. Dai led a Special Unit team for four years."

Alicia seated herself up front, alongside their silent Japanese driver. It was just after 6 a.m. in Tokyo, with a bland dawn lightening the eastern skies. The buildings were still in shadow, dark bulks without form. The sidewalks and streets were relatively quiet, the morning bustle still an hour or so away. Alicia took the twenty minute drive to think.

She wasn't entirely sure where she was with her life. The running always had to end sometime, and it had ended when she realized Matt Drake was a man worth her time, worth changing her ways for. The team and its missions had then governed their lives, the constant traveling and hunting from one end of the world to the next. Improbably, it was the sudden long break that had taken her out of her comfort zone, made her sit back and evaluate everything she was doing.

She didn't *have* to do this. None of them did. It was a way of life, sure, but it didn't have to be a lifestyle choice.

But what else was there? How long could this team stick together? The month off had reaffirmed nothing for her, only given voice to more questions.

For now, there was no alternative. Dallas had to be avenged and Hayden, Kinimaka and Molokai had to be saved. She felt intense sorrow for Dallas and even for Kenzie. Though they didn't like each other, she knew how hard it was to lose someone you cared about. And Kenzie had become a valuable team member.

Alicia was happy with Drake, and happy with the team, but loose threads still lay all around them. The Blood King. The Devil. And now the Tsugarai. Who knew what evil monster might raise its ugly head next?

Mai announced they were here. Alicia followed Karin and Dino out of the car, surveying the area carefully with a hand on her gun. Mai had warned them always to be ready for an attack. Ninjas didn't just act under cover of night.

They pressed through a door and up a flight of stairs to a large room. There were bars on the windows and blinds. Meagre decorations made the place look more spartan rather than humanizing it in any way. There was a refrigerator, a table and several chairs. To the right a steel door stood, opened by a keypad, probably the armory. A man waited for them, a man Alicia knew well.

Dai greeted Mai with a hug and then turned serious. "Grab refreshments now if you want them," he said. "We have a lot to go through."

Alicia took the can of Pepsi Max Drake offered and found a seat near the window, setting her weapons down and adjusting her body armor. It was already hot and stuffy up here but one of the panes was broken, offering a modicum of fresh air. She cracked the tab and drank, waiting for Dai to begin.

"What do you have?" Mai asked.

"The Three Sacred Treasures are a Japanese paragon," he said. "A part of the architecture of our history. It is unfathomable that Japan would ever be without them. That said, and as the more well-informed might imagine, the ones on display are fakes. The real Sacred Treasures would never be put at risk. They are brought out occasionally, when a new emperor is crowned and only then under extreme guard. Your enemy, the Tsugarai, mentioned them, so we have to assume they are going after the real things."

"I would say so," Drake said.

"Well, that might be a problem. Because the real treasures I mentioned—the ones they only bring out for an emperor's coronation—those are fakes too."

Alicia made a face. "What?"

"Two of the three real Sacred Treasures were lost long ago, so long nobody can remember. The mirror was passed down through the Tsugarai clan until it came to Gyuki in his youth. Soon after, it too disappeared. It is thought Gyuki knew the whereabouts of all three treasures, but if he did, he took it to his grave."

"Which is where you come in." Luther nodded at Mai.

The ex-ninja nodded. "They seem to think, because I was Gyuki's worthiest student, that he must have passed some information on to me. He was grooming me for leadership, therefore I should know all of his secrets." Mai shrugged. "The Tsugarai won't believe anything I say."

"And those of you that were abducted?" Dai asked.

"As we said," Drake shifted impatiently, "they came for Mai. When they found it impossible to take her, they took what they could."

"What exactly are these Three Sacred Treasures?" Karin asked.

Dai drank from a bottle of water. "They're comprised of the sword, named Kusanagi. The mirror, Yata no Kagami. And the jewel, Yasakani no Magatama. They represent three primary virtues. Valor, wisdom and benevolence. More importantly they represent the three biggest areas of influence: Force, knowledge and wealth."

Karin frowned. "Why are those more important?"

"That brings us to the big picture," Dai said. "There's so much more in play here than you understand, than most of the world understands. It's all highly secretive, to the point of death. If you're caught spreading rumors about this you are killed, your family are killed and anyone even remotely connected to your bloodline are killed. Not only that, but everyone around you, connected to your sphere of influence, is also killed."

"So by telling us this—" Mai began.

"Yes, I am risking my life."

"Then stop," Mai said. "I can't let you do that. And I won't risk Chika and Grace."

Dai nodded. "I respect that."

Luther sat forward. "I don't get it. If you reveal this now who the hell's gonna know?"

"Any number of reasons," Dai said. "Somebody's always watching. Listening. When you are told something earth-shattering you should look surprised. If that's not apparent, it will be assumed that you already know. It is of Japan's royal bloodlines, that is all I can say."

"Let somebody else take that risk." Dino nodded.

"Right," Drake said. "So what do we have? Three Sacred Treasures that we assume the Tsugarai are being paid to find. Gyuki knew where at least one was hidden. Mai can't remember anything specific. Hayden and the others are still abducted and, more than likely, being held at the Tsugarai compound."

"A stretch," Luther told him.

"Maybe. But where the hell else would they go? We're never gonna fight our way through a hundred of those bastards."

"The last count was one hundred and fifteen," Mai said. "Trained warriors. Plus staff and elders. And I have no idea who leads them since I killed their last grand master."

"I'm assuming you have a plan?" Alicia asked Dai, seeing the way the ex-cop was directing the conversation.

"Yes, a dangerous one. The simple truth is: We need more information. On the treasures, the fakes and the bloodlines. On the Tsugarai and their role in this. And especially on Gyuki. Possible locations. And why these treasures are so important."

"You don't know?" Karin asked in surprise.

"I'm a cop, not an archaeologist."

"I thought, with you being Japanese . . ."

"I'm a fairly normal person with a hard job and a family. I don't have time to look into ancient Imperial artifacts. And I can't remember what I learned at school. Can you?"

"I have a pretty good memory," Karin admitted.

"Then strap yourself to a laptop and get googling," Dai said. "I have arranged a meeting with an old informant for this afternoon. He's been in deep with the Yakuza for some time and knows where everything's buried. He doesn't give a shit about protocol. And he once worked closely with the Tsugarai. He's our man."

"Great." Drake looked pleased. "When do we leave?"

"Not us. Me. He will only talk to me."

"That sounds dangerous," Mai said.

"It is. He wants to meet in a bad part of the city, among gangsters and criminals. He feels at home there. Always did. He'll come through for us, if I get out alive."

Mai shook her head. "If it must happen, you're not going alone. I'm going with you."

"We all are," Drake said.

Dai grimaced. "You think eight Special Forces soldiers walking into a mafia-run bar is gonna end well?"

"That does sound like the start of a bad joke," Alicia admitted.

"Oh, it would be," Dai said. "A fatal one. I can probably take Mai. She'd fit in. She knows the Tokyo underworld and they might know her. I can make that work."

The Japanese woman stood up. "That's settled then. When do we move out?"

"Now," Dai said. "Right now."

CHAPTER NINE

Mai found and bought some old clothes along the route to the bar and changed in the back seat. She donned a baseball cap and sunglasses. She secreted small weapons around her body, the type that didn't show. By the time Dai pulled up alongside a high curb she was ready.

She peered out the window. "You take me to all the best places."

"I did warn you."

A burned-out car stood across the road. Most of the businesses were boarded up. Those that were open had sturdy metal shutters over their windows and were accessible only through barred doors. Mai saw two people—men standing around a street corner, talking. Both had handguns stuffed into their waistbands.

"Let me guess," she said. "The cops don't come here often."

"Not without a serious reason. This is Yakuza territory."

Mai stepped out of the car, which was parked in front of a placed called Mak's Casino. It should be renamed, she thought. Mak's Dive was more appropriate. Shabby green boarding ran above a double set of darkly tinted doors. Looking down, she saw fresh blood spread along the trio of steps that led up to the entrance.

"You ready?" Dai asked

"You know me," Mai said. "Just another Thursday."

Like the rest of the team, the long layoff had introduced a new dynamic to her life. Her feelings for Luther had grown. She was closer to him now than anyone in her life except Drake. She didn't want to lose him. Emotions like that made you question mortality—it brought up issues you never previously entertained. And Dallas had just been murdered right in front of her. She didn't know how close he and Kenzie had been, but she felt deeply for the Israeli.

Still, the job was clear. Hayden, Kinimaka and Molokai needed help.

Dai led the way, pushing through the front doors into a dingy lobby. Two men approached, machine pistols slung over their shoulders, but quickly recognized him and let him pass. Dai looped an arm across Mai's shoulders and hurried her through. They didn't expect trouble, but it was best to be careful.

Inside, the casino was dimly illuminated. Ceiling lights were low except for those that shone down on the tables scattered around the room. The walls were mostly in darkness, made up of plush sofas and low-slung tables where waitresses delivered drinks and snacks. Dai made his way between two blackjack tables.

He stopped in front of a sofa. A tall, scrawny man sat there with a girl under each arm. He was scarred and dirty looking. When he grinned, Mai saw yellow teeth and a glazed light in his eyes that spoke of serious drug use. If this man had been Dai's informant when he was in the force, she wondered how he'd managed to live so long.

"Meet Danzo," Dai said. "A friend."

Mai nodded. Danzo noticed her for the first time and rose quickly, instantly forgetting the two women seated beside him.

"Hey," he said with a yellowy grin. "What's *your* poison?"

She'd been around drug users and sleazeballs often enough to know his question was fully loaded, encompassing all evils. Before she could speak, however, Dai jumped in.

"I don't have long," he said. "Let's get this done, shall we?"

"Sure." Danzo sent the women away before settling back down. "I'd heard you'd gotten a new bitch. This her?"

Mai clenched her fists under the table, badly wanting to lash out, but kept her face calm. Her emotions were locked inside, as they had been since the Tsugarai bought her from her parents long ago.

"She's my bodyguard," Dai said. "So I'd watch your fucking mouth."

Danzo raised an eyebrow but sank back into the leather seat, apparently letting it go. Mai took a moment to scan the room. Security guards were everywhere, all carrying machine pistols over badly fitted suits. Most were bald, their heads as reflective as the ceiling lights. Players leaned over as they shook dice or checked cards, revealing that they also carried weapons ranging from guns to knives. Clearly, this wasn't any ordinary establishment.

"I want paying." Danzo leaned forward. "The information you're asking for—it's lethal. You pay me now or I walk."

Dai nodded. "I agree," he said and reached inside his jacket.

"I thought you were undercover," Mai said.

"Depends on the day of the week," Danzo said. "And the action I'm getting."

"You enjoy this life?" Mai scanned the casino again.

"I've known worse."

She guessed that was the truth. Danzo was clearly an addict, a cop who'd gone too far and not been given enough backing from the department when he wanted out. It wasn't all Danzo's fault. It was the chain of command above him.

Dai handed over a bundle of cash. "What do you have for me?" he asked.

A waitress approached, carrying a silver tray that held three tumblers of black bourbon. With a steady hand she proceeded to place them on the low table. Mai took a moment to smile at her in gratitude and saw that the woman was already staring at her with some kind of recognition.

"Let's get on with this," she said as soon as the waitress had gone. "I have a feeling we don't have long."

Danzo nodded, but still took a moment to swallow half his bourbon. "All right. First of all, the royal bloodlines. Japan has its emperor and its royal family, which is known around the world, but there is a more ancient bloodline, dating back to far earlier dynasties. This line, or *lines* to be exact, stay in the shadows. They are an old royal lineage, made up of about seven families, constantly vying for superiority. They control everything. Mafia. Gambling. Entertainment. Building control. The banks. It is all under their purview, ruled from afar."

"You're saying Japan is controlled by a shadow government," Mai said. "That's not unusual."

"Not like this," Danzo replied. "These families are from the old dynasties, the oldest money on the planet. There are three at the top right now, the Japanese and the Thai families, and one from Brunei. Four others are challenging them. It has always been this way. Enormous battles fought in secret with everyone affected told ridiculous, utter lies."

Mai inclined her head. "It is the same around the world."

"Maybe. But now the secret Japanese royal family is struggling for the first time in its existence. And the Shingen family—a dynasty of hated samurai—is growing in power. The Japanese family is desperate. Their current leader, a woman named Mochizuki Chiyome, already sees her power diminishing. There have been scandals and large property losses, probably engineered by the other bloodlines. She's seeking to reassert herself and make the others pay dearly. So dearly, her lineage won't be challenged again for a thousand years."

"Which brings us to the Three Sacred Treasures," Dai said.

"Yes. First it was only Zuki seeking them, but now the other families have found out and are also in the hunt. Zuki hired the Tsugarai, so she is still the favorite, but the Tsugarai don't know where they are. And they have but a single unsolvable clue."

Mai perked up. "They do?"

"Yes, a haiku. Apparently, their leader, a man called Gyuki, recited the poem often. He shared most of his life with a woman that later betrayed and murdered him. She was called Mai Kitano."

Mai narrowed her eyes. "Betrayed?"

"I don't know the details, just what I've been told through the years. It was said that this Mai Kitano would know of the haiku and what it means."

Mai hid her surprise and looked back through her memories, finding many that she didn't want to revisit. Gyuki had been a savage master and a bully. He'd shown delight in turning a young, innocent girl into a ruthless assassin.

"You say you heard the haiku often," Dai said. "Can you recall any of it?"

"Beneath Himiko's place,
"Yomi's Mirror will wait,
"For those who know me."

Danzo sat back and finished his drink once he'd stopped speaking. Mai recalled the words as he spoke them. Gyuki *had* recited this haiku often in her presence but she'd blocked *everything* from those horrible days, not just the bad stuff. Before she could consider the lines anymore, Danzo continued.

"I don't like the atmosphere in here," he said, raising her antennae.

"It's full of criminals and cutthroats," Dai said. "I guess it's always pretty tense."

"People are staring." Danzo looked nervous. "That waitress, I think she knew you. That you're a cop. I have to go."

He made a move. Dai reached out and grabbed his wrist. "You stay," he said quietly. "You stay until you've told us everything."

Danzo's face twisted with worry. "The Sacred Treasures are the ancient symbols of force, wealth and knowledge. It is said they contain portions of the very first meteorite that ever struck the earth, though I don't know how. A rock billions of years old. They were re-framed by the greatest swordmaster that ever lived, Masamune, around the year 1300."

"If they were re-forged using the first meteorite," Dai said, "that alone makes them priceless."

Danzo continued, "It is also said among the Tsugarai that, when all three treasures are brought together, they will point the way to a fourth, an incredible mythical prize the like of which has never been found."

"Really?" Mai asked with a little skepticism in her voice. "I hear there's been some pretty incredible artifacts found recently."

"From what I hear . . ." Danzo whispered, "this will dwarf all of those."

58

Mai tuned him out for a moment, still reeling from the fact that Gyuki continued to manipulate her life. Even now, years after his death. The Tsugarai knew she'd been his closest student, his confidante, that was why they'd come to grab her. They couldn't solve the haiku's riddle, so assumed she could. That act had resulted in Dallas's death and the abduction of three of her friends. It had also put the rest of the team and her Japanese family in danger.

Gyuki, she thought. *You were always a monster. Why can't you just die?*

As she stared into space, she became aware that Danzo was right. Several pairs of eyes were staring. The noise level had lessened. A thicker air of tension permeated the room.

"Dai," she said. "I think we really need to go."

"It's okay," Dai said. "They wouldn't believe we're police. Not here."

"I'm not thinking that," she said. "What if that waitress recognized us because the Tsugarai put our descriptions out?"

Dai blinked at her. "Fuck me. I never thought of that."

Danzo's face creased in terror. "No," he said.

Mai stared at him. "Not quite the badass you thought you were, eh?"

Before she'd finished speaking, Dai had started to run.

CHAPTER TEN

Mai was hyperaware. Nobody made a move toward them or tried to stop them, but everything was very wrong.

What would make a busy room of cutthroat criminals wary, willing to spill information?

The Tsugarai. Only them.

She chased after Dai, heading for the exit. Danzo was with them. The doors opened outward. Mai cast a glance at the guards, but they made no move. Someone had warned them off.

The shit was about to hit the fan.

They burst into the street, faced with rundown stores and barred windows. Their car sat at the curb to the left. Mai studied the shadows, the alleys, the rooftops. Nothing moved. But that didn't mean they were safe. Dai reached the car first, Danzo a step behind.

A figure rose up from its far side, handgun pointed at them.

"Stop!"

Dai ducked. Danzo threw up his hands and started around the car, toward the gunman.

"I didn't know. I—"

A shot rang out. Danzo's words were cut off by a bullet through the face. Mai shouted desperately at Dai.

"The alley!"

The Tsugarai wouldn't kill her, but they wouldn't hesitate to take him out. Dai spun around and ran into the nearest alley. Mai dashed after him. The man with the gun tracked her movements, speaking into a concealed mic.

Dai splashed through pools of stagnant water and leapt over mounds of rubbish. The alley wasn't long. They emerged from the other end. Saw another dingy street. Figures stared out of windows, perhaps hearing the gunshot, disappearing when Mai looked up at them.

"It's the Tsugarai," Mai said. "I know it."

"We can't let them catch you," Dai said. "Your friends' lives would be forfeit."

They sprinted left and then down another alley. Mai saw nothing ahead and tried to check the rooftops above, but all was darkness up there, the black vault of the night just another shadow. For ten minutes they ran, weaving through dangerous and almost pitch-black Tokyo streets. Beggars reached out to them from patches of shadow. Drunks and drug-users wandered into their path. Mai thought she saw a dark figure leaping across the rooftops above. She thought he might be carrying a sword.

"What's the escape plan?" Dai finally asked.

"Hibiki," she growled back, "that was *your* job."

"I provided the narc."

"Well, we have good information," she said. "A starting point. We just have to get out of here."

There was a skate park ahead, a large concrete playground. It was bordered by railings, but the gates were wide open.

"Come on." Mai led the way.

"How is that going to help?"

Mai checked their surroundings. "It's what's on the other side."

She'd spotted a university campus, a place that had its own security and somewhere the Tsugarai couldn't blend in, but Mai and her old friend certainly could. The entrance lay just beyond the skate park.

They ran. Mai saw figures converging from the right. As they approached the railings the figures were twenty feet away; all wearing the signature jackets and face masks of the Tsugarai. They carried swords and guns, and had knives sheathed at their waists. Mai made sure she was between them and Dai.

Her boots struck the concrete hard. The night air whistled past her face. Mai was sweating. They left the stench of the alleys behind as they ran through the open area. The railings rattled behind them as the Tsugarai ran through the gates.

"Not enough time." Mai saw they were closing fast. "We have to slow them down."

Dai glanced at her. "Keep going," he said. "I'll buy you some time."

Mai's heart hit the floor. There was no way she'd allow Dai to sacrifice himself for her. "They'd kill you."

"But you'd be safe. And Chika, and Grace. That's what matters now."

Dai slowed, his mind made up. Mai had seen the fatalistic look in many a soldier's eyes, many times. It was the sign of a man or woman summoning the courage to die whilst saving their friends. The Tsugarai were mere feet away, drawing their swords as they ran.

One slashed down at Dai, aiming for his head.

Mai tackled her friend around the waist, forcing him away from the calculated stroke, feeling the air of the blade's passing just millimeters from her own head.

They hit the concrete and rolled, disentangling immediately then rising to their feet. The Tsugarai were coming at them. Mai dodged a blow and came in from the left, winding her opponent. She smashed a second attacker point blank in the nose, breaking it. A third blocked her attacks. Dai went down to one knee but managed to evade a knife thrust. Mai saw already that the six Tsugarai were too much for them.

Did that mean more ninjas were coming? Their protocol was to send out a small investigative team, followed by a dozen more warriors if a lead panned out. But there was no time for anything now. Not even time to survive.

Two men were behind her. She chopped down at the wrist of a man trying to stab Dai with a knife. She spun and kicked him in the chest, sending him staggering. She grabbed Dai and pulled him away, the two of them sliding down a skateboard ramp and gaining precious seconds of time.

The robed Tsugarai leapt after them.

Mai grabbed her friend's arm. "Move it!"

They were ten feet from the rear of the park, thirty from the university's gates. They'd never reach safety without some kind of distraction. Mai's head was calm, her body ready to fight. They started forward together, watching the Tsugarai converge.

"Any ideas?" Dai asked.

"Just stay alive," Mai repeated the mantra she'd often heard Drake use. "One second more. And then another. Don't give in."

They broke for the far fence, the university's lights dead ahead. The Tsugarai came at them in a black, silent wave. Raised swords caught the light. Mai felt her feet touch grass. A car drove past, along the road, ten feet away. Then a pair of boots struck her in the spine, sending her flying. Dai tumbled beside her. They were stopped hard by the very fence they'd been trying to run through.

Mai hit the steel bars, bruising her face. She shook the pain away. Dai groaned at her side. The Tsugarai stood over them.

"Kill him," one said. "Take her."

"No." She struggled. She looked across at Dai as he braced for the sword that was already descending toward his skull.

"Please . . ."

The sound of gunfire was a confusing but welcome sound to her ears. Welcome because bullets shredded the Tsugarai, sending their lifeless, bloodied bodies stumbling back into the park. Swords fell. Bodies fell.

Mai turned to see who'd saved them.

Alicia thrust her head through the bars. "Bet you're glad we followed your candy asses now, aren't ya?"

CHAPTER ELEVEN

Back at the safe house, Mai listened as the team tried to come up with a plan.

"This haiku," Drake asked her eventually. "Do you have any idea what it means?"

Again she sifted through her memories, carefully navigating through the harmful parts of her past. "It didn't mean anything at the time. It was just one more lesson. A repetitive lesson, yes, but that was often the case. I remember dozens of haikus. Gyuki was twisted, a man that believed he was born of the underworld. He loved that idea. That he was an avenging demon or something, sent to earth as the underworld's fighter."

"I get that he gave you the clue," Drake said. "He was grooming you to take his place. Teaching you everything would take years. But do you have any idea what it means?"

Mai recited it once more: "Beneath Himiko's place, Yomi's Mirror will wait, For those who know me."

"I guess we start googling Himiko and Yomi," Karin said.

"Not necessary," Mai said. "I know what that means."

Before they got into it, Drake walked over to the machine to make himself a coffee. Dahl and Kenzie sat on the other end of the sofa to Mai, talking quietly.

"How are you?" Kenzie asked the Swede.

"Me? I'm good. I'm worried about you."

"I'm hurt. Crushed. I feel guilty because I brought him into all this."

"Whatever you are," Dahl said, "you are not responsible for Dallas's death. You didn't make the Tsugarai kill him."

Kenzie placed a hand on Dahl's arm. Mai turned to stare in the opposite direction, feeling a little shame for listening but unable to tune their conversation out.

"And you? I know you're hurting," Kenzie asked Dahl.

The Swede took a while to answer. "My children are in Sweden," he said. "They are safe. I hope they are happy."

Mai felt her throat close with emotion and stood. She found herself right behind Karin as she took a moment out with Dino.

"You want to tell them now?" Karin was saying.

"No. I don't know. Maybe after all this. Maybe before something else kicks off."

"Oh, well, that's bloody clear then."

"If we're leaving the team," Dino said, "we should give notice."

Mai breathed in sharply with surprise. Karin head and turned to her. "Hey."

"Sorry," Mai said. "I didn't hear a thing."

"Thanks," Karin said. "It's not definite yet."

"Not my business." Mai walked across to the window, leaning against the wall as Drake returned to the sofa. "Where were we?" he asked.

Mai spoke up. "Gyuki's haiku was constructed entirely for me. As I said, he thought highly of himself, that he was born of the underworld. The last line 'for those who know me,' is telling. Sometimes he spoke of Himiko, the sorceress and queen of the dead, as his mother. In his youth, Gyuki told me time and time again that he used to worship at one particular shrine."

"Himiko's shrine?" Dahl asked.

"Perhaps. But the shrine of Yomi, the Underworld, is at Sakurai. Gyuki's birthplace."

"You think he hid the mirror there?" Karin asked.

"The haiku tells me that," Mai said. "It tells me nothing else."

"And what's the purpose of this meteorite?" Luther asked her. "The old one."

"Could be nothing," Mai said. "Or it could have something to do with this mythical fourth treasure that Danzo mentioned. I don't know."

"Sakurai it is then," Dahl said, sitting forward with purpose. "When do we leave?"

"That brings us to the big issue," Drake said. "There's no way we're leaving Hayden and the others behind whilst we chase these treasures. We have to rescue them from the Tsugarai."

"From their camp?" Dino asked. "How the hell do you propose we do that and find the treasures before all these other royal families?"

"We split up," Dahl said. "But then you've already decided that, haven't you?"

"Who's going?" Alicia sked.

"Just Drake and I," Mai said softly.

Alicia glared. "No fucking way."

Luther coughed, looking a bit taken aback. "Gotta agree with her."

Mai glanced at both of them without emotion. "It has to be us two," she said. "We work together flawlessly without even speaking. We know each other's thoughts, moves and decision-making capabilities without conversation. That's a quality we'll need to infiltrate the Tsugarai. I *have* to go, because I know the camp, its surroundings and its warriors. I know how they think and plan. I choose Drake as my partner."

"You two? On a covert mission? Days and nights together?" Alicia said. "Why do I feel paranoid all of a sudden?"

Mai was watching Luther, knowing he too would be uncomfortable at the idea of Mai heading into deep cover with her former lover. Not only that, she'd already told him Drake had been the love of her life. Alicia probably sensed that too. It was a tough moment.

"Hey," Drake spoke up. "Stop being a pair of arses. We'll fettle these Tsugarai bastards and be back with you in a few days. With Hayden and the others too."

Mai knew it wouldn't anywhere near that easy, and so did the others. Alicia couldn't bring herself even to pretend to smile. Luther was staring at a wall. Everyone else in the room kept their views to themselves.

Still, there was no doubt in Mai's mind that she was doing the right thing. And she had a plan.

"I guess I'm leading the treasure hunt," Alicia said finally.

Luther looked at her. "And why's that?"

Kenzie scratched her head. "I can't see why."

"Because I'm the only one here who's successfully found gold on more than one occasion and Kenzie, you're the only one that habitually steals it. I'm best qualified."

Luther shifted in his seat. "God help us."

"If that's the case," Mai said. "I have to tell you this. Dai, my sister and Grace are out of the loop now. Totally out. You don't ask for their help or contact them in any way. Do you understand me?"

"Relax, Sprite, I got this."

Mai didn't think she had. It was rare anything got through to Alicia without something hard attached.

"I'm very serious," she said. "Don't ignore my words."

Alicia walked over to her, standing so close that Drake started to move in. "I got it," Alicia said softly. "Hibiki, Chika and Grace are out. I got it."

Mai nodded, knowing she'd pushed it as far as she could. The trouble was, once she and Drake were out of the way Alicia would become a machine, intent only on her goal. For some minutes there was no more talk, so it seemed the team had agreed to her suggestions without much discussion.

She took a moment to walk away, into another room where she could be alone. She sat down on the edge of a box, tucked her midnight black hair over an ear, and pulled out a cellphone.

Searching through the contacts she found a number and dialed.

"Hello?" a female voice answered.

"Grace?" Mai said, keeping her voice low. "It's so good to hear your voice."

"Hey!" Grace's voice rose several octaves in excitement. Mai smiled to hear it, the undisguised emotion helping to lift her anxious heart.

"How are you?"

Mai listened for a few minutes, letting Grace run through the most important events that were happening at school and in her personal life. Eventually, when Grace was done, Mai tried not to hate herself as she brought up the past.

"I'm sorry to do this," she said. "I really am. I wouldn't bring it up again if it wasn't a life or death situation. But . . . but—"

"Go on, Mai. I can handle it."

Grace's accepting tone only made it worse.

"You remember Gyuki don't you? I know, he was a monster. A brute. He ruined both our childhoods."

"You saved me from him," Grace said. "You rescued me and gave me a new life."

Mai bowed her head. "I have to go back. The Tsugarai

have three of my friends. All these years I've only wanted to forget about them, to stay off their radar, but they came for me. And now . . . now I have to get back inside that camp."

Grace was silent for a while, processing it. Some time later, she said, "How can I help?"

"Don't worry. I'm keeping you well away from all this. The rest of the team have strict instructions to leave you alone. In fact, if they do contact you let me know straight away. I promise, I'll hurt anyone that involves you in this."

"You're gonna hurt yourself?"

Mai winced. The humor was quick, deserved and telling. "I have only one question. Back when you were Gyuki's student and the Tsugarai's warrior, was there anyone else you trusted? Someone that might help us now? Somebody that might want out?"

Grace's reply came faster than expected. "Yes, yes very much. We talked often about escape in the early days but then I think they threatened her family and she went quiet. I can send you a description, but her name is Mariko."

"And you trusted her?"

"I did. But that was years ago. They could have broken her by now."

Mai thanked Grace and said her goodbyes. She had no illusions. This was going to be the hardest mission of her life.

CHAPTER TWELVE

Hayden's wrists and ankles screamed with pain. Her mouth hurt. Her right side ached from lying on it for too long. Next to her, jammed up close, were Kinimaka and Molokai, similarly bound. They'd been shoved into a shipping container and then something resembling an overlarge coffin—basically a big wooden box with thin padding. A lid had been put on and nailed down. The sound had been ear-splitting. Hayden and the others had no room to move in any direction.

She fought down a surge of anxiety and stress. Something terrible told her they would suffocate and die here. But the air didn't run out. Somewhere, probably behind the padding, this box had airholes.

It was hours before she sensed something again.

Their box was swaying, fixed to the floor but rolling up and down. They were on the seas, somewhere off Hawaii. They were being transported somewhere.

They couldn't talk. Someone had stuffed old rags in their mouths and then duct-taped their lips closed. Their hands were tied at the base of their spines. The pain grew as the journey went on. Nobody came for them.

Hayden knew it was days later when the ship docked. The swaying eased and then stopped all together. Hours passed. Finally, they heard the sound of nails being extracted and then the lid was removed. A darkness just a few shades lighter than pitch black greeted them, along with the sight of several shadowy figures leaning over.

"That's them?"

"Yeah, hurry. Boss wants 'em out of here quick."

Hayden screamed behind the gag as her body was lifted, as her joints complained. She and her two companions were dumped onto a pallet on their backs, strapped down and then transported out into the night by a forklift.

The forklift was loaded into the back of a van.

Under cover of dark they were transported from the unknown docks for several hours. This time, their bonds allowed a small amount of movement, enabling the three of them to ease tired and aching muscles. They couldn't speak. They could only await their fate.

The van slowed, turned sharply and then seemed to drive over a rutted track. Hayden's head bounced off the pallet's rough wooden timbers more times than she could count. Mercifully, they stopped after a few minutes and then their world was silence.

Hayden's ears pounded in the stillness. Every bond rubbed at already broken skin, making her want to scream. The waiting was worse than the traveling.

Seconds stretched out into minutes. There was no noise, not even the sound of the van doors opening. Her mind flicked back over the last hours as she waited. It had been a well-timed, well-planned attack. She recognized the garb her attackers wore. She'd seen it before, years ago.

Kinimaka groaned. Molokai remained silent, which to be fair wasn't all that unusual. She felt the big Hawaiian's body stiffen when the van's back doors rattled.

And then they were flung open.

Hayden stared at three dark figures, shrouded by black skies. Did the sun not shine anymore? She hadn't seen sunlight since they walked along Waikiki Beach. She braced herself as the three figures jumped up into the back of the van and untied their bonds.

There was no fighting back now. She could barely stretch her legs and arms. As the men came closer, she saw hard Japanese faces and the familiar clothing. She tried to ask for water, but her mouth wouldn't open, her voice wouldn't work. She was dragged off the back of the van first by her ankles and allowed to fall into the dirt. She was rolled to the side as Kinimaka and Molokai received the same treatment.

After that their kidnappers stood over them. "Stand up," one said with a thick Japanese accent.

Hayden struggled and failed. Kinimaka didn't even bother. Molokai managed to get to one knee. Their captors fed them half a bottle of water each. It took another three attempts before Hayden managed to gain her feet.

"Walk," the man growled.

She shuffled a little. Some feeling was returning to her limbs and the water had helped. For the first time she got a look at her surroundings. It was an open space; fields and low hills. There was a forest to her left. Ahead, she saw the Tsugarai compound as she'd expected she would. It was a few acres of low-slung buildings and huts. Around it, fields were full of the food they ate, and a wide stream bordered the northern land.

It was all picked out by low-voltage floodlights dotted around the compound. Slowly, Hayden and her companions were led along a dirt track to the bottom end of the compound and pushed through an open door into what appeared to be a barn illuminated by flickering torches set to both sides. The floor was dirt, the walls ill-fitting wooden timbers. The roof was thatched.

At the very center six thick, wooden poles were set, driven into the ground. Hayden, Kinimaka and Molokai were made to sit with their backs to the poles. Their hands were tied around them, bound with thick rope, but otherwise their bodies were unshackled.

If she was being honest, Hayden didn't mind this new development. Her limbs were feeling strong again. The water had revitalized her mind. All she needed now was some food. Five minutes later it came in the form of bread and cheese. After that, their mouths were taped again, and they were left alone.

Hayden turned her head to Kinimaka. "You okay?" she mumbled.

Mano nodded. Molokai nodded. It had been a hard journey, but here they were, still strong and willing to fight. Already, they were testing their bonds. With her fingers Hayden found a heavy knot and tried to loosen the rope.

Soon, they heard movement outside. Figures passed the gaps in the timbers and then the door rattled as a padlock was opened. By the light of the flickering torches, Hayden saw eight men enter, shadows thrown wildly in all directions as a gust of wind swept past them. She was left staring up at the man that stepped forward.

"What do you know of the Three Sacred Treasures?" he asked. "What will Mai Kitano do? What does she know of the treasures? What do you know of the royal bloodlines, of Gyuki? These are the questions we want answers to."

Hayden studied the man. He appeared to be in his mid-thirties, with a scarred face and hard eyes. Some greasepaint still clung to his cheeks, attesting to the fact that he'd been in Hawaii and hadn't arrived back that long ago. Or possibly he'd just completed another mission. The men behind him glared without speaking, no animosity nor goodwill or pleasure in their eyes.

The only emotion Hayden saw was a limitless amount of solid, driven purpose.

"You are prisoners of the Tsugarai, and I know, through

74

your own experience, that you know exactly what that means. You will not be rescued. There is no hope. Your only source of comfort is compliance. Now," the man turned to his brethren, "remove their gags."

Hayden grimaced as the tape was ripped from her mouth, taking skin with it. She wanted to ask for water but wouldn't give this man the satisfaction of withholding it on purpose.

"You first," he said to her. "Answer any question."

"I know nothing of treasures or bloodlines," she said. "In fact, I don't know what the hell you're talking about."

Both Kinimaka and Molokai nodded in agreement.

"Once we capture Kitano, your lives are forfeit," the man said. "You would do well to gain some goodwill with me."

"What's your name?" Hayden asked.

The man shrugged. "I am Kenshin, the new grand master. I know you've been here before. I know what happened. That doesn't matter. For you, there are only answers to be given."

Hayden shrugged. "I don't know what to tell you. I don't know what Mai will do. The only thing I know about Gyuki is that he was an absolute bastard. Oh, and a grand master too."

Kenshin took a step back. Hayden braced herself. Three men darted in and, though she scrunched her body up as best she could, delivered severe blows to their bodies. Hayden felt all the breath escape from her, leaving her gasping. Her lungs were on fire. Her boots drummed the floor, kicking up dust. The blows kept on coming until Kenshin spoke up.

But that didn't stop the pain. Hayden gave up trying to breathe. Her head lolled. It was several terrifying seconds before she managed to draw breath, before the black spots stopped dancing in front of her eyes. Her chest and stomach screamed out in pain.

"Where will Mai Kitano go? What will she do? Where are the Three Sacred Treasures?"

When she didn't answer they came at her again. They hit Kinimaka and Molokai again. Hayden tried to compartmentalize it, to rise above the pain. It wasn't happening to her; the situation wasn't as serious it really seemed.

They would leave this barn alive.

Kenshin walked up after the eighth beating. He squatted down so that his eyes were level with hers. "This is but first contact," he said. "A little softening on the first night. Tomorrow, it will be far worse for you."

He rose, turned and led his men out of the barn. Hayden and her friends were left alone, wracked with pain, but with their mouths un-gagged.

In her experience, she guessed Kenshin was hoping they would talk and reason with each other overnight. Come to an agreement where they would spill the beans. Also, he might have men close by, listening.

"Well," she said quietly after a while. "Any ideas?"

CHAPTER THIRTEEN

Zuki padded through her palatial home, heading for the training room where her weapons' master waited. She'd been trained in every form of martial art since an early age. She was Dan level in all of them, a master of swords, of nunchuks, daggers, axe, sickle, spear, shuriken and crossbow. She was a master of defensive weapons too, of shield and halberd. Her mentor had guided her through all levels, through every eventuality. He had made her fight in rain and snow, in blazing heat. He had made her fight naked and alone. He had made her fight the strongest men, the fastest women, and the best of the best. There was nothing left that could surprise her.

Zuki faced the foremost instructor on the planet now, waiting for him to speak.

"Swords," he grunted.

He was a man of few words, which Zuki appreciated. She stripped off her robe and moved over toward the weapons' rack. She wore ultra-tight, second-skin compression leggings, a sports bra and a Threadborne T-shirt, the latter made of HeatGear fabric. Movement was absolute. She couldn't be hindered when she fought, and this outfit gave her freedom of movement and confidence.

She chose a glimmering katana, a forged battle sword, and turned to face her instructor. At that moment, her cellphone rang. Zuki grimaced but raised a hand.

"I am sorry, Sensei. I have to take this."

He bowed. She dug the phone out of her robe and answered. "Yes?"

"This is Kenshin. You asked for updates. We failed in our attempt to capture Mai Kitano but did take three of her friends. Hayden Jaye. Mano Kinimaka. And another we don't yet know. We're still searching for Kitano."

Zuki held her temper, knowing the Tsugarai were the one and only group of people on the planet she should respect. "What did your captives tell you?"

"We have only just started. They still think they have a choice."

"I see. Well, break, chop and flay whatever you like. We need answers, but they are expendable. Kill them as soon as you can. Use them against each other. The men might break if you torture the woman."

"I know warfare," Kenshin said. "And I know my torture. It will be done."

"Whatever they say, I need to know if they're telling the truth. I need Mai Kitano."

"Yes. And we will keep a watch on the other members of her team as soon as they resurface. They are hiding now, but once they reappear around Tokyo, they won't be able to escape our thousand eyes."

"Good. Stay back. They might lead us to the treasure."

"My thoughts too."

Zuki ended the call, understanding that she'd been a little disrespectful to Kenshin. The grand master would be fine with it. He knew the great reward for capturing Kitano and finding the treasures. She replaced the phone and faced her mentor once more.

"Sensei?"

"Let's begin."

*

Two hours later, she returned to her office, dripping with sweat, her body aching from the workout, both bruised and cut, but comfortably confident. Her martial arts and weapons training were supreme. It gave her the confidence to succeed in other areas. It gave her honor and value, incredible self-esteem. She could move forward now against all those that sought to destroy her family and her family's legacy.

First, she showered. She redressed in loose clothing. Then, she sat at the window of her large, high office, staring out at the lights of Tokyo. The city was a shimmer of color blended with darkness. From up here it seemed to pulse with an inner life, a beat all its own. She regarded Tokyo as her city. It would never be taken away from her.

The struggle with the other two big royal families would continue. She'd heard reports that they too were seeking the treasures, which pointed to a traitor in her own household. That traitor would be weeded out. He'd be flayed alive and parts of him sent to all the families. Of course, she had her own spies too. She knew as much about them as they knew about her. She knew where they played, slept and ate. Where their children went to school.

Bloodshed had rarely been spilt between the secret royal families. Their battles were usually a few steps removed, confined to gangs, banking, territory disputes or something similar. This time though, Zuki could sense something was coming. Something big, bloody and final. The samurai family were disrespecting everyone. The Cambodians and Malaysians were gearing up for war, even going so far as to pull their men in close and sacrificing several far-ranging businesses. The royal family of Bhutan were silent, betraying nothing. Zuki knew that most of Asia was on a knife edge.

And even those that didn't know why, sensed something.

Of course, she was satisfied that she'd thought to secure the services of the Tsugarai. Oddly, that was her biggest advantage despite the vast amount of men, women and lands she owned. Zuki had never been one to employ advisors, she preferred hands-on leadership. She wasn't a woman to let others make decisions for her.

Briefly, she wondered if that was why her family's legacy was in danger.

A moment later, she forced the negative, toxic thoughts away. They exhausted her. They manipulated her. If she identified them early, she could get out from under them and focus on clearer, productive emotions.

Her mind clear, she concentrated on the Three Sacred Treasures. There was the mirror, representing knowledge which, according to the legends, was said to reside in Yomi, the Land of the Dead. There was the jewel, representing wealth, hidden in Ryugu-Jo, which was said to reside in the Undersea. And there was the most famous one of all, the sword, representing force, called Kusanagi, said to reside in the Land of the Gods. All were said to contain some part of the first meteorite. And she'd heard recent whisperings that, once combined, they might even lead to a fourth, far more valuable, treasure.

Far more valuable? What could be more valuable than Japan's most famous symbols of heritage? What could move 127 million people with thousands of years of history more than this custom?

Zuki let it all run through her, sorting the noxious thoughts from the harmless ones, deciding upon the path her family would march down to secure their glorious future.

CHAPTER FOURTEEN

Alicia took in everything that Mai told them. She absorbed information about Gyuki, his past, the shrine where he worshipped and how he'd mentored Mai. She listened when Sakurai was mentioned and the Land of the Dead. She knew she was leading the largest contingent of the Strike Force team into imminent danger.

But one thought ran constantly through her mind: *Fucking Kitano's taking Drake, alone, on a covert mission.*

They would be together for days, alone. Working as one.

Alicia wasn't an insecure woman, far from it. She wasn't jealous to a point. She wasn't clingy or overbearing. But there was something about Drake and Mai that harked back to the old days; that put her on edge.

They had a great history, and they both still loved each other in their own ways.

Lately, Luther had been taking up most of Mai's time, a fact which Alicia respected him for. Taking on the Sprite was a tough, risky job. You'd have to spend entire days talking to her about cosplay and shit. About anime. About video games. Alicia couldn't imagine a harder scenario.

Poor Luther.

Even worse now. He'd have to watch his new fatal attraction slinking off with her ex. And he'd have to do it with a smile.

Same as her.

When she got chance, she took Drake aside. "You listen to me," she said. "For as long as you're with her, if the pork sword pops up to say 'hi,' that's the last time it will ever pop up. Is that clear?"

Drake grinned. "Clear."

"I'm not joking. If it even thinks about sliding out of its sheath and into hers, it's mincemeat."

Drake winced. "Jesus, Alicia what do you think—"

"Don't talk to me," she said and swaggered away.

She thought, if anything, that would do the trick. Of course, she knew Drake wasn't about to be unfaithful. She knew Mai wouldn't try to force anything. But it was best to let them know exactly where they stood.

"Luther." She walked up to the big American. "I gave Drake the hard word. You'd probably be wise telling the Sprite where she stands."

Luther grimaced. "I don't think that's wise."

"You scared of her?"

"She's a formidable warrior, but not in that way. I feel our relationship is deeper than warnings and ultimatums."

Alicia regarded him. "Then you're dumber than you look. Don't come crying to me when your new girlfriend accidentally sends you pics of her getting jackhammered by some dude. Just saying."

"That's strangely specific," Luther said.

"Yeah, I guess. I might have accidentally sent a few myself once."

Luther shook his head and walked away, trying not to smile. Alicia put her feelings aside and took in what was happening. Her team was making ready to move out. Drake and Mai were doing the same. The safe house was a hive of activity. Everyone knew what to do. Alicia busied herself sorting through the weaponry.

An hour later, the Strike Force team had parted and were on their way to double destinations.

Alicia sat aboard a private airplane. The trip would be about forty minutes. They weren't wasting any time. Clouds scudded by outside their window as the small plane journeyed its way west toward Sakurai. Dahl, Luther, Kenzie, Karin and Dino were quiet along the way, no doubt processing everything they'd gone through since the attack in Hawaii.

The plane touched down and taxied to the main terminal. A car was on hand to transport them to the sleepy town of Sakurai. The team exited the car and donned jackets made of a light fabric to cover up their armament and body armor, but nothing could hide the implacable set of their faces and the severity of their eyes. They were on a mission. Enemies were going to die. The Strike Force team wouldn't rest until they found their friends and annulled the threat hanging over their team.

A threat tied to Gyuki and this shrine in Sakurai.

Alicia talked as they walked in a tight group through the streets.

"It's the mirror we want," she said. "As well as pointing the way to the other treasures, it's a bargaining chip. Be ready for anything. Gyuki may have left traps and so might the original owners. Oh, and this is the underworld so look out for zombies. I hate those fuckers."

Dahl sighed at her side. "Worse than sand spiders?"

"Shit, no. I'd take a zombie any day."

"So I've heard," Kenzie said.

Alicia stopped on the edge of a retort. Kenzie should be immune from catty banter at least for a few days. She followed sloping, worn streets. Badly made curbs ran on both sides with gutters that stopped and started at random. Small shops lined the way, selling everything from bed linen to magazines and paintings. It surprised Alicia that here, miles from what she thought of as the norm, a familiar round, red bordered, thirty-miles-per-hour round speed sign stood in the street. The shopfronts were random and covered in Japanese writing.

They followed the tree-lined streets for a while, using Dahl's GPRS phone to hone in on their target. Those people they saw in the street gave them a wide berth, but nobody detected anyone hostile.

A short while later Dahl slowed down. "Just ahead," he said.

They walked around a bend where a stand of thick trees blocked the view. In front now, stood the shrine Mai had told them about. Gyuki's boyhood worshipping place, where he used to think of himself as having been born of the underworld, and of Himiko.

"This is it?" Kenzie asked.

"Himiko's shrine," Dahl said.

"And we only need to find a mirror," Dino said with a hint of sarcasm.

"We're looking for the Land of the Dead," Karin said. "In the old texts I've been reading it's described as a world of darkness, comparable to hell. I'd say we should look underground."

They approached the shrine. Alicia shivered a little, recalling that it was here where the madman Gyuki worshipped, ate and possibly even played. They were following in the footsteps of a clever, guileful psychopath who had killed thousands. The shrine was impressively large with broad, gabled roofs. Its Torii, its gate, was ornate and crimson in color; in Japanese culture representing the division between the everyday and the divine world. The main sanctuary was also crimson in color, its sweeping roofline clean and clear-cut.

Alicia climbed the steps to the entry door. Dahl and Kenzie scouted the area but found nothing untoward. If they were being watched, the watchers were very good. Of course, the watchers could well be the Tsugarai, possibly the best surveillance tacticians in the world.

Alicia couldn't fight what she couldn't see.

"Into hell?" Dahl asked.

"Into hell," Alicia said.

CHAPTER FIFTEEN

Inside, Alicia saw polished wooden floors and round orange pillars. The shrine was so clean, every surface gleamed. They moved forward, no doubt breaking a dozen laws of etiquette, but they couldn't worry about that now. Alicia never worried about it.

She waved at different areas, sending the team in search. She saw bronze lanterns, multicoloured vases and teak gongs. She saw ema—wooden plaques bearing prayers or wishes, and Komainu—the lion-dogs and guardians of the shrine. It was intensely quiet in here, the air suffused with a sense of peace. She walked down the main hall, heading for the rear.

"Look for anything that represents Yomi," Karin said through the comms. "Words. Symbols. Pictures. Anything."

"How does Yomi look in Japanese kanji and kana?" Dahl asked.

"I'll ping the characters to your phones."

Alicia checked and held the phone out in front of her, looking to match the characters. She'd already seen several mirrors. She realized that without concise direction, they were stabbing in the dark.

"I'm not seeing anything," she said.

"I've been reading up further," Karin came back. "Apparently, scholars believe that the word Yomi was actually derived from ancient tombs in which corpses were left to decompose. It was clearly defined as existing below the earth. I believe what we're looking for is a crypt, or a tomb."

Alicia wondered where a man like Gyuki would do his worshipping. She soon found it. A large statue of Himiko herself, the seductive sorceress, barely clad, sat upon a black throne.

One step led up to the throne. Alicia bent low and saw that it was worn smooth, even delved where countless knees had rested over the centuries. She imagined Gyuki himself doing the very same thing, possibly even before he'd become the twisted head of a murderous machine. She looked up at Himiko.

Does that bitch have a snide smile on her face?

Alicia grinned, looked down and then it hit her. Gyuki's haiku! It practically told them where the bloody mirror was hidden.

"To me," she said into the comms.

The team gathered and Alicia reminded them of the haiku. "It's at the start," she said. "Beneath Himiko's place."

Dahl stepped forward but Karin held out an arm to stop him. "Wait, what are you doing?"

"With Hayden and the others missing? Whatever I fucking well have to."

Dahl did pause then to check with Alicia. "You sure?"

She forced down her misgivings and nodded. "Beyond doubt, Torsty."

The mad Swede unleashed himself on the statue along with Luther and Kenzie. Alicia didn't fail to register that these three were the most likely to trash a statue. She put Dino and Karin on watch and dove right in alongside them.

The entire structure was wooden, a wooden throne built upon a wood base. The statue itself was some kind of metal. Luther and Dahl hacked away at the base for some time, cracking timbers all the way around. Alicia was heaving at the back when the statue started to tilt.

"Fuck, wait, her ass is in my mouth!"

Used to the off-color comments, Dahl and Luther continued to push and pull so they could dislodge the statue. Alicia dove out of the way, rolling into a wall as the admittedly heavy piece of steel crashed down where she had been.

She glared at the men. "Didn't you hear me?"

Dahl sighed as Luther shrugged. "You talk a lot, Alicia," the Swede said.

"You shout a lot too," Luther added.

"But there is a tunnel under here." Dahl pointed at the hole where Himiko's statue had been.

Alicia clamped her mouth shut as Karin and Dino came into sight around the fallen statue. They were followed by a distraught-looking man wearing yellow robes. He was tall and thin and ringing his hands in misery.

"What have you done?" he said in English. "What have you done?"

"I'm sorry," Alicia acknowledged gracefully at first.

"What have you done?"

"Our fucking friends are in danger." She felt her anger rise. "So fuck off."

"Wait," Karin said. "We were talking to this guy when you started hacking at the statue. He told us there's another way into the crypts."

Alicia closed her eyes. "Shit."

"Yeah, you should've asked." Kenzie nodded, suddenly in agreement with anyone but Alicia. "You've ruined that statue now."

"Me?" Alicia fumed.

"You're in charge." Kenzie shrugged.

Karin caught Alicia's eye. "How else do you think Gyuki made it in there?"

Alicia tried to hide her embarrassment as Dahl and Luther walked toward Karin. "We'll use this entrance. Grab your stuff."

"We will pay for the damage," Alicia said, "and the restoration."

"First day in charge." Kenzie grinned. "First fuck up."

Alicia knew she wasn't going to let it go. Shit, when Drake and Mai found out, she'd never live it down. She spent several minutes placating the robed man and promising to put him in touch with someone that could help.

Hayden would know what to do.

Shit, I'll ask her when I see her.

Then Dahl and Luther were shining flashlights into the pool of darkness they'd uncovered beneath Himiko's statue.

"Shouldn't we use the tunnels?" Karin still fretted.

"The haiku reads: Beneath Himiko," Dahl said. "This will save us time."

Alicia didn't have quite as much faith in Gyuki's directions but followed the mad Swede. She'd have preferred to interrogate the old man—if Gyuki had been here in the last two decades he might have some information. But Dahl was already descending into darkness, waving his flashlight to and fro.

The air grew cold and clingy, cloying. It wrapped them in a second skin. Alicia found herself surrounded by the dark, a dirt roof above her, hard-packed earth below. On closer inspection the roof also had many planks of wood inserted to make it stronger and large timbers shored it up along the way.

Nevertheless, soil trickled down in places as the timbers groaned.

"Nobody's been here for a while," Dahl whispered, pointing ahead.

Alicia saw spiderwebs. "After you," she told most of the team.

Darkness and silence enfolded them as they advanced. A noise came to them. Dahl stopped abruptly. Alicia heard a low susurration, as though someone was whispering. When she looked back, she saw the robed man, staring down the hole they'd made in his shrine, looking after them with a knowing, smug look on his face.

Then he disappeared.

"I don't like this," Alicia said.

"Look out for traps," Karin said. "I've heard a lot about this Gyuki. The man's a monster."

It was a poor choice of words. Alicia shivered. The walls were moving, trickling soil and water always active. The roof was groaning. The floor was alive, insects scuttling this way and that, annoyed that their lifelong home was being disturbed.

Dahl led the way, followed by Luther. They came to a place where the walls had been boarded over and the floor covered. It appeared to be a minor refuge, somewhere someone like Gyuki might take a rest. Pray? Eat? Alicia thought the tunnels they'd circumvented might be very long.

"Good call," she told Dahl. "Coming this way."

Twenty minutes later they reached another refuge, this one a little different. The walls were made of stone. In fact, Alicia saw, this tunnel had been hewn through the rock in ancient times. They were inside a cave system now. Old drawings had been scrawled into the wall, representations mostly of animals but also of the night sky. Alicia saw much fresher daubings too. Symbols added, characters written.

Karin made them wait whilst she deciphered them using a tablet. The signal wasn't good, it wavered in and out and she had to move back up to the tunnel to get clear of the rock. Finally, she shook her head.

"Something like 'danger'. The word Himiko is pretty clear. And I think that line," she pointed, "says 'I am Gyuki. Beware. All who pass this point die at her hands.'"

"Loony," Dahl said. "Mai mentioned that he believed he was born here. That he belonged to the underworld. If that's so, I guess we're walking into hell."

Alicia shuddered, looking around at the ungiving walls that surrounded them, listening to the whispering dark. If she strained her ears, she could have sworn she could hear somebody talking, somebody far away.

"Come on," Dahl said. "We're getting close."

Alicia's only thought was: *To what?*

CHAPTER SIXTEEN

The cave system took them down, so they could imagine they were headed into the bowels of hell. Alicia found herself sweating hard. It wasn't even cold down here. Some unknown heat source was staving off the chill.

An inferno?

Alicia needed to quit that line of thought. It was distracting her and no doubt several of the others. Even Luther looked jumpy.

Down they walked, minutes passing like hours. Ahead, Dahl stopped, bringing the whole line to an abrupt halt. "Trip wire," he said. "Hard to spot, at ankle height. Looks like it leads to the right-hand wall there."

"Probably triggers a cave in," Alicia said.

One by one they spotted and avoided the trip wire. The next obstacle was a pit as they crossed a section of soil. It wasn't deep, maybe nine feet and shored up with timbers, but it was deep enough so that a man couldn't climb out. Soon after that they returned to the cave system.

And now there were more symbols and even paintings on the walls, each one showing Himiko at various stages of her life. Himiko receiving one hundred bronze mirrors from Emperor Cao Rui, a recorded historical event and one more reason Gyuki may have chosen to hide the sacred mirror down here. Himiko as a shaman and a sorceress. Himiko practicing black magic and riding a demon. Himiko as a queen.

Dahl used his flashlight to point them all out, proceeding very slowly now. They found old rugs and a straw mat, evidence that somebody had slept down here. Possibly for many days. Barely a two-minute walk beyond those, Dahl came to another death trap.

A twelve-foot-wide ravine lay in front of them, at the bottom of which flowed a black river. The drop was over one hundred feet, the waters surging down there as they entered the narrow ravine. Several planks were already laid across the gap.

Dahl rolled his shoulders and then chose one, stepping out onto it. Alicia gasped out loud as it snapped, breaking in the middle.

"No!"

She jumped forward, but was woefully short. Dahl tried to back up as the part of the plank he stood on fell forward at an angle and started to slither down to certain destruction below. His boots slipped. Alicia reached out again, fingers grazing the edge of the plank.

"Dahl!"

It was no use. Dahl pinwheeled his arms, falling purposely back toward the bank. Karin was closer, but only managed to scrape her fingers along his backpack. Dahl hit the plank with his spine as it lost its fight with gravity and started to slide down.

Luther's reaching hand somehow managed to snag the Swede's backpack, which halted the man's fall. When all of Dahl's weight was gripped only by Luther's right hand, the American yelled out in pain.

"Hold me, I can't hold him."

Alicia fell across him, her entire body vertical to his horizontal one, pinning him tight to the rock floor. A second later someone clambered over her back, leaning down to support Luther's arm. By the cursing and the accent Alicia knew it was Kenzie.

Two minutes later they were kneeling, heads down on the bank. Dahl let out a long breath before speaking.

"Thanks," he said, "from the bottom of my heart."

"No probs, bud," Luther said. "I know you'd do it for me."

Alicia eyed Kenzie. "Good job."

The Israeli nodded and then winked. "Can't wait to tell Mai you waited less than a day to jump her boyfriend."

Alicia couldn't hide the smile. It was probably driven by pure relief. "To be honest," she said, standing up, "it doesn't normally take me that long."

They surveyed the scene. Obviously, they assumed all the other planks leading across the gap were also rigged to break.

So how had Gyuki traversed it?

"There," Luther said finally. "The planks that shore the roof up are doubled up right there."

Alicia walked over with Dahl and Dino. It seemed Gyuki had rigged the trap and then camouflaged the real planks on top of others. Slowly, they dragged them clear and laid them across the twelve-foot gap.

"They're still only two feet wide," Karin said. "Be careful."

The team made it across without incident. Alicia shone her flashlight ahead, noting its light being swallowed up by an over-arching darkness. The ravine appeared to transition the start of a natural cavern. Slowly, the other members of the team joined her and started to illuminate the vast, dark space.

A wide plateau of rock met jagged walls and then a curved ceiling high above. Water dripped and trickled down from the heights. Roughly twenty feet ahead, a set of stone stairs led up to a platform, and on that platform sat the rectangular shape of a coffin.

"Was Himiko's body ever found?" Alicia asked.

"No," Karin said. "I remember reading there were disputes that she even existed. That she was actually Chinese or Korean. If Gyuki found Himiko's body, he sat back on one more national treasure."

"Not surprising," Alicia said. "And now the haiku makes even more sense."

Dahl closed his eyes. *"Beneath Himiko,"* he whispered, unable to hide a shudder.

"I don't believe in evil," Luther said, "that I can't see, fight or kill. I don't believe in demons and hell. Let's go see what we're dealing with."

The big American strode across the cavern. As he approached the platform with the raised rectangular dais, he slowed. Alicia walked shoulder to shoulder with Kenzie and Dahl, backing him up.

And then, they saw what he saw.

"Fuck me." Alicia whispered.

Lying on the steps, deep in shadow, were several sets of skeletons. Alicia could tell they were old. Several limbs had crumbled away. As much as they were able, they lay shoulder to shoulder as if they had simply lain down to die. Luther approached more steadily, looking for footprints in the dust that covered the floor.

Which they now knew was bone dust.

They paused at the foot of the steps. The platform with its rectangular coffin was eight feet above them, picked out by their flashlights. Alicia swept the coffin with her beam, looking for markings, but saw none.

"No footprints anywhere." Kenzie had completed a circuit of the platform. "And this appears to be the central point of this rock plateau."

"Been a while since anyone was here," Alicia said. "Maybe Gyuki was the last."

"If that is Himiko," Karin said, "she will have been shunned. To the ancients, she was a sorceress. All kind of curses will be associated with her."

Alicia glanced at Kenzie. "Off you go then."

The Israeli smiled. "I'm already cursed a dozen times over," she said. "One more won't hurt."

But Luther was already ascending, his heavy boots leaving marks in the grayish dust that covered the steps. There was no sound other than their breathing as the team started forward. Alicia was careful to step over the skeletons, trying to avoid looking at the skulls' eyeless sockets that seemed to follow her everywhere. *Just like the fucking Mona Lisa,* she thought. *The eyes follow you.*

Luther reached the top first. Dahl was next. Alicia came up on the far right. She studied the rectangular slab of rock and its cover made of stone. From first inspection she couldn't tell if it had ever been moved. Luther wrapped his fingers under the rim and felt the weight.

"It'll slide," he said. "Do we want to slide?"

"I think we have to," Karin said. "Or we did all this for nothing."

"We could always continue down the tunnel," Dahl said.

"No, there's nothing," Kenzie said. "The far side of this plateau is a solid rock wall."

Alicia slipped her own fingers under the rock slab. Before she pushed, she gave Karin a glance.

"Anything else we should know about Himiko?"

"Nothing beyond the curses, booby traps, poisons and walking dead, no."

"That's good then."

On the count of three, most of the team hefted the cover and pushed it in a diagonal direction. It wasn't too heavy and soon they managed to lift it free and set it down alongside the large slab. Alicia, and everyone else, had been holding their breaths whilst they uncovered whatever they might find but now, seeing nothing swirling through the air except dust motes, they breathed again.

Alicia stepped to the lip of the stone coffin.

Dahl was beside her, his presence uncannily reminding her of the time he leant over a coffin long ago, staring down at the bones of Odin.

The first thing she saw was a partially wrapped skeleton. Once, it had been covered by a white robe, but time and insects had eaten most of the material away. The skeleton was small in every way, and surrounded by jewelry: beads and amulets, small representations of weaponry.

At the center of Himiko's chest however, where the bony fingers of her hands still interlocked, was an octagonal mirror with a small handle, set into a round, obsidian frame. The glass of the mirror still shone when Kenzie's beam passed across it. The frame appeared to be rough and irregular. The mirror was entirely black, symbolizing this place, Himiko's legend and Gyuki's heart. It was a fitting symbol for the Land of the Dead.

"Yata no Kagami," Karin said. "The sacred mirror. It is so ancient, even the Japanese can't agree on its origins."

"Who's gonna grab it?" Alicia asked.

There was a silence. Taking the mirror would mean pulling it from Himiko's dead fingers. Alicia didn't relish the task. Kenzie patted her on the shoulder.

"I really think it should be our leader, don't you?"

Alicia ground her teeth together. "Leaders delegate."

"Nah, they show the way forward," Luther said.

"Don't you start too," Alicia growled, then, gingerly, leaned out over the coffin. Something scuttled among the bracelets, something small and thin. With an effort she ignored it, seeing Himiko as the main threat. The long-dead woman's ribs were beneath Alicia as she reached in.

Carefully, she pushed two skeletal fingers to the side, took hold of the mirror and pulled it away. As she took firmer hold the mirror almost slipped out of her grasp, threatening to fall and shatter Himiko's ribs.

She held on, sweating hard. Everyone was concentrating on the mirror and Himiko's chest.

And then Karin said: "Shit, have you seen that? Where the hell is her head?"

For the second time, Alicia almost dropped the mirror.

The skeleton ended at the neck. Everyone spun around and shivered as a sudden, cold gust of wind swept through the cavern.

CHAPTER SEVENTEEN

Drake and Mai drove overland for several hours before parking up their car, concealing it and walking away. They were about ten miles from the Tsugarai compound and were already in the middle of nowhere, but they couldn't risk detection.

They grabbed backpacks and hiked across green fields. So far, their journey had been one of focus. They'd barely spoken. Drake felt a bit off-kilter, being alone with Mai again. It was as though he'd been transported over a decade into the past when Mai and he had worked on several different missions.

"How long?" Mai asked.

"Until we hit the danger area?" Drake said. "About two hours."

The sunlight was waning above, which they'd timed to perfection. By the time they reached the Tsugarai compound it would be full dark. Tonight would be all about getting the lay of the land and finding out if there were any weak spots in the defenses, any exploitable areas. They also needed to source a safe place to make camp.

"Is this strange?" Drake blurted as they navigated a deep fold in the land, following a winding river.

"What?" Mai replied.

Drake tuned out the chattering waters as they splashed and flowed over the rocks. "You and I, alone again. On a mission."

Mai shrugged. "If I were Alicia, I would treat that as a challenge and become aggressive. But it is odd, Matt. We haven't even been alone together in years."

"Yeah, I thought so. Are you okay?"

"With life? Yes, are you?"

"I don't know," Drake admitted. "Something's missing. Alicia and I, we can't seem to live without a mission. We took six weeks off, some of it in paradise, and all we thought about was the next op."

"Your bodies healed though."

"True. And, partially, our minds. We got past the traumas. But . . . what's next?"

"If you don't like it . . . quit."

"And what would you do if I quit?"

Mai stopped on the grassy bank and turned to him. "That's a very good question. I don't know. I'd have to give it some thought."

"To my mind we *are* Team SPEAR. The originals. You, Alicia, Dahl and me. Just because it has a new name doesn't change my viewpoint."

Mai was close. Too close. Drake found himself searching her eyes and then started walking again, moving quickly. He continued in silence for a while, following the GPS to their destination. When they came to within a mile, they found a deep area of the forest and dug in, erecting a two-man tent and then burying supplies. When they were done, they camouflaged the whole area, shielding it from patrols and prying eyes.

Drake checked his clothing, weapons and body armor. Everything was perfect. "Are you ready?"

"To go back to the Tsugarai compound? Never."

Drake nodded, letting her walk past him anyway. Mai had spent the worst years of her life here. It was a testament to her courage and determination that she'd come back.

"Sorry," he said. "Wasn't thinking."

Mai didn't respond. They crept through the trees a step at a time. Satellite surveillance and high-level drones had determined that there were no early-warning devices planted in this forest. The Tsugarai had always been old-school, preferring to rely on thousands of years of tried and trusted methods of observation.

The trees began to thin out. Mai dropped down and crawled the last few feet. Drake followed and soon they reached the end of the tree line.

A silver moon illuminated a landscape that may not have changed for a thousand years.

To left and right, about three hundred yards distant, Drake saw several buildings set out in haphazard fashion. All constructed of wood, they ranged from small huts to dwellings and to long, low barns, like hangars. The fields were neat, tilled. The gentle slopes that surrounded the area were also tidy. A series of floodlights lit various areas at night and Drake saw many yellowish lights flickering in the windows.

"Has it changed?"

"No," Mai said. "Maybe an extra building or two. That's it."

"You say there's a central area. A gathering place."

"Yes." She pointed. "That's where I killed Gyuki and saved Grace. And where Gyuki used to love subjecting me and others to countless humiliations during our training. He was a monster."

Drake knew she'd never lose those memories. He nudged her now. "Look, something's happening."

Doors were opening. Using field glasses, both he and Mai observed in silence for the next few minutes. They saw about two dozen members of the clan exiting what appeared to be their homes before heading to the gathering place. They all carried weapons and wore robes with hoods.

"They're preparing for a mission," Mai said. "It's what we used to do. They'll be getting their instructions from the new grand master in the square and then moving out. Could be gone for hours or days."

"Transport?" Drake asked.

"There's an airstrip and a helicopter pad over those hills, well camouflaged. Also, that building there—" she indicated a wide barn "—houses many different types of vehicles; something for every mission."

"We can't tell if Mariko's among them," Drake griped. "But this will make our entry easier."

They waited until the Tsugarai had moved out and then identified a shallow ditch in the ground, probably an old stream, that they could use to get closer to the buildings. Mai went first. Drake followed, keeping as low to the earth as possible. Within an hour, they were lying face down at the side of a low-slung barn.

"Do what I do," Mai told him. "From now on, if we're not equal to these shinobi, we're dead."

Drake nodded, watching her roll out of the dip until she came up against the side of the barn and then slipped into deepest shadow. He listened. All was okay in the silent night. He copied Mai. They crept down the length of the barn, stopping at the front. Ahead, Drake saw a row of smaller dwellings. To the right he saw the gathering place Mai had mentioned.

"They sleep three or four to a house," Mai said. "We'll try the windows first."

It was an optimistic decision. If they were hoping to see Mariko sat on a bed or even staring out at them, they were unfortunate. Looking through windows was dangerous at best. It added chance to the odds that were already stacked against them. They saw men and women, young and old; resting, reading, asleep or talking, but they only had Chika's description to go on as to what Mariko looked like.

On the plus side, they identified that the men and women slept separately and that there were eight female dwellings. Four appeared to be reserved for older women.

Mai sank into shadow and faced Drake. "Four to choose from. What do you think?"

"Couldn't tell," he said, "though I'd put my next bacon sarnie against it being anyone in shack four. Didn't Chika say Mariko would be twenty-four or five now?"

"Yes."

"That leaves three shacks. What—"

At that moment Mai sprang at him. He went down, shocked, landing on his back. Mai bore down on top of him, pushing his body as far into the grass as she could. Her right hand came up and covered his mouth. Her eyes were inches away.

He got the message.

Seconds later, a two-man patrol passed by. Their boots crunched along the gravel just a few feet from Drake and Mai's unmoving bodies, but their focus ranged afar rather than near. Drake didn't even see them. Another minute passed by before Mai let him up.

"You okay?" she asked eventually.

"I will be, so long as Alicia doesn't find out you jumped me on the first night."

He knew Mai well enough to see that she hid a smile at that. "You do feel firmer," she said. "Maybe it's the armor."

Drake rose to his knees. "What I was about to say is that leaves three shacks. Judging from what Grace told us Mariko will be in that one." He pointed. "Which ties up with what we saw through the window."

"There are four women inside," Mai said pointlessly. He already knew that.

"No toilet though," he said.

They found a good place to hide; Mai shimmying up a drainpipe to a low-hanging roof from which she could see the entire compound. Drake joined her a few seconds later and settled down to wait out the night.

"She might never come out," Drake said.

"I know."

"She might be on the mission."

"I know."

"She—"

"I know," Mai interrupted. "I know all the ifs and buts options. But what other choice do we have?"

Hours passed. It was getting on toward dawn before Drake heard the first sound of movement from the hut they were watching. It was the unlatching of the door and then the shuffle of feet.

Mai used night-vision glasses to scan the subject. They were equipped with high-end facial recognition software that sought out the person's face and matched it against several pre-known requisites. Unfortunately, they only had Grace's description and a sketch, but Mai's glasses flashed up an 88 percent match.

"It's her," Mai said. "Go."

Drake hit the ground first, moving as silently as he could. As soon as his feet touched earth Mariko appeared to sense it, whirling toward him and pulling two wicked looking knives from beneath her robes.

Then, she attacked.

CHAPTER EIGHTEEN

Drake reeled away as a dagger slashed through the air close to his face. He ducked as a second dagger plunged toward his ribs, managing to roll aside. But Mariko was fast, as fast as anyone he'd seen, and she wasn't taking prisoners. Before he stopped rolling, she was on him, slamming an elbow into the side of his neck, before pulling him onto his back and raising both her knives.

"Wait." Drake raised an arm.

Mai landed on Mariko's back, sending the other woman sprawling. One of the daggers fell away. Drake grabbed it. Mai followed up with two rib strikes and then held her own dagger close to Mariko's throat.

She clamped the woman's mouth, leaned in close to her right ear and whispered, "Grace sent us. Do you remember Grace?"

Drake wasn't surprised to see Mariko knew English very well. Learning languages was as much part of a shinobi's training as silent assassination.

Mariko let her body relax and nodded. Mai didn't let up. "We need your help," she said. "And we want to help you."

Drake watched the surrounding area and checked his watch. They were in good shadow here, close to the back of the hut, and there were no more approaching patrols. The trouble was, dawn was due in about twenty minutes.

"Let's hurry this up," he said.

Mai sat up warily, knife still close to Mariko's throat. The other woman rose too, sitting with her back to the hut. Without being asked, she dropped the other knife.

"You are Mai Kitano," she said with a hint of awe in her voice.

"You know of me?"

"They whisper of you. The older women."

Mai looked like she didn't quite know how to deal with that information. "Oh. Well, Grace told me all about you. Do you want to leave this place? Do you want your freedom?"

"I'll never be free unless you kill them all."

"I'm free," Mai said. "Grace is. The masters have already given you the tools to stay out of their way. We can put you on the right road. And anyone else you want to bring with you."

Drake winced at that. It hadn't been part of the plan, and introduced a more severe degree of danger. But this was Mai. She knew the horrors Mariko and others like her were forced to put up with, and she wanted to help them.

"This is about the three prisoners isn't it?" Mariko asked.

Mai nodded. "Yes. Our friends."

"You're here for them. Not me."

Mai hung her head a little. "I should have destroyed this place a long time ago," she said. "When I took Grace and killed Gyuki, the Tsugarai merely waited and then paid off the right authorities, continuing as if nothing had happened. I think, now, we have to change that."

Drake was counting down the minutes. They were already risking it, traveling back to their tent in the new dawn. Every passing minute made it harder.

"We have to go," he said.

"Will you help us?" Mai asked.

Drake saw the conflict on Mariko's face. The need to escape was there. But the hold the Tsugarai had over her was clear too.

"You will shut them down?" she asked.

Mai replied instantly: "I promise."

Drake knew there was no plan to do that. Shit, was it

even possible? They'd need an army. A bloody big one.

"That's my first condition. The second is tough also. But if you show me you can do the second, I will help you and your friends."

"What's the second?" Drake asked.

"My—"

Suddenly, there was a flurry of activity. Drake saw boots flashing past as he hit the ground, face first. Eight robed figures ran by, heading for the central square. In the distance, he heard the approach of a helicopter.

"Mission's over," he said. "They're coming back. We're out of time."

"The second condition is my family," Mariko said. "Some years ago, the Tsugarai became even more of a brutal entity. In addition to buying children and turning them into killers, they started to threaten those children's families, proving they could do so at will by showing them up-to-date photographs. They said if we ever try to escape, they will torture and kill our entire family."

"You want us to get them to safety?" Mai asked.

"Yes, and then I will help you."

"Where are they?" Drake asked.

"Tokyo," Mariko said. "The northern districts."

"We literally just came from there." Drake thought about the ironies and obstructions in life.

"I can give you their address. You return and find me in three days. Same time, same place. Then we will have a deal."

Mai glanced over her shoulder at Drake. His eyes said it all.

Are you sure?

"We're doing this, Matt, so get on board with it. Now, move."

CHAPTER NINETEEN

Hayden heard very little through the night. She tried to get some sleep but found it hard to drift off with her hands tied behind the pole at her back. She found it even harder when Kinimaka snored.

She looked over at the Hawaiian. Molokai was staring too.

"He can do that *now*?" Molokai said. "That's unreal."

"That's Mano Kinimaka," Hayden said. "He'll never change, and I really don't want him to. How are your bonds coming?"

"They're not. After they took us out earlier for the toilet break someone made them tighter than ever. Can't feel my fingers."

"Shit."

Hayden wrestled her own as she spoke. "They're gonna kill us," she said. "Either when they realize we have zero information or if they capture Mai." She paused for a moment and then said, "Do you have any dependents, Molokai?"

"Well, no. All my adult life I've spent fighting, torn from one war zone into the next. Luther is my only living relative. Our parents were killed in a car accident decades ago."

Hayden thought of Drake. His own parents and his wife had shared a similar fate. "I'm sorry to hear that."

"We had little choice, growing up," Molokai went on. "It was either grow too tough for the bullies to pick on you or become victims of a flawed system. We chose to fight. Eventually, we enlisted."

"To keep fighting."

"No. To escape the gangs and criminal enterprises that were forcing us to join them. In our neighborhood, there was only one way out."

Hayden took a deep breath. She didn't want to feel sorry for Luther and Molokai, not right now, but they'd grown up hard and they'd had no choice. Molokai had become a bomb tech and Luther a Special Forces leader. Now, all they knew was fighting, the Army, and the harsh world it revolved around.

They stayed in military service because they had nowhere else to go. They didn't know how to do anything else. They thought they were moving forward, but all they were doing was circling back around.

The night passed slowly. They heard running feet and saw the shadows of dark figures running through the gaps in the timbered walls. They saw deep night and heard absolutely nothing, not even a distant animal call. They thought they heard whispering near the dawn but couldn't be sure.

Kinimaka woke then nodded off again. Hayden moved regularly to ward off the numbness in her backside and the pain in her spine. She couldn't do anything about her wrists. Her mouth was dry, her throat parched. They were being fed just two small meals per day and allowed a few swallows from a bottle of water each. This hut was their home and their prison. It was the place where they suffered. She sat and stared into space, through slats she now knew so well, at the latched door, at the thatched roof, at the brown mix of dirt and gravel that made up the floor.

It was cold here at night, but they'd been given no coverings for their arms. When Kinimaka finally woke, Hayden tried to engage him a little.

"Hey," she said softly.

Kinimaka grunted. "I didn't snore, did I?"

"No. You slept soundly like you always do, Mano."

He took a moment to glare at their surroundings. "It isn't a dream then. We're still here."

"Not quite the Four Seasons, is it?"

Kinimaka smiled at the memory of the hotel where they'd recently stayed. "Nah. That was where we heard Kono was pregnant."

"A good day. You were so happy."

"I hope I get to see her baby."

Hayden bit her bottom lip, wanting to reach out but unable. "We're not alone in this, Mano. The entire team will be coming to rescue us."

"Can't rely on that," Molokai said. "It's best to believe we're alone and rely on our own skills."

Hayden could see why he would think that way. Molokai was a loner, used to depending on himself, happy with his own company. Over the last several years, the biggest thing she'd learned was how you *could* rely on friends that loved you.

"We do both," Hayden said. "And we hold out, no matter what."

Dawn was rising faster, its crimson hues slanting in through the gaps in the walls. Hayden welcomed it for the warmth it brought, but regretted it because sunlight would also bring something else.

Kenshin, the grand master.

The sound of gravel crunching made her clench her fists. She took a deep breath. Today was not going to be easy.

"It's all about surviving." Molokai was looking at her. "In any way you can. I've been in this position before, and I'm guessing you have too. Don't show them fear, or love, or regret. You can't help but show them pain, but you can store that motherfucker today to return to sender tomorrow."

Kinimaka gave her an open, loving look, the last he would give her before they put on their game faces and faced the day. The door rattled. The padlock came off. Kenshin walked in with four bodyguards, his expression a little wistful this morning.

"Mai Kitano," he said. "The secret royal bloodlines. What do you know?"

Hayden locked eyes with the man, unwilling to show an ounce of emotion.

"And what is Strike Force?" Kenshin said. "The name on your IDs. A very secret group? Even more covert than SPEAR?"

More silence followed. Kenshin eventually sighed then signaled to his men. "Get the toughest. We'll start there."

They moved in fast. Two bent down to untie Molokai whilst two more covered him with handguns. The big man didn't resist, but he didn't make it easy for them either. They started by taking away his robe.

Kenshin stared at Molokai's face, crisscrossed with old leprosy disfigurements. "I see you're no stranger to pain," he said, "but you had your chance today."

The guards moved in, slashing at Molokai. They cut his wrists, his arms, his thighs. They darted and withdrew. Molokai withstood it for only a short while before striking out. When he did attack, a bullet thudded into the dirt close to his bare toes. Molokai froze. The knife assaults continued. Molokai grunted and occasionally cried out. He staggered and leant forward, but he didn't fall to his knees.

"For fuck's sake, stop this." Hayden couldn't help but try. "He doesn't know anything. Think about it. You took us unawares on vacation. We didn't even have weapons on us. Do you think that's normal for a team on a mission?"

Kenshin waved at his men. "Maybe you know nothing of the bloodlines. But Kitano knows something. Maybe she told you."

"I know nothing of the Sacred Treasures and Gyuki. I know Mai hated him. I know she killed him. Nobody questioned her further."

"I need to know if you will stick to that story when your friends are dying in agony. I'm sure you understand."

Kenshin nodded at his men. From the side of the hut they walked to fetch several thick, hard bamboo sticks. Molokai squared up to them.

"Attack," Kenshin said.

CHAPTER TWENTY

Alicia descended the stone steps, putting several feet between her and Himiko's headless body. Everyone followed her except Karin and Dino, who elected to stay and study Himiko's skeletal remains.

Dahl shone the flashlight around the wide cavern. "No massive balls rolling toward us," he said. "That's a decent sign."

Alicia glanced over. "There are times when I'd completely disagree with you," she said, "but down here, I have the same opinion."

"What do you have?" Kenzie leaned in, wanting to see the mirror.

Alicia held it up. The object was surprisingly heavy, a perfectly octagonal mirror set into a round frame, edged by a jagged piece of the world's oldest meteorite. It felt rough under Alicia's fingers, rough but polished at every edge.

Karin came down the steps to join them. "Can we talk about Himiko's head?"

"No," Alicia said. "We bloody well can't."

"Well, it didn't just roll out of here on its own."

"We have the mirror," Dahl said, "and we're short on time. There are two more Sacred Treasures to find. Can we concentrate?"

Alicia nodded and turned the mirror over. It was pure black on the back and smooth where the maker had rubbed and honed the meteorite surround. As Alicia looked closer, she saw the reason for the level surface.

"There's writing on the back," Dahl said.

"Two haikus," Karin said, peering closer. "Let me get some photos of that."

Dahl shone the flashlight closer as Karin snapped some pictures of the Japanese characters written vertically down the back of the mirror. Alicia knew she'd have an app on her phone, something that would translate the haikus, but they needed to escape this cave system first.

"We have everything we need," Alicia said. "Let's move out."

As they started to retrace their steps, Kenzie spoke up. "I'm gratified we found the first Sacred Treasure," she said. "Not only will it stick it to the Tsugarai, but Dallas would find it poetic."

"We'll get them all," Dahl said. "The ones that killed him."

"That will be a good day."

"Speaking of the first treasure," Karin said. "This mirror, Yata no Kagami, represents knowledge, or wisdom, which is probably why it has those haikus on the back. Its name translates to *eight-sided-mirror,* an obvious reference to its shape. Forged by a deity it was said to have passed to Amaterasu's grandson's hands who, also with the sword, Kusanagi, set off to pacify Japan. Nobody alive or dead knows how old it is, but in 1040 it was thought to have been burned in fire. Clearly though, the master swordsman, Masamune, at some point reframed this artifact with the meteorite."

"Why so secretive?" Dino asked.

"Due to the Shinto priests' long-standing refusal to show the Sacred Treasures, nothing can be confirmed. Even in 2019, when Emperor Akihito abdicated from the throne, the Three Treasures were shrouded inside boxes."

"Because they don't have them," Dahl said.

Karin nodded. "But to reveal that to the public at large would lose the government, any government, enormous face. It could end them. The uproar would feed many dissenting voices and lead to panic."

"Somebody mentioned a fourth treasure?" Luther said as they walked.

"Yes, but that's a complete unknown," Karin said. "Perhaps the new haikus will help."

"We'll soon see," Alicia said. "We're approaching the exit."

It felt good to breathe fresh air again and be able to turn the flashlights off. The group climbed up out of the hole and back into the shrine. Several people stood around, faces grim and sad, staring at the people who'd defaced their local sanctuary.

Alicia hid the mirror and reiterated what she'd already told them about compensation. She knew it wasn't perfect, but it was all she could offer them. Quickly, they left the shrine behind and returned to their vehicle.

"I sure hope those haikus tell us where to go next," Luther said. "Because, if not, we're done."

Alicia noticed that Luther seemed a little on edge, more nervy than normal. Her own feelings were somewhere along the same lines. Drake and Mai had been gone over a day now, and whilst she trusted the Yorkshireman, she knew his weaknesses.

Mai was one of them.

Luther was probably aware of it too. She wondered if they should talk, maybe get drunk together, but then dismissed the idea. She'd never been one for heart-to-hearts.

But then Luther fell in beside her. "You okay?"

"There's nothing to worry about."

"I know, but . . ."

"Yeah. You can't help but wonder if their mission's gone more horizontal than vertical?"

Luther winced. "I think that's a bit harsh."

"Yeah, probably best if we don't talk about it, eh?"

"Probably."

They reached the vehicle and climbed in. Luther took the wheel. By the time they left the village behind, Karin, who'd been trying to match both haikus to her translation app, spoke up.

"It's gobbledygook," she said. "I think some of the characters, the kanji and kana, are very old, possibly even a separate language, so I'm not getting the right translation."

"Shit," Alicia said.

"I'm emailing Dai," Karin said. "He'll know somebody who can help."

"Is that a good idea?" Alicia turned in her seat. "Remember the Sprite was very pushy about how she wanted her family kept out of this."

"It's just an email," Karin said, "and if we want a fast answer, Dai's the best bet."

Alicia didn't like it, but Karin was right. They couldn't afford to waste time. Karin sent the email, calling Dai to make sure he saw it straight away. Alicia was confident Dai would have the contacts. She was less confident about involving him further. Never mind Mai, if anything happened to Dai and his family, *Alicia* would never recover.

Their vehicle reached the airfield where the CIA plane waited. As soon as they boarded, the pilot asked them for a destination. Alicia told him to hold his horses for a little while.

They took their seats. They ate sandwiches and drank water, checked their phones for messages. Dahl sat beside Kenzie, in front of Alicia, trying to take her mind off Dallas.

Alicia felt sorry for the mad Swede. He was in enough personal pain without the Israeli adding some of her own.

But she did feel for Dallas. She felt worse that she hadn't made a better effort to get to know him.

A little while later her phone rang. Dai Hibiki's name flashed up on the caller ID so Alicia switched it to speakerphone.

"What do you have?" Dahl asked.

"You were right. In writing style alone, these haikus far predate the previous one that Gyuki taught Mai. It's clear now that Gyuki knew where the mirror was hidden and concocted a haiku of his own to start the quest. The haiku engraved on the back of the mirror, in the meteorite material itself, is written in a much older language. We're having trouble translating it all."

"Do you have anything?" Luther asked.

Dai paused. "Do you really have one of the Three Sacred Treasures in your possession?" He sounded breathless, reverent.

"Yes," Alicia said. "And when we rescue our friends you can kiss it, but for now tell me: Does this haiku tell us where to go next?"

"It's the jewel next," Dai said. "Wait, let me read you the English translation from the Japanese as close as we can get it."

Alicia rolled her eyes at Dahl and Luther as Dai rustled a piece of paper.

"*The Noted Magatama,*

"*In Ryugu-jo,*

"*The red coral beneath the Devil's Sea.*"

Alicia spread her hands. "What the hell does that mean?"

"We don't know with any certainty," Dai admitted. "But you can start flying toward Tokyo. I'll explain our thoughts."

Alicia took a minute out to send instructions to the pilot. Almost immediately, the engine note grew louder and the wheels began to roll. Everyone ignored the pilot's suggestion to buckle in.

"The noted magatama," Dai began. "Well, magatama are curved, coral-shaped beads that first appeared in prehistoric Japan. From 1000 BCE they were used in decorative and ceremonial jewelry. The most *noted* magatama is the Yasakani no Magatama, the sacred, imperial jewel, and one of the Three Sacred Treasures."

"Perfect," Alicia said. "What do the other lines mean?"

"We're researching Ryugu-Jo as we speak. But the Devil's Sea is located off Japan, off Tokyo. There is one problem though."

Alicia coughed. "Only one?"

"Okay, two then. First, it sounds like the jewel is underwater. Second, that water is called the Devil's Sea."

"Don't tell me," Dahl said. "It came by that name for a particular reason."

"Also called the Dragon's Triangle. The area is probably best described as the Pacific Bermuda Triangle."

Alicia hung her head. "Not again."

Dai went on, "As you know, there are areas in many oceans with stories like that. The Japanese call them *ma no umi*. But it is the Bermuda Triangle that gets the publicity. Many ships have been lost in the Devil's Sea through the years within an area that the Yokohama Coast Guard Office officially classify as a special danger area. Over a dozen ships lost in perfect weather. When the Japanese government sent a ship to investigate, called the *Kaiyo Maru,* it too disappeared. The authorities have now labelled the area a danger zone, as it's said several military vessels have also vanished in the area, though there's no direct corroboration of that."

Alicia took a breath. "And let me guess, the red coral is directly, unequivocally, absolutely in the very middle of this bloody Triangle?"

"Well, the Japanese red coral, I'm now reading, should have been classified as an endangered species, but industry lobbyists got in the way, stating they'd rather manage the coral themselves. Japanese and Taiwanese fisherman have been collecting it for years, but since the '80s their harvests have reduced dramatically. Coral poachers have wiped out much of the red coral across the Pacific."

"But not in the Devil's Sea?" Dahl asked.

Dai didn't answer at first. "I don't know," he finally said. "I hope the place's reputation put them off. Better than that, I hope they came to poach and vanished forever. But nobody has officially mapped the Triangle. Not this century or last. If the coral's gone, we're absolutely fucked."

Dahl opened a bottle of water as the plane banked to the east. "Then we find someone," he said. "Dai, you mentioned Japanese and Taiwanese fishermen who've been harvesting coral for hundreds of years? Families like that—they will know the seas. They'll know the coral and where it's most likely to grow. And, seriously, they'll know the Triangle."

"I hope so," Dai said, echoing Alicia's own thoughts. "I'll check back as soon as I can when we've translated the second haiku, the one that legend says leads to a mythical fourth treasure."

Alicia found herself with both fists clenched, her head back, feeling about as useless as she could imagine. Here in Japan, an outsider's ID didn't work, a gun didn't work, word of mouth didn't work. You had to know the place inside out. You had to be accepted.

Sorry, Mai, I tried to keep him out of it.

But without Dai, they were dead in the water.

CHAPTER TWENTY ONE

Hours later, in the predawn of a new day, they were on a large fishing boat, heading out of Tokyo harbor toward the area known as the Devil's Sea. The air was cold. A drizzle fell from the slate gray clouds. Alicia, huddled in the boat's surprisingly large wheelhouse, stared out of the wide windows with the rest of her team. The horizon rolled steadily before her eyes, offering no distracting sights other than an alternating view of the sky and the sea.

To her right, Dahl drank coffee. Luther was sitting on his own at the back of the big cabin-like structure. Kenzie, Karin and Dino were positioned around the wheel.

They were guided by a man Dai had put them in touch with. The man, named Jun, had been promised a year's wages to take them to the only place he knew where the red coral still grew in the Devil's Sea. Through Dai, on the phone, he had translated that it lay in the very center of the Triangle, right where the majority of boats mysteriously vanished. Alicia hadn't been surprised.

With the mirror tucked safely away, they'd embarked on this next journey to find the jewel following age-old instructions, a haiku written on the back of the Sacred Treasure, engraved into a part of the first meteorite ever to strike the earth. Alicia just wished Drake, Mai and the others were with them.

"How long?" Alicia asked Karin. None of them spoke the fisherman's language and, since they couldn't bring Dai himself, they were reduced to apps or gestures. Karin pointed at her watch and eventually received an answer.

"One hour."

Alicia turned her back on the unappealing view and navigated over to Luther. "How's it going?"

The bald man looked down at her. "Mai and Drake? That's not the issue for me. It's their safety I worry about now. It's Molokai's, Hayden's, and Mano's safety. It's how they're standing up to the inevitable torture. It's Mai and Drake trying to infiltrate the toughest, deadliest body of warriors in the world."

"With inside information and help," Alicia reminded him. "That's the only way it becomes possible. And they have that."

"We hope."

"I know you want to help them, to save them," Alicia said. "It's your nature. I know they're on your mind even when you're in trouble because I feel the same. We need to keep faith in their abilities."

"Faith? That's not a word I ever thought to hear cross your lips."

"It's a word," Alicia said. "Don't get cute, Luther, it doesn't work for you."

"Mai would disagree."

Alicia threw him a wicked look. "I doubt Mai's disagreed to anything in the last twenty-four hours or so."

"Fuck you."

"Not today, mate." She looked around as the boat turned on a wave, altering its course. "I sure hope this guy knows where he's going."

Dahl stood in a corner of the wheelhouse alongside Kenzie. The only thing he wanted to think about was the mission, the friends that weren't with them and how they might find the jewel in the Devil's Sea, but Kenzie needed attention.

"I failed him."

It was the first time she'd spoken of Dallas since he'd been killed. Dahl put a hand on her shoulder. "That's not the real Kenzie speaking. That's a girl struggling with grief. It's not how you think, act, or make decisions. The Kenzie I know understands it wasn't her fault. None of us could have saved him. The Tsugarai are to blame."

"If I hadn't brought him into the team he wouldn't have died."

"Again, that sounds like a girl making excuses to stay locked in her grief. It's not true. Dallas made his own decision. He might have died elsewhere."

"He stayed with me . . . because he wanted more."

Dahl drew away. "I don't know about that but, Kenzie, you didn't kill him. You have to know that."

The Israeli leaned against the wall, arms folded. "I'm working on it."

Dahl squeezed her arm, trying not to get too close. He didn't want to send any signals that might be misinterpreted. His marriage might be over, but he still had the children to worry about; he wanted time to be single. They'd been thrown into this mission against their wills, forced by the Tsugarai and the unknown royal family that had decided to seek out the treasures. He hated the arrogance of that, the disregard for human life shown by someone he'd never even met, some distant king or queen who, with a click of their fingers, ordered the ruin of innocent lives.

And yet, in today's world, Dahl knew, it happened on a daily basis. He knew Dai had been checking into the royal bloodline angle and called him up now, asking questions.

"It's a difficult and deadly line of enquiry," Dai told him.

"If it were easy, everyone in the world would know. You've encountered these shadow families before, so you know better than most. They're supremely protected, hidden behind dozens of layers of deniability. I haven't even scratched that surface yet."

"To stop this, we will have to root out the source."

Dai let out a long breath. "Because it's you, I know you know the massive significance of what you're saying. Dynasties this powerful, this wealthy, have existed since before the shoguns came to power."

"They've never come up against us before," Dahl said. "Keep at it, mate."

"Of course."

Dahl was a man of action. Right now, he wanted to either chase, punch or hunt somebody down. Standing here in this cabin, sailing between one unknown horizon to the next, was making him antsy.

Then the fisherman started talking.

Alicia walked over to Karin. "What's he saying?"

"Are you kidding? You think I learned Japanese in the last half hour?"

"Maybe. You're supposed to be a genius."

"From his actions, I'd say he's nervous and unsure. From the few words I can make out, he's . . . lost."

"Oh, bollocks. Out here, that's not good."

Fifteen minutes ago, they'd entered the mysterious area known as the Devil's Sea. The waters had remained calm, the area deserted but also creepily tranquil. The waves didn't roll, the horizon never changed, and the ship plowed on as if to nowhere. A silence had descended over the boat along with an odd gray sky, laced with streaks of crimson.

Karin had no choice but to enlist the help of one of the captain's sons. The two of them were checking the diving gear below decks, but had to be brought up. Both were young and skinny, wearing open shirts and jeans. Both seemed confident in the room full of soldiers in the center of the Pacific Bermuda Triangle.

"What's he saying?" Alicia asked.

"He hasn't traveled this way for many years," the tallest son answered. "Give him a few moments." He spoke some calming Japanese words to his father. At least, Alicia hoped they were calming. The other son placed a hand on the man's left shoulder.

Jun, the captain, steadied himself.

"He is worrying about the stories, the legends also. He says that every time he has been here the sea has never behaved this way."

Alicia tried not to gulp as she turned her gaze to the window. From left to right and dead ahead it was glassy smooth, with the appearance of a hard concrete surface.

"He's never seen anything like it and neither have I," the son said. "And he was born on a floating village on the sea. I've been fishing all my life."

"The sky?" Dahl said. "What is that?"

They all looked up. The crimson was spreading, streaks becoming large swathes. Alicia caught the oldest son's attention.

"Does he know where he's going? Where the red coral is?"

A minute of conversation passed. Finally, the oldest son turned to Alicia. "Yes, but he does not want to go."

She knew it wasn't worth arguing, wasn't worth mentioning the money or offering more. This man had both sons aboard and an inherent feeling for the seas. He was also old enough to harbor an age-old fear of this place.

"Can you take over?" she asked. "We're out of options and, if we don't do this, so many people will die."

"I don't know. Let me see if I can help."

Alicia stood and watched, unable to influence the outcome, feeling alone there in the wheelhouse of the fishing boat. Leadership, she decided, wasn't all it was cracked up to be. If these fishermen decided to get the hell out of here, they would take any chance she and her team had of reuniting the Three Sacred Treasures and saving Hayden, Kinimaka and Molokai's life.

The son turned to her, his head down. "I'm sorry," he said. "We can't go on."

CHAPTER TWENTY TWO

Zuki spent the morning catching up.

She was aware that most of her household thought of her as a spoilt, privileged brat. The truth was, she didn't know how to be anything else and when her family died, promoting her to head of the household, these lesser qualities she possessed helped her gain and then retain control. As with any leader, her main goal was keeping her head of security close and employing a willing team of whisperers throughout her domain.

The Tsugarai had long since decided she was indeed the brat they'd always assumed and treated her that way. But, for now, she needed them.

"How far along are you with the prisoners?" she asked Kenshin, their leader, as she sipped tea and nibbled on fruits.

His reply was harsh, perhaps more severe because of the crackling phone line, perhaps not. "All three are soldiers. I don't expect you to understand what it takes to break a soldier."

"What it takes? Are they naked? Do they have electronics strapped to them? Do they have all their fingers and toes?"

"That is not how it is done."

She knew they hated her, that they disrespected her, and that they thought themselves untouchable. In truth, they probably were. She decided to play the brat they assumed her to be.

"I have soldiers in my household. When I get bored I send them down to the dungeons to die slowly. It takes less than a night to extract everything from them. I've never met a soldier I can't break."

"You haven't met Matt Drake or Mai Kitano, or the other members of their team. You haven't met Hayden Jaye or Mano Kinimaka. And . . . you haven't met me."

Zuki stretched out on a chaise longue, staring out the ceiling-to-floor window in her bedroom. Her body was covered by a sheer, silk kimono, her flesh luxuriously wrapped, but her toes were bare, blood-red nails pointing at the glass. "You think I couldn't break you, Kenshin?"

"You are a royal cherub," he said with disdain. "You know nothing of hardship, of being a soldier, and you know nothing of me."

"I care to wager that I could break you in a day, in more ways than one. Come face me, after you find the treasures. Come deliver them to me and we will dance, you and I, in more ways than one."

She enjoyed the baiting, the rising tensions, the underlying passion. Kenshin was right, she didn't know him, but she'd spent her entire life getting everything she wanted.

As expected, Kenshin ignored her. "The other team, led by Alicia Myles, has located one of the treasures. They are currently seeking the second, a perilous and enormous undertaking. If she succeeds, we will take both treasures from her."

"You're tracking this Alicia Myles?"

"Of course. By radar and by drone."

Something new occurred to Zuki. "Are you tracking me?"

Kenshin remained silent, trained to reveal nothing that he didn't have to. Zuki walked over to the window. "Can you see me now? What color is my kimono?" She was aware she was talking to one of the foremost killers in the world, with perhaps the most skilled team of cutthroats at his back. The thought excited her.

"Do you have any other questions?" Kenshin asked.

"Just one. Would you like me to take my kimono off?"

Kenshin hung up the phone. Zuki laughed, enjoying even that tiny show of power. She believed she enjoyed interacting with Kenshin because he hated her and refused to acknowledge her superiority. Curious, she did remain at the window for several minutes, studying the far and middle distance for any sign of a drone or prying eyes.

She saw nothing except her driveway, a snaking route through trees and high hedges, leading to a two-lane highway that descended into northern Tokyo. She could see the roofs of houses, even some windows. She could see distant huddles of buildings where the masses lived. The wide Sumida River that ran through the city.

Mostly though, her deep black eyes saw and reveled in her own kingdom. The gardens and fields below. The walls of her home. The staff toiling away. The east and west wings. The guards who called servants to carry out her every whim.

To her mind, the interrogation wasn't going well. This Hayden and her friends should be experiencing her wrath by now. Mai Kitano was still the key to all this, and nobody knew where she was. Zuki wondered if the Tsugarai were the right group of mercenaries for the job.

She wandered back to her seat and sprawled out, calling in a servant to pour more tea. When he'd backed out of the room, bowing, she returned her mind to the previous point. Her main issues were the other royal families. The two main bloodlines were researching, trying to track down the family of the person that had brought the Sacred Treasures to the Tsugarai in the first place. Zuki thought that a valid line of research, and it bothered her. The other problem was that even the upstarts were hunting now; the samurai clan in a noisy way, offering ridiculous rewards for information. To Zuki, it felt like the whole of Tokyo was searching for the Three Sacred Treasures.

But no, she was first. She had the lead.

What if the Tsugarai decide to betray you?

It was paranoia, she knew, but all good leaders suffered from a healthy dose of paranoia every single day. It was healthy because it kept you alive.

She couldn't align with anyone. The other royal bloodlines had always been enemies. They wouldn't support her. But this last few days, Zuki had been leaning on certain crime syndicates around the world, pressing all the right buttons to ensure competent backup wasn't far away.

China had special killing teams of its own. So did Israel and one country she considered an ally: India. Japanese mythology had always embraced Buddhist traditions. Originating in India, Buddhism spread through most of Asia, intertwining many of the two countries' traditions. An intertwining that was respected to this very day. Zuki had half expected the Sacred Treasures to be in India, but so far that belief was proving unfounded.

Zuki had arranged a deadly gang to come to her aid, over and above her own personal guards that numbered in their low hundreds. She felt protected, even from the samurai and the Tsugarai. But she needed to do more. Put the other bloodlines off balance, upset their concentration.

She called her man in the Yakuza, ordering a hit on several of her competitors' businesses.

"Casualties?" the man asked, questioning whether the attacks should be carried out in normal hours or at night.

"I don't care so long as my orders are carried out."

"They will be."

Three more phone calls made sure her rivals would be knocked off-kilter in the next few hours. Zuki stretched on the chaise-longue, contemplating a bath before returning to the affairs of head of state. A bath sounded good, so she summoned one of her slaves to run it medium hot and then to massage her shoulders after she slid into the warm, foamy water. Soon, she relaxed. If the Tsugarai did their job right she'd be the undisputed leader of Asia, a legend of her bloodline, and be given more power than even she'd held in her lifetime.

Soaking in the bath, she turned her mind to what she might do with all that power.

CHAPTER TWENTY THREE

Drake and Mai arrived in northern Tokyo just after mid-morning. Time was already against them. The female shinobi, Mariko, had insisted she would help them rescue Hayden only after her family were safe. They didn't waste even one minute leaving the compound and returning to Tokyo.

Again, Mai found herself asking for Grace's help. "We spoke to Mariko. She agreed to help after her family is safe."

"So the Tsugarai's answer to losing candidates through brutality and increasing lack of respect for the old ways is to threaten people's families? That, I can believe."

"I am sorry to ask, Grace, but in all the years you spent with Mariko, did she mention her family? Where they lived? Their name? We didn't have time to get it out of her."

"Yes, of course. She spoke about her family a lot." Grace went quiet, thinking. "Maybe she knew I would remember."

Drake watched Mai note down the family name and the place where they lived. Watching the Japanese woman, he saw the toil it put on her to enlist the help of the girl she'd saved from a Tsugarai conspiracy. Mai would take it personally, much harder than Grace ever would. Mai ended the call with a quiet, heartfelt word of thanks.

When she looked up, Drake felt a surge of emotion. The pure sadness in her expression moved him. Without thought, he moved in to hug her. Mai wrapped her arms around him and held tight.

"She's a great kid," he said. "And she'll be fine."

"I would die if anything happened to her."

"It won't. She's safe. And so are Chika and Dai. The only people we have to worry about are those back at the compound."

She held on for a few more seconds before pushing him away. When Drake looked at her again, he saw the old Mai. The strong woman he'd once fallen for. Being alone like this made him want to ask a boatload of questions.

They found a taxi to take them to the right area. When they'd both settled in the back seat Mai turned to him once more.

"It's not just Grace," she said. "It's the Tsugarai. They won't leave me alone. Matt, they *bought* me. From my parents. Sometimes . . . I just feel like . . . they still own me."

Drake had heard these thoughts before and understood. A traumatic, horrendous experience was best left behind. The more you put it in your rearview, the less it affected you. For Mai, the Tsugarai kept on coming. He was worried it might affect her mental health.

"You know me," he said. "A plain speaking, open, candid Yorkshireman. I know it's not what you want to hear—but we're in it now. To the end. It only stops when we get Hayden and the others back."

"The Tsugarai—"

"We will end them," Drake said. "This time we will end them."

Mai's eyes were open and unguarded. Drake saw a wetness there. He leaned in. "Your parents had no choice. But Mai, you escaped, and you saved them. You saved Grace and killed your tormentor. Remember that. This is just one more step on the journey to never having to worry about them again."

Mai leaned in too and, for one moment, full of feeling, hope and gratitude for each other, their lips brushed. It was the spark of surprise that made Drake draw away and Mai smile.

"Alicia is a lucky woman."

"Luther too. Well, not quite . . ."

Mai cleared her throat. "It's okay, I know. Luther is a good man."

Drake reached out and took her hand in his own. "We will finish this, Mai."

The taxi dropped them off outside a two-story dwelling in the middle of a busy street. Drake paid the driver and stepped out. The car drove off, leaving them amid a sea of humanity, pedestrians walking in all directions. Drake could barely hear Mai but understood from her gestures that they should cross the busy street.

They found a crossing and walked up to the house. Mai knocked. They waited, shoulder to shoulder until one of Mariko's parents answered. After Mai talked them inside, she and Drake got down to the business of sharing the painful reality of the life their daughter was leading, and enlisting their help to pull her free of her captors.

They were long hours. Drake helped to the best of his ability, but it was Mai that got through to them, recounting stories from her own experience and stressing how much Mariko valued their safety and wanted out. They perched on the edge of an old sofa and drank water or tea, watching with sadness as Mariko's parents grew to understand the plight both they and their daughter were in.

"Can you guarantee the safety of our daughter?" Mariko's father asked.

Mai bit her lip. "I cannot. It may be that she is already in too deep and, in the end, does not want to leave. But a showdown is coming with the Tsugarai. I can't in all honesty say who will survive."

She looked over at Drake with a somewhat fatalistic expression. It hurt him more than he cared to admit.

The Tsugarai cut her deep, leaving a wound that might never heal. So deep, she still believes they might be instrumental in her death.

"My parents are safe now." Mai said. "We can take you to safety. Then, we will bring Mariko to you. But you have to come with us now."

Drake watched the old couple struggle with the suddenness of it all. Nobody wanted to be uprooted with a moment's notice, but any parent would move mountains to help their child.

"How do we know you're telling us the truth?" the father asked.

Drake took that one. "We have no other reason to be here," he said, "telling you all this. Truth be told, we're gonna try to keep you safe. I don't think you guys are compromised but I'm guessing 90 percent of Tokyo's bad guys are looking for us."

Mai waved it off. "Normal day," she said. "Are you ready?"

They weren't, but they came. Drake moved to help them at first, before seeing they were fully able and preferred to stay together. They took ten minutes to pack a few things and then walked toward the front door.

"Check the street," Mai told Drake. "I don't want to take any chances."

"Clear," he said after a moment. "Let's go."

CHAPTER TWENTY FOUR

Alicia paced the wheelroom in frustration. The old boat caption, Jun, refused to continue. The sea was a mirror, flat and eerie, and the skies were the color of fresh-spilled blood.

Kenzie walked in front of her. "There's a reason this place is called Devil's Sea," she said. "We just chose to ignore it."

"Doesn't matter," Alicia said. "We need the jewel. It's the second Sacred Treasure. Without it, we have no bargaining chips."

"Well, we have one. The mirror."

Alicia clenched her fists. "We *need* that jewel. If you can't be productive, shut the hell up."

"Hey." Kenzie prodded her shoulder. "I have as much invested in this as you do. Remember Dallas? Those Tsugarai bastards murdered him in the street. If anyone should be angry here, it's me."

Alicia caught Kenzie's wrist and gripped it tight. Eye to eye, the two women seethed. Dahl came up behind Kenzie, laid a hand on her shoulder, and pulled her aside. Alicia closed her eyes.

To a point, Kenzie was right. But Alicia was still in charge here and she wouldn't let Hayden or Drake down.

The boat continued to drift, heading nowhere as its captain looked at her for guidance. Karin was pecking at a laptop, watched by Dino. Luther looked like he wanted to grab the captain and force him to act. Alicia buried the urge to tell the big man to do just that.

"Try again," she told the man's oldest son. "We can't be far from the red coral. We're hours out of Tokyo."

To his credit, the boy tried but the old man's face was blank. He kept gesticulating at the unnatural seas and sky. Alicia opened the door to the wheelhouse and sniffed at the air. There was no breeze at all.

Luther came to her side. "I'll force him to take us," he whispered.

"It's not right. It's—"

There was a sudden shout from Dino. Alicia looked over and then glanced to where he was pointing to the rear. Her eyes widened.

"Oh, shit. That's not good."

She hadn't known what to expect. Hadn't known what manner of creepiness her eyes would find following them. But it was a bank of swirling black cloud so wide it took up their whole rear horizon.

"Is that a storm?" she asked.

Jun squawked at his sons, waving them to various controls. The storm bank was coming in fast, eddying and churning. Alicia saw streaks of lightning inside it, silver flashes that marched along the skyline.

The oldest son caught her attention. "It's a boat wrecker," he said.

Alicia breathed out. Where could they go? Apparently, the Devil's Sea area was dotted with several islands. Maybe they could take shelter there.

Karin spoke up. "I think I can find it," she said. "The red coral."

Alicia fixed on her. "What?"

"It's endangered, right? Everything classed as endangered is tracked. There'll be a radio beacon or something sending a signal to a satellite. If I can hack into the website, I can find it."

"Best do it quick," Alicia said. "That storm's getting closer and it'll probably take our signal booster out."

"Booster?" Dahl said. "It'll take the bloody boat out."

Already the vessel was underway, motoring across the glassy surface, the sea's stillness even more unnerving with the maelstrom at their backs. The boat picked up speed. Alicia eyed the clouds as they came closer.

"We're not fast enough."

Karin slapped the laptop. "Got it. The beacon's flashing in an easterly direction—" she waved a flat hand "—quite close to an island called Miyake Jima. Just off the coast actually."

Alicia stomped up to Jun and pointed, barked an order in his face. The captain was already scared, but now looked terrified.

"Tell him," she told his eldest, "that if he doesn't take us, we will tie him up and lock him downstairs. We know where the red coral is now."

After relaying the information, the eldest son stepped away. Alicia had her hand on her gun, watching him in case he went for a concealed weapon, but he just laid his hands on a wooden rail. Jun gripped the bridge of his nose, glanced at the approaching storm and then in an easterly direction.

He spoke rapidly.

"Okay, okay," the son translated, "we can go that way as there is no better way. We die if we go back, we die if we go on. So . . . we die."

Alicia felt the first swelling waves rock the boat. It was going to be a stomach-churning ride.

"How long to this Miyake Island?" she asked.

"Thirty minutes," Karin said. "Give or take."

Alicia found something to hold on to. The waves came.

The laptop slid away. Dino leapt to catch it but fell sideways and knocked his head against a chair leg. Dahl grabbed a rail with one hand and Kenzie with the other, keeping her stable since she still had the faraway look in her eyes.

A howling wind swept past them, gusting through gaps in the wooden structure and cracks in the windows. The skies darkened, heavy rain started to fall. Alicia was reminded of the Bermuda Triangle off the coast of Florida and all the legendary stories associated with it. Ships and boats used to go missing all the time.

Karin had told them that, like several other places around the world, the Devil's Sea or Dragon's Triangle as it was also known, was hard to explain logically. From the thirteenth century there had been reports of lost ships and, even back then, over 40,000 crew members missing. In the nineteenth century came reports of a mysterious lady sailing a vessel in the Triangle. Research vessels were later lost and ghost ships had been found drifting with no sign of their crew.

Who could explain that?

Alicia held on as the storm worsened. The boat rocked from side to side, hit by swells. She checked her watch. Only fifteen minutes to the island and the coral they needed. She took her mind off the present, still examining details about the Devil's Sea in her head. The Japanese term originated from an archaic Chinese fable about dragons existing beneath the sea.

Before her, the horizon rolled. Lightning flashed, illuminating black seas. It wasn't late in the day, but Alicia saw only darkness brought by the storm. Jun wrestled the boat through it, trying to maintain a course, helped by his sons. Alicia watched all three.

"There," Karin said. "An island."

"Is that Miyake?" Alicia shouted.

Jun nodded without looking at her. Alicia studied it as it came closer, a small, barren looking rock protruding up out of the Pacific. Just then a heavy gust of wind battered the boat, sending her staggering. Luther grabbed her, saving her from falling into an open toolbox overflowing with rusty wrenches, hammers and screwdrivers.

She nodded her thanks, then whipped her head around to Karin. "Where's the coral?"

"That cove," she said. "Head for that. The coral is just near the reef."

"Can we sail into the cove?" Alicia asked nobody in particular.

The tallest son turned around. "Yes. Our keel is not too big. We can do that."

Then the oddest thing happened. Alicia noticed their surroundings lighten. The clouds broke, allowing daylight to flood through once more, and the seas stopped heaving. There was no more wind. Everyone aboard the boat turned to stare at each other.

"What the hell happened?" Alicia asked.

The oldest son translated his father's words. "It was a dragon coming for us. It passed by."

Alicia shivered. When she checked she saw that the track of the storm had indeed moved away to the east. They'd only been caught by the tail end. Now, as they approached the island, they took a collective breath.

"We're here," Karin said

"Over the coral?" Dahl asked.

Jun stopped the boat's engine as if to agree. One of his sons moved away to brew tea. Another reached into a cupboard for something stronger.

"Fisherman's courage." He grinned when he saw Alicia watching him. "Want some?"

"I don't drink and dive," Alicia said with the slightest of smiles.

Karin set about pinpointing the exact position of the coral as Alicia, Dahl, Dino and Luther found their wetsuits and changed into them, then pulled on their full face masks with comms. A soft breeze caressed the decks now and a strong mid-morning sun beat down. This Dragon's Triangle deserved its legendary status, she decided, even if it was all down to the kind of unpredictability they'd just witnessed.

"We ready?" she asked Karin.

"In three minutes we should be right over the coral. Then it's a matter of searching."

"Speed is important," Alicia reminded them. "No tossing it off down there."

The men shook their heads. They were ready.

CHAPTER TWENTY FIVE

"Whilst we wait," Karin said. "Remember the haiku that brought us here: The Noted Magatama. In Ryugu-jo. The red coral beneath the Devil's Sea."

"Got it," Dahl said. "This is Ryugo-jo. The magatama is the jewel. No worries."

"We don't know what's down there," Alicia said. "But I seriously doubt the elders just threw the jewel overboard. Remember the mirror? Ryugo-jo is the undersea. Check everything."

Five minutes later they were slipping overboard. Alicia didn't enjoy diving and kept her excursions below water to a minimum. But this was one dive she couldn't escape from. There was so much resting on the outcome.

They swam down, reaching the seabed in a matter of minutes as it inclined toward the island's shore here. They had strong flashlights and nets, filter systems and tech to navigate the seabed. Karin fed them information through their comms system, telling each person where they were and which direction they had to go.

Alicia came down just behind the reef, enjoying its beautiful colors before reaching the bottom. A shoal of fish swept past her, disappearing into the darkness. Pools of mud mushroomed up from where she swept her hands through sand and silt. The flashlight illuminated large patches in front and below her. She kept her head down, swimming in a straight line, occasionally pausing to search through the sand. Rocks protruded from the seabed, some so large they blocked her way. Every time she stopped to examine them but, so far, had found nothing of importance.

Twice, Dahl reported possible findings. Both times he came up empty. Luther and Dino were searching in other directions, their progress slow but thorough.

Alicia came across the red coral fifteen minutes later, growing on a large boulder, covering its surface. It was a good marker, shining bright in the torchlight, waving gently in the passing current.

"Coral located," she reported.

Karin gave her a few words of encouragement. Alicia didn't need them. She figured the coral was here before the jewel, so mentioning it in the haiku meant it was a pretty solid marker. She slowed now, taking her time swimming around the boulder, which was a good twenty square meters in circumference. It was covered in a green moss too with the silvery flashes of darting fish flying by every second. She kicked at the seabed. She knelt to search around the boulder's underside. She scraped at the moss, taking care not to harm the endangered red coral.

And then she thought: *It's not here.*

Because of course, it wouldn't be. It would be close, but not this close to the coral. She spoke to Karin and together they plotted an area that surrounded the coral. Soon, all four of them were swimming around the location.

Forty minutes later, Dino spoke up. "I think I've found something."

Alicia swam over as quickly as she could, hoping nobody saw her attempts at a fast swim. It wasn't a pretty sight. Eventually she found Dino, Luther and Dahl.

"Took your time," Dahl said.

"Missed the bus," she fired back and then nodded at Dino. "Show me."

The Italian-American had found a gap under the reef

opposite the red-coral-covered boulder. It was a small arch, big enough to admit one man crawling. When Alicia pulled herself down she saw a stony structure on the other side.

When she focused her gaze more clearly she gasped. "Is that a . . . ?"

"A dragon, yes," Dino said. "They built a dragon down here."

"More likely it's an old structure that was submerged long ago," Dahl said. "The person who hid the jewel was aware and thought this a perfect place for it."

"So there are dragons beneath this sea," Alicia breathed. "Just as the old legends say."

"All of this is really interesting," Karin said over the comms. "This place, Ryugu-jo, literally translates as 'Dragon Palace Castle.' It is the undersea palace of Ryujin, the dragon kami of the sea and listen to this . . . a direct quote: 'Ryujin's palace is built from red and white coral.' I think you're in the right place."

Alicia shone her flashlight through the gap in the reef. "Who's going first?"

"The smallest." Dahl looked at her.

She turned her head to Dino. "After you then."

As Dino set off, Luther gestured at her. "*Is* he the smallest?"

"Oh, sorry, I thought Torsty said youngest."

Dino's flippers disappeared through the hole. Alicia went next, making sure her suit didn't snag on the coral or get scraped by the rocks. They swam almost along the sea bottom, sometimes placing their hands on the bedrock to pull themselves along. Soon, they came to the stony structure that resembled a dragon.

It was constructed of stone blocks, some small, some large, and some quite intricate. The neck was short, the body bulging. There was no tail, but a ragged rocky stump attested to where it had snapped off years ago. The head was intact down to the eye sockets and sharp looking teeth the size and shape of big stalactites.

Dirty sand and silt drifted around it, making it a murky vision. Alicia saw a silver eel emerge from one of the eye sockets and dart away. A shadow passed over her head and she looked up to see some kind of shark gliding above her.

"Of all the fucking things," she complained. "I've never been fond of animals."

Dahl was also looking up. "Don't worry. I don't think it wants you to take it home."

Alicia ignored the Swede and the shark, and turned her attention to the stone dragon. "What do we think?"

"It's a palace," Karin said. "There should be a way in."

Dino was already swimming under the broken tail, circumventing the overlarge stomach. Alicia and Luther swam in close to their side, studying the fine joints.

"It's very well put together," Dahl said. "No wonder it's survived intact for so long."

Alicia swept her flashlight around, now seeing an undersea stack that rose up to the left of the dragon, close to the head. It resembled a mini-mountain and it too was covered in red coral. She was about to swim over there when Dino called out.

"This could be a door."

They all swam to his side. Alicia saw nothing at first, but when she shone her light closer to the dragon, she saw that, instead of staggered seams around the stonework, there were two perpendicular lines. Above them sat what could only be a lintel, helping to carry the weight above.

"No handle," Dahl said.

"It would be a bit obvious," Dino said. "I only noticed it

because I was checking every single seam."

Alicia was impressed. "I was keeping an eye on the shark to be fair."

Dino planted his feet on the seabed and pushed individual stones. Nothing worked. He dropped to his knees and felt along the lower seams, pushing, heaving and trying to dig his fingers in. Luther tried the same along the lintel's lines.

Still nothing.

Alicia fought down a wave of frustration. "Karin, any ideas?"

"Still reading," came the answer. "This Ryujin character is the dragon itself. He symbolizes the power of the ocean. He lives in his palace under the sea where he controls the tides through the use of *magical jewels*. This *has* to be the place."

"Agreed," Alicia said and looked up at the structure. "Maybe he's not home."

"Interestingly," Karin said, "Ryujin is said to be one of the ancestors of Japanese imperial dynasty. This whole thing is about old dynasties and bloodlines, isn't it?"

"Yeah," Alicia said. "Anything else?"

Karin said, "Do you see any carvings?"

Alicia saw Dino and Luther look around. The younger man said, "Yeah, a few along the bottom."

"It says sea turtles, fish and jellyfish were servants of Ryujin. And that he created the jellyfish by crushing all its bones in a fit of rage."

"Whoa, I saw that image," Dino said, adjusting his position. "Here."

He planted his feet, took up a solid position and pushed at the stone displaying the carving of a jellyfish. Dahl swam down and helped. As they pushed, the stone moved inward and then the entire door area collapsed. Alicia saw a person-size hole appear in the side of the dragon.

She swam down, taking point. She passed through the frame and found herself inside a tunnel that angled only one way.

Down.

Slowly, Alicia swam down the vertical shaft, surrounded by blackness. The only light now came from the small flashlight strapped to her forehead. They swam in silence, wondering what might be waiting for them under the belly of the dragon.

Alicia was relieved when the tunnel ended and she swam into a larger space. Using the flashlight again she determined that there was only one onward path.

A tunnel to her right led away from the dragon, under the stack she'd noticed earlier. This tunnel angled upward quite sharply. Alicia allowed the water to carry her, pulling at the sides of the tunnel to gain momentum.

By the time they broke surface inside a large, pitch-black chamber none of them were surprised. Alicia trod water and swept her flashlight from left to right. The others did the same, strobing the undersea cavern.

A set of rock steps led up out of the water to a slick platform above their heads.

Alicia climbed onto the first step and drew her gun.

CHAPTER TWENTY SIX

They climbed up the stone steps and sat down to rest. Water ran off their slick suits, pooling on the floor. Alicia removed her flippers and then her mask, pronouncing that the air was good. Together, they ate a few energy bars.

As expected, their comms system was useless.

Dahl rose first to explore the cave. "Nothing out of the ordinary," he said. "The steps lead to a high outcrop where——" he climbed higher, straining up to see "—we have another tunnel. I suggest we get started."

Alicia followed the Swede, taking care to step warily on the slick rock with her bare feet. Soon, they were ascending a narrow passage, the steps worn by time and moisture. Dino fell first and then Luther, both managing to catch themselves before doing any damage. Alicia followed Dahl up through the ill-lit darkness.

"It's an undersea cavern formed inside the rising rock mount," Dahl said. "I can only assume it was found by accident, but a perfect place to conceal the jewel. Nobody would ever find it without the start point only Gyuki could give."

"Or each successive leader of the Tsugarai," Alicia amended. "Which, in a different world, would have been Mai."

"Yes." Dahl nodded. "That's a very odd thought."

"Oh, I'm full of 'em."

At the top of the winding stairs they came to another cavern. Dahl stopped, crouching with his gun in hand. Alicia drew her own weapon, not knowing what to expect, and sidled around the big Swede.

Before them, littering the floor, looking stark white and crumbling in the torchlight, lay piles of old bones.

"That's not good," Dino said as he emerged.

Alicia saw skulls and empty eye sockets staring forever in a single direction. All sorts of other bones too, and tattered clothing. Dahl scanned the area.

"It seems clear," he said. "But stay frosty."

Alicia counted the piles but stopped when she got to a dozen. There were too many. "What is this?" she said. "And, more importantly, what did it?"

"Ancient mariners," Luther said. "They found the jewel, or almost did. They got this far and . . ."

"Just dropped dead," Alicia finished. "Yeah, right."

"They seem very old." Dahl was on his knees, peering at the skeletons. "Maybe whatever did this is long gone."

He picked up an old, dull sword, studying the handle. Alicia tapped his shoulder. "C'mon, Torsty. This isn't the time to find something for Kenzie's birthday. It's onward and upward, it seems."

"Maybe they did it to each other," Dahl said speculatively as he rose. "Old pirates and cutthroats and all that."

Alicia thought it most likely. It took another ten minutes of walking before they came to a third large chamber. Inside this one a flat plateau of rock led away from them. It curved at its far end. They shone their flashlights into the blackness at the edge of the plateau but could not penetrate its inkiness.

Dahl walked forward. "It's an outcrop," he said, going to his knees. "Most likely over an enormous drop."

Alicia joined him. "There has to be something else."

"There is," Luther said. "Look."

Alicia watched him aim his flashlight on full beam into the darkness. The edge of the light picked out something.

148

Together, the four of them concentrated their beams until they could make out a far rock plateau similar to this one.

And on it, an altar.

"How big's the gap?" Dino asked.

"Too big," Dahl said. "But look at that."

Angling his flashlight up and to the right, Alicia saw an incredible sight. The skeleton of a huge dragon had been sculpted into the cavern's right-hand wall, the carving stretching clear across the gap. The ribcage stood out in sharp relief, the knotted bones connected, as did the tail and the sloping neck. The head itself angled down toward the far plateau, a bridge connecting the carving to the rock outcrop.

"Bollocks," Alicia said.

Dahl shrugged his pack off, letting it fall to the ground. "No point all of us trying it," he said. "This is my kind of terrain."

Luther stopped him. "Wait, I'll go."

"You done much climbing or parkour? Any buildering?"

"I have no clue what two of those things are."

Dahl walked over to the right wall without speaking again. Reaching up, he took firm hold of the dragon's tail and hefted himself up. The jutting bones appeared to be about six inches thick, offering good handholds and small ledges for the feet. But still, the penalty for one mistake was steep.

Very steep.

Alicia glanced into the abyss below, seeing nothing but murky darkness. Maybe the ocean swirled down there, maybe it was solid rock at the bottom. She said nothing, clenching her fists and holding her breath as Dahl made his way up the dragon's tail.

Where the tail joined the body, the deadly fissure

started. Dahl gripped the spine of the beast, resting his boots on the lower ribs and, facing the rock, inched his way across. Tension fell across the group, filled the cavern. Alicia was sweating, Luther mouthing silent assurances.

At the halfway point, Dahl slipped.

CHAPTER TWENTY SEVEN

Dahl's left foot slid off a smooth rib, the momentum sending his whole body swinging to the left. Alicia saw his fingers grip hard, heard a whoosh of air, and then Dahl was scrabbling for purchase. His right foot slipped left and right along a six-inch ledge. His fingers held onto smooth rock, struggling for purchase—a knot of stone, a groove in the cliff face. His left leg was still in space.

His entire body was dipping to the left.

Luther ran without thought, without losing a second. He hit the rock face hard, grabbing hold of the tail bone and hefting himself up. His feet found purchase and his fingers grabbed the spine, allowing him to sidestep at a quick pace.

Dahl fought to keep hold of the ledge with his right hand, but it was super-slick and offered no firm handhold.

Luther reached him in seconds and grabbed his flailing right hand. Gripping tightly, he hauled Dahl back to the cliff face. He held him steady until the Swede managed to swing his left leg back in. Alicia let go of the intense breath she'd been holding the entire time.

Both men were now clinging to the wall.

Dahl made a move, placing each foot more carefully and searching for grooves in the rock. Luther followed his every step. Dino was poised near the tail, ready to leap up and help if he was needed. Within a few minutes though, both Luther and Dahl reached the far plateau without any extra incident.

Alicia saw them exchange a few words. Dahl rubbed his ankle and clenched his fingers. Luther made a move toward the altar which she could barely see.

"What is it?" she yelled, waving her flashlight about.

"A comma!" Dahl yelled back and held it up for her to see.

As Luther and Dahl focused their lights, Alicia and Dino saw Yasakani no Magatama, the Sacred Jewel of Japan. It was entirely underwhelming; a dull jade color and shaped as Dahl said, like a comma.

"I don't see anything sparkling!" Alicia shouted over.

Dahl muttered something that Alicia couldn't hear. Probably just as well. She could see the altar a little more clearly now, as Dahl and Luther shone their lights on it. The sides were decorated with carvings of dragons, and more significantly she saw a mirror engraving that resembled the first Sacred Treasure. She also saw the depiction of a sword.

"Does the jewel have two haikus on the back?" Dino shouted.

Good question, Alicia thought. That would be the clincher.

Dahl nodded before answering. "It does."

The Swede pocketed the jewel before Luther and he made their way back, taking great care. This time Luther's foot slipped off the smooth rock but he managed to catch himself. When they were across, Dahl took out the jewel.

"Two out of three," he said. "How about we get the fuck outta here?"

The return journey was painstakingly slow. Nobody wanted to get injured on the way back. Alicia concentrated harder than she'd ever concentrated before. The burden of leadership forced her. How the hell did Hayden and Drake manage it so easily? She felt responsible not only for herself, but for everyone else and for the decisions *they* made. Was that her duty? To second guess them? To offer a better alternative?

What would Drake do?

Well, to start with, he'd get them all back to the boat in one piece. She checked regularly, but everyone was soon swimming along the bottom of the ocean once more, away from the dragon structure and the red coral.

The ascended through murky waters, trying their comms once more as they neared the boat.

"We're out," Alicia said. "Karin, you up there?"

"All good."

Alicia breathed a sigh of relief. It might be a cliché, but she'd been half wondering if something might have happened up top. Soon, they breached the surface and climbed into the boat. The sun was high, shining down on them at last. Alicia angled her face up and closed her eyes.

"That's nice."

"It's getting on," Dahl said. "Let's head back to Tokyo and figure out our next move."

"My thoughts exactly," Alicia said and followed the Swede below decks. Soon, they were all gathered around as the captain started to make way. Dahl placed the jewel at the center of a table.

They leaned forward. Alicia saw a dull green rock, probably the same as a million others around the world. The difference was, this one had two haikus on the back.

Karin set about translating them, again with Dai's help.

Alicia looked up as the captain's eldest son entered the cabin. "Everything okay?" she asked.

"We don't think so. We are being followed."

Alicia was acutely aware they were still in the Devil's Sea. "By what?"

"By a flying eye. And there is a blip on the radar, mostly out of sight, but keeping track of us."

Alicia, Dahl and Luther headed above decks and studied

the sky. Far to the right and a few hundred feet in the air they saw a familiar silver shape.

"A fucking drone?" Dahl said.

"Tracking us all along," Luther suggested. "Probably by boat on radar. The Tsugarai want the treasures as much as we do, and they must know we already have the mirror."

"Keep tracking the boat," Alicia told Jun's son. "Let us know if it comes any closer. How far to Tokyo?"

"Couple of hours," the son said.

"Put your foot down," Alicia said. "Or whatever you do on a boat."

The big vessel picked up speed as soon as the son disappeared. Alicia spent a few more minutes studying the drone. "Do you think we can shoot it out of the air?"

"Unlikely at this distance," Dahl said, "but I'm very happy to give it a try."

"I'll do it." Luther said. "Used to be a marksman way back when. You two concentrate on that haiku."

Alicia nodded and left him to it. Together, she and Dahl made their way below decks and back to the cabin.

"Any luck?" she asked Karin.

"Yeah, the translator's got this pretty much nailed down by now. As you know, there are *two* haikus written on the back of the treasures. One leads to the next location, just like the mirror led to the jewel, but the second haiku appears to be different. The second haiku is much harder to translate, written in an older language, and appears to be one big haiku broken down into three parts."

"You hadn't managed to translate the first part before we got to the Devil's Sea," Alicia reminded him.

"I know. Well, now we have both. The part from the mirror and the part from the jewel, which, legend says, is supposed to lead you the mythical fourth treasure, whatever that may be. Okay, here goes:

"Through stars I fell,
"The Chalice in the Shield,
"The Treasure of Orion.
"Old rock stabilizes Planet,
"Old Rhythms maintained,
"For Healing, For Wishing, For Purification,
"We Saturate Space."

Alicia stared open-mouthed at the phone. "What the hell does all that bollocks mean, Dai?"

"I told you—"

"Yeah, but—" Alicia shook her head. "I think we should shelve the great mystical treasure for now and concentrate on the third sacred one. Agreed?"

Dai coughed. "Of course. Well, as you know the third Sacred Treasure of Japan is the sword. To find it we have to decipher this new haiku:

"The Heavenly Sword of the Gathering Clouds,
"In Takamagahara,
"The Shrine of Kami-ari-zuki."

Again, Alicia made a face. "That's not helping."

Dahl laid a hand on her shoulder as Karin smiled. "I think it is," she said. "But I'll let Dai continue."

"Thank you. Well, the first line simply points to the great sword—Kusanagi. It is the legendary sword that has killed monsters and treacherous warlords through the centuries. Much later, it was remade by the greatest swordmaker the world has ever known—Masamune, so that the meteorite surround could be incorporated. The second line translates as the Land of the Gods, which is where we will find the sword. The third line is a little odd."

Alicia cocked her head. "Odd?"

"Yes. The closest relation we can find is the phrase *Kan-na-zuki,* which in the Japanese calendar is the tenth lunar

155

month. It means the Month of No Gods. It's just struck us now as odd, that the Japanese calendar would have a Month of No Gods, since there are roughly eight million of them."

"Right," Alicia said, "We'll keep heading back to Tokyo whilst you chew on that. Karin, any suggestions?"

"No, but I can research too." She turned back to her laptop, already pecking at the buttons.

"How long to Tokyo?" Alicia asked the room.

"Less than an hour," Dino said.

"Let's see how Luther's getting on with that drone."

As they climbed above decks there came the sound of gunfire. Then, Jun and his sons yelled in shock and fear. Luther ordered them to take cover.

Alicia drew her guns.

CHAPTER TWENTY EIGHT

Up on deck, it was sunblasted, hot and heaving. The waves were becoming more pronounced, the wind blowing harder. Alicia gripped a rail and stared port side. A vessel very much like their own was closing in. It was a dark gray color, with two cabins and a raised bow. Men leaned over the rails, aiming their weapons.

Alicia guessed it was about thirty meters away.

Shots blasted high and wide. The seas were unpredictable, the wind volatile. She used field glasses to check faces and clothing, recognizing the garb of the Tsugarai.

"Shit, they found us."

"I doubt they ever lost us," Luther said. "We found two of their treasures. We did all the work. Now, they want them."

It certainly seemed that way. Alicia wished she'd heard something from Drake and Mai. She wished she knew how Hayden and the other captives were doing. "It's useless taking potshots," she said. "Conserve your ammo. We may need it. Stay low."

She could see the faint outline of Tokyo Bay ahead, probably forty minutes distant. The other boat was closing on an intercept course. She sought out the best places to hide and take aim and put Dino, Luther and Dahl there.

She headed to the wheelhouse to speak to Jun.

"When we get to the dock just put it anywhere," she said. "I suggest you vacate pretty quickly too, or they might ask you questions. Get your sons and lie low for a couple of days."

Jun nodded as his eldest translated. Alicia left them to it. The Tsugarai's vessel was much closer already, the bullets pinging off the boat rather than flying into space.

Alicia touched her comms. "Be ready. They're coming."

The gap between the boats narrowed. Soon, their enemies had to take cover as Dahl, Luther and Dino opened fire. One man wasn't fast enough, taking a slug to the back and sprawling across the main deck. Nobody rushed to help him.

Alicia watched him bleed out. She was crouched behind a low storage unit, where a fisherman might store supplies. She raised her head enough to get a feel for the scene.

The other boat came alongside. It didn't drive or maneuver; it hit hard, striking their own boat with its bow. Both boats shuddered. Rails cracked. The boats scraped together, metal and wood rending. Alicia fell sideways, striking her head on a hard surface. She saw stars. She pushed herself up, expecting to see men jumping from one craft to the next.

It wasn't happening. The other boat's crew were also on their backs, thrown off their feet by the hard contact. The boats continued to scrape together until Jun turned the wheel hard.

Alicia fired three shots, pinning two of her enemies down. Bullets were fired back but went high and wide. A heavy swell hit their boat, knocking her the other way. She put out a hand to steady herself, lost a gun and scrambled to retrieve it.

The swell sent them hurtling back into the other boat. They struck it amidships with the sound of tortured metal. More railings snapped. A huge dent was made in the structures of both boats. For a second, the Tsugarai craft leaned above their own, then smashed back down into the seas as it rode another wave.

Straight back into them. Alicia could barely hold on. Dino rolled toward the edge of the ship and a place where the railings were intact. He caught himself and Dahl rushed out to help him back into hiding.

Alicia managed to fire several shots as the boats collided once more. She saw a Tsugarai figure clutch his chest and fall, slipping down the boat and into the heaving waters. Jun somehow caught hold of the wheel again and steered them away from the other vessel, still on course for Tokyo. A strong wind howled through the cracked windows and across the boat's bows. The Tsugarai's boat wallowed for a moment, its bow nosediving. Waves washed across the decks, scooping up two men and sweeping them overboard.

"Put your bloody foot down!" Dahl yelled at Jun.

The fisherman nodded frantically, face drawn with stress. They opened up a gap of perhaps ten meters, but the other boat was faster. It was going to catch them long before they reached harbor.

Dahl ran to Alicia's side. "Thoughts?"

"I was thinking we throw Kenzie at it. Might sink the bloody thing."

"We're carrying nothing powerful enough to sink a boat."

"Yeah, I know that, Torsty. It's up to Jun to pilot as best he can—zigzag in front of it—and us to keep them pinned down. Move to the rear."

Dahl, staying low, crawled to the back of the ship.

Luther dropped beside Alicia. "Heard anything from Drake and Mai?"

"Not a thing. Don't worry, could mean anything."

"That's what I'm worried about. I'd prefer to know they're okay."

"Shut up, you pussy. Go help Dahl."

As Luther moved off, Alicia hid her eyes. She was feeling

the same, worrying for both of them. Unlike Hayden, Kinimaka and Molokai, they both had an easy means of communication. Still, it hadn't been too long since they parted. Maybe they hadn't even found Mariko yet.

As their boat bounced over the waves, assaulted by a crosswind and endless spray, the Tsugarai craft inched closer. Men wearing cloaks, their hoods drawn back, were already lying at the bow, taking aim. Others were perched in advantageous positions. Alicia reckoned they had about five minutes before the boats closed together again.

She checked Tokyo Harbor. It looked much larger on the horizon now, the bridge that spanned it looming closer and the sweeping docks taking shape. But they were still twenty minutes out.

"Call the cops," she told Karin. "Tell them we're coming in hot. See if they can get choppers out here."

"If they detain us, we're done. We can't afford that kind of delay."

"I know. I'll think of something. Wait," she said, unsure of herself. "Ignore me. We can do this."

She took a deep breath, hoping she'd made the right choice. If not, this mission, their friends and their lives were forfeit.

CHAPTER TWENTY NINE

Drake and Mai left Mariko's parents' house, walking swiftly across the road toward their car. This was a run-down neighborhood, thick with pedestrians and cars. Drake knew the Tsugarai would have every criminal, from the lowest vandal to the highest kingpin, searching for them. It would only take one set of eyes to recognize them and a third of Tokyo would be on their tails.

Mai wore a black baseball cap, keeping her head low. Mariko's parents wore thick jackets and carried plenty of bags in their hands. They kept to a fast pace, stopping only at the curb. Drake watched for a break in the traffic.

It didn't come quickly. He cursed under his breath. Only when a group of youngsters forced their way out into the road did the vehicles slow down.

Drake signaled to the others. "Move."

Hounded by slow-moving vehicles that refused to completely stop as pedestrians walked through them, surrounded by petrol and diesel fumes, they traversed the road and reached a taxi Drake had called. The taxi was random, something to throw off any would-be followers. The driver eyed them. Drake climbed into the front as the others took the back seat.

Drake gave the driver an address. The driver nodded and pulled out into traffic, ignoring cars and pedestrians alike, forcing his way along. Drake kept a close eye on him, saw him staring at Mai in the rearview and then glancing askance at him. He wondered if a photo had gone out. Taxi drivers would make a perfect surveillance team.

Nevertheless, the driver spent the next hour getting them to the address, where another car waited.

Drake paid and leapt out, hurrying toward a black four-door sedan. This was good. They were on the north side of Tokyo, from where they could drive back to the Tsugarai compound.

Mai was at his heels. "We good?"

"I think that taxi driver clocked us, love. Don't hang around."

They stowed the bags in the trunk and jumped into their car. Mariko's parents looked and sounded as if they regretted coming along and Drake didn't blame them. There was a safe house on the way north where they'd be protected for a few days.

"Mai," he said. "Take a video on your phone. Ask them to record a private message for Mariko, something to prove they're okay. Then we can go help Hayden and the others."

Mai pulled her cellphone out and turned around, speaking in Japanese. Drake drove out of the car park, right past the taxi driver who was talking on his own phone. Their eyes locked. Intuition told Drake something was very wrong.

He stepped on the gas, pulling into traffic and swinging across three lanes. But how could they escape the taxi driver network? They were everywhere. He drove as fast as he could, heading north out of town, aiming for Highway 5, which was the biggest tributary he could see on the satnav and may be a way of getting lost.

Three miles later, his heart sank.

He'd passed a police car at speed half a mile back. Lights flashed and sirens rang out as the car started in pursuit. Mai used her phone once more, trying to somehow route a message back to the Japanese police that they were a

Special Forces team cleared to act in most places around the world. There were code words that she could use.

But two minutes later, Drake told her to hang up the phone.

"Two black sedans," he said, "just came alongside the cop car. The passengers said something to make it fall back. There are three more sedans now."

Mai looked through the back window. "I see them. Tsugarai?"

"Has to be."

With no need for subterfuge, Drake stamped on the gas pedal, now close to the big motorway that would take them north. A junction was coming up fast, but so were the sedans. They cut through the traffic like killer sharks, carving it up, leaving accidents in their wake. They didn't care. The gap closed to eight car lengths.

Drake hit the off-ramp, making the car bounce. Mai and the others jolted left and right in the back, hitting heads and shoulders. The tires skidded, making the car slew, but Drake held on to it, powering up the ramp toward the motorway.

"Should be more space on there," he said. "Shit, they're fast."

They were fast because they were reckless, forcing two more cars into barriers as they powered closer. Drake suddenly realized the motorway might not be such a good idea after all.

Just as they raced onto it.

He cut in front of a petrol tanker, gaining time, then drove across two lanes. The sedans were momentarily trapped by the tanker, but sought a way around it. There was another police car in the fast lane. Drake tried to signal it, but the driver saw him and fell back, slowing hard.

The sedans flew around the tanker, causing havoc, cutting in front of half a dozen cars. Two of those cars panicked and swerved, crashing into each other. One rolled along for several rotations before coming to a stop on its side. Most of the other traffic pulled up or crawled around.

"At least those people will be okay," Mai said, still watching out of the back window.

"Me and the cops are gonna have a fucking word when this is all done," Drake fumed.

"Not all of them," Mai said, reminding him she and Dai had once worked for the police force. "We just got unlucky."

"Same old story."

He swung out to pass an SUV just as a sedan powered up to their rear. It didn't stop, and smashed into them.

Drake fought the wheel. The car slewed to the left, hit the SUV and rebounded. He couldn't stop the front end hitting the middle barrier, striking with its right headlight and then spinning. It spun once and then came to a hard stop, tilting up on two wheels before crashing down.

Drake was already flinging open his door, revolver in hand. He fired two quick shots at the sedan that had taken them out, smashing both side windows. Mai dragged Mariko's parents out of the far door, keeping them low.

Drake ran around to the front of their car, sighting over the hood. Two Tsugarai, dressed in the familiar brown leather tunics, jumped out of their sedan and rolled. He fired, catching one in the shoulder and the other in the thigh. They moved out of sight, groaning.

Five more sedans raced up.

"Look!" Mai cried out.

He saw the big petrol tanker cruising up on the inside. Without considering other options, he sprinted toward it, aiming his gun at the driver and waving him out. He had to reach it before the other sedans got here and so did Mai. Drake fired the rest of his mag at the stopped sedan, nullifying its occupants, and yanked open the door of the tanker.

"Out," he told the driver.

After the man jumped clear, Drake climbed into the driver's seat and pushed open the door for Mai. She and Mariko's parents climbed in, the old man and woman with some difficulty. Drake couldn't worry about them now. He was trying to save lives. Before Mai had the door closed, he was pressing his foot down, getting the tanker moving.

It was sluggish. Worse than that, it was a huge risk. Would the Tsugarai fire on the tanker? He didn't think so. They wanted Mai Kitano. Drake and Mai were part of the Strike Force team trying to find the Imperial Regalia. That was all the Tsugarai and their patron, Zuki, knew. Assuming they hadn't captured Alicia and her team, Drake had to believe they were needed alive, especially Mai.

The tanker picked up speed. The sedans followed, no doubt clarifying their orders. He weaved through traffic without taking his foot off the gas, trying to build up momentum.

Two minutes later, Mai spoke. "This isn't gonna work, Matt."

He nodded. "I know."

"We can't stash Mariko's parents with them on our tail. And we can't return to the compound."

"I know."

"Where's the petrol hose on this thing?"

Drake's eyes flew wide open. "You gotta be fucking joking, Mai."

"We're between the Tsugarai and a royal shadow-queen. Our friends are being tortured. Others are in trouble. I don't have a choice."

With that, she opened the door at fifty miles per hour, stepped out onto the ledge and hauled herself up onto the roof of the petrol tanker.

Drake flinched. "I'll try to keep it steady!"

Mai lay flat on top of the tanker, gripping one of the two rails that ran down the sides. The surface was cold, smooth and a little slick. She'd already spotted the hose, close to the back and to her right.

Sheer across the other side.

Of course it is. Mai inched her way down the length of the tanker, pulling herself along with the rails, every movement bringing her closer to the back end. She kept her head and body as low as possible; trying to stay hidden from the following sedans. Of course, they might have seen her climbing out of the cab, but she didn't think so. They had been driving in a single line, at the same speed, awaiting new orders, or so she presumed.

She neared the back. It was crunch time. Drake kept the tanker steady. She had him on the comms.

"We good?"

"Straight as a die here."

"I'm crossing over."

She pushed herself off from the left side, momentum carrying her across the tanker's smooth roof to the right. Mai swiveled her body as she slid, reaching out with both arms and grabbing the opposite rail as it came up.

Maneuver done, she took stock. The hose jutted out about three feet below her. She would have to hang off the tanker's side to unhook it. She touched her comms. "Is there some kind of safety switch for this hose?"

"Yep, you want it switched off?"

Mai affirmed and then, without waiting, clung on to the rail and swung herself off the edge of the speeding tanker. The tarmac whipped by beneath, the wind grabbed her hair and struck her body. Mai reached out for the hose.

At that moment, someone in the sedans must have spotted her. Two veered to their left, putting her in full view. The others sped up, powering to the tanker's rear.

"Keep it steady," Mai told Drake.

"All good here."

Mai held on with one hand, pulled at the hose's handle with the other, and then leaned away from the side of the tanker. She aimed the hose high, with an arc that would spray down into the following sedans.

Then, she started pumping fuel.

CHAPTER THIRTY

Alicia held on tight as their boat skimmed across the waves, pursued hard into Tokyo Harbor. Dahl and Luther were swapping bullets with the Tsugarai at the stern. Slugs pinged off the boat's transom and cabin. Jun, the captain, was coaxing every ounce of speed from his boat but it wasn't enough.

The Tsugarai's vessel was creeping up, passing their stern, trying to come alongside once more. Together the two boats plowed through the churning waters, exchanging gunfire. Karin and Kenzie were inside the wheelhouse, protecting Jun and his sons. Dahl and Luther were at the back. Alicia was crouched amidships, trying to clip the pilot or one of his helpers. So far, she'd shattered the glass of their wheelhouse and taken out one of the men, but the boat kept coming. Tsugarai warriors lay down covering fire from atop the structure and around its sides.

They were maybe eight minutes from the docks.

The other vessel inched up. Suddenly, one of the ninjas jumped over, crossing from one ship to the other. His boots hit the deck and he managed to stay upright, pistol in one hand, sword in the other. Alicia was closest and rose to meet him, but gunfire pinged off every surface around her, forcing her back down.

The warrior ran hard toward Luther, who had his back turned.

Alicia keyed her comms. "Enemy on your six, Luther."

The big American spun and shot the man in the chest without flinching. He, Dino and Dahl then crawled back from the stern. Luther picked up the discarded gun for ammo on the way.

Alicia shot two more Tsugarai as they leapt between ships, sending both tumbling into the roiling waters. With only about five minutes to go before docking, the Tsugarai changed their tactics, lining up and firing volley after volley into the fishing boat, sweeping the decks with bullets.

Alicia could only take cover. Dahl and Luther too. Slugs slammed into the wheelhouse, first destroying the glass then the entire framework. Alicia heard screams from inside. The boat powered toward the upcoming docks. She heard boots hitting the deck of their own boat. She saw blood leaking from out of the wheelhouse and spreading across the decking.

"Get down!" Kenzie screamed across the comms. "Get down now! *We're gonna hit the fucking docks!*"

Alicia grimaced. This wasn't good. She tucked in her weapon and held on to something solid, scrunched her body up into a ball as best she could. Boots were tramping toward her, Tsugarai warriors coming to kill her, but she couldn't fight them now. If she let go she would surely die.

Seconds passed like hours as she waited for the devastating impact. Her whole world was reduced to sound: the engines of the fishing boat, the roar of the Tsugarai's vessel, the sound of men approaching, distant screaming that could only be coming from the docks.

A boot came down close to her head. Alicia saw dirty black leather. She looked up, saw a grim face staring down at her, a machine pistol aimed at her skull. Alicia pulled one arm back, revealing the pistol she held, and shot the man in the chest. He flew backward just as their boat crashed into the docks, the metal craft smashing into concrete and scraping along the side.

There was a devastating sound like nothing she'd ever heard. Their boat shuddered deep from its highest point to its keel. They plowed through lined up sailing boats, tearing them apart, the Tsugarai vessel still alongside. There was no let up, both boats destroying everything they crashed into and scraping the ungiving concrete. Their own boat reared up out of the water, its bow now up onto the dock itself, still scraping along and turning sideways. The Tsugarai craft fell away, losing momentum.

At last, their boat slowed.

Alicia's grip was unbreakable. Her finger joints screamed with pain. She couldn't stop her legs flailing, but luckily ended up with few bruises. As the boat shuddered, she knew she had to get up.

She rose fast, still clinging to the bulkhead. A scene of terrible devastation met her eyes. The boat was still traveling, albeit slowly. To her right, much of the cabin and rear had collapsed, shedding itself across the docks. Timber from many other boats had been strewn among it. To her left at least two Tsugarai had been hurled like rag dolls by the impact, crashing into ungiving objects and breaking apart, leaving red smears in their wake. Behind, Luther and Dahl were also standing, guns in hand.

That left the damaged wheelhouse.

Alicia waited one more second, eyeing the Tsugarai and their boat. It drifted about forty feet to their port side, dead in the water, men scattered around its deck. But they were still active over there, checking their colleagues and scooping up weapons.

"We're beside the dock; they're not," Alicia said into her comms. "Let's take advantage of that right now."

She darted into the wheelhouse. Kenzie was on her knees over Jun, patting the older man's face. The two sons were sitting with their backs to a broken wall; one holding his elbow, the other his right temple. Karin was lying face down, groaning, struggling to sit up.

Alicia caught her under the arms. "Are you okay? We have to move."

Karin nodded. Alicia turned sharply at a scuffling noise, but it was only Luther, Dahl and Dino arriving. She helped Kenzie with Jun and soon all nine of them were exiting what remained of the wheelhouse and climbing the bow up toward the dock. It was a steep ascent, but adrenalin helped them do it in seconds.

Alicia hopped onto dry land, thankful for that at least. They had to be quick. They were exposed to gunfire up here and the Tsugarai craft drifted ever closer. The ninjas aboard, not happy about having to wait, were jumping from their craft to another and then another, leapfrogging boats to get closer to the docks. Alicia counted at least a dozen of them already en route.

She dragged at Jun and one of his sons, sweating, dirty, bloody, shouting at them to move faster. Dahl had the other son across his shoulder. Luther and Dino watched the rear as Karin ran ahead.

"Sirens," she shouted. "Hurry!"

"We'll reimburse you," Alicia whispered to Jun. "Just tell them you were forced to take the boat out. We'll find a way to replace the boat."

Approaching the end of the dock they saw flashing blue lights to the right. Behind, eight Tsugarai were giving chase, too far behind to cause concern. It was the approaching cops that could make the most trouble. Still, the Tsugarai kept coming. Alicia made the decision to run toward the cops, drop Jun and his sons off, and then melt away. The buildings were thick and plentiful at the rear of the docks, leading into some of Tokyo's most dense districts.

Alicia grabbed Karin's hand. "You have the treasures?"

"Safe and sound in my pack."

It was time to get lost. Alicia ordered them to leave the fishermen and dart left between a fishing warehouse and a container yard. Smells assaulted them, from a thick diesel stench to the sickly aroma of tons of fish. The streets were rubble strewn and slick with rain. The sun beat down from the west now, heading toward its horizon. Alicia led the way, picking between streets and vehicles, and skirting fences. They didn't look at the people they passed, just kept their heads down and their feet moving. Behind, sirens still beat at the air. They ran from shadow to sunlight as they threaded through narrow alleys and parkland.

Finally, Luther slowed. "I think we lost the cops."

Alicia turned her head. "I doubt they were ever on our tail. Too much shit to deal with and the Tsugarai too."

"What next?" Karin asked.

"Well, we have two haikus to decipher and nowhere to go." Alicia hadn't stopped moving, heading for a tight network of busy streets. "Somehow, we have to stay out of sight. The Tsugarai won't stop hunting."

"Yeah, and I'm pretty sure that's a drone," Dino said.

They glanced at the sky, seeing a silver unmanned aerial craft up there, circling the tops of buildings. Another joined it and came toward them.

As they crossed a road, Alicia saw a taxi driver slowing, staring at her face. Somebody in a crowd frowned at her and pulled out their phone.

She swallowed drily. "The Tsugarai own this city," she said. "Through Zuki, I'm guessing, the royal. They have the cash to find anyone. How the hell are we going to stay unnoticed?"

"We're not." Dino pointed as the silver drone descended toward them as if picking them out.

Sirens sounded only two or three blocks away.

We can't escape this. Too much surveillance. Too many eyes. Even the fucking cops . . .

Alicia looked at Luther and Dahl. "Any ideas?"

"Just stay free. Stay alive for one more minute," Dahl repeated an old mantra. "You never know what might come up."

Alicia led them deeper into Tokyo, crossing streets and using alleys to try to throw off the drones. She had a feeling their enemy was closing in, waiting up ahead. She had a feeling the Tsugarai were already laying out a trap.

They just had to figure out a way to not fall into it.

CHAPTER THIRTY ONE

As Mai pumped fuel, aiming the flow at the following sedans, Drake saw something else coming closer. Something smaller and speedier, darting toward the fleeing tanker.

Motorbikes.

Black clad riders were upon them. Drake counted six, all wearing impenetrable black helmets. Already, they were darting around the sedans, heading for Mai, who was exposed and almost defenseless hanging on to the side of the truck.

Drake made a quick decision and turned to Mariko's father.

"Can you drive? Good, then take the wheel and stay straight. No sudden moves." He mimed it out as best he could. At first, Mariko's father looked terrified, shrinking away from the wheel, but the desperation in Drake's eyes must have penetrated his fear.

Drake made a face. "There's no option here."

He pulled the comms device from his own ear and attached it to the other man's. At least that way, Mai and he could warn each other of potential pitfalls. Then, without waiting any longer, Drake opened his door and climbed out into a howling wind.

He clung on to the side of the truck, boots set steady on the door frame, then lunged for the top rail running the length of the tanker. His fingers gripped, but the wind tugged at him, blowing his legs toward the back of the vehicle. Drake heaved with all his strength, pulling himself on top. Ahead, Mai was waving the hose back and forth, soaking the cars as the bikes came closer, making the road slick with gasoline.

Drake took a moment to gain his balance, then ran down the middle of the tanker as it barreled straight ahead. He reached the back in seconds, taking a moment to glance down at Mai.

"How's it goin', love?"

She didn't answer but looked grateful for his presence. Drake saw all six bikes now approaching as the five sedans spread out across the motorway. As soon as the men on the bikes fired, Drake drew his handgun and squeezed the trigger. His first shots went wide; there was a lot of motion between the tanker, his arm and the speeding motorcycles. Fortunately, his enemies had the same problem. Bullets fizzed through the air.

"Drake!" Mai cried. "We're moving into the next lane!"

He nodded, grateful for the information. His next few bullets pinged off one of the bikes' wheels, making it skid and go down. The rider tumbled away. Mai was still pumping gas.

Drake didn't carry a lighter, but he was always prepared and unclipped a small phosphorous grenade from his belt. "Cut that thing off!"

Mai replaced the hose and clung tight to the side of the tanker as a volley of lead flew by her shoulder.

Drake flung the grenade, watched it arc through the air and hit the ground, setting fire to the trail of gas. Very quickly, the entire motorway flared up behind them, flames reaching eight feet high and spreading left to right. Two sedans veered but were caught in the conflagration. The sound of their tortured wheels struck at the air. A third sedan pulled to the far side of the road, but it too then erupted in bright flame, sending it crashing into the barrier.

Drake didn't let them rest as Mai climbed back up on to the roof of the tanker, emptying mag after mag into the remaining sedans and trying to pick off the bike riders. One motorbike caught fire but kept coming, the unaffected rider maintaining speed on his fiery steed. Another rider skidded away, tumbling into the back of a sedan.

Riders were speeding up, trying to hide under the shadow of the huge tanker. Mai grabbed the safety rail and leaned over, head aimed down at the deadly tarmac, and shot one through the visor. The others veered away.

Drake fell back as sedan passengers fired up at him. One appeared to have a machine pistol and unleashed a salvo that made Drake hug the surface of the tanker's roof for long seconds.

When he looked up again two empty bikes were spinning away to the left. That only meant one thing. Two men were on the tanker.

He scrambled across, only to meet a fast-rising punch to the face. He fell back, stunned, unable to grasp how they'd managed to climb so quickly. But then he remembered who they were dealing with as two Tsugarai jumped onto the roof of the tanker. They were met headlong by Mai Kitano.

She stood her ground, punching and kicking. They blocked but didn't fall back. Drake grabbed his handgun and steadied the barrel. One of the ninjas whirled away from Mai and came at him. Drake saw a blow heading for his sternum and blocked it.

He didn't see the one coming from the right. It connected hard with his temple, knocking him to one knee. His opponent kicked Drake's gun out of his hand and sent it tumbling across the roof where it snagged against the far safety rail. Drake gasped as the ninja landed on him with two knees, striking down. He blocked the blows and rolled, throwing the man off, toward the edge but he jack-knifed his body into an almost impossible maneuver, somehow ending up at Drake's ankles.

He came in fast again. This time Drake was ready, raising his boots so that the man's chin struck them. Drake used the precious seconds he'd gained to scramble away and jump to his feet.

He reviewed what they were up against.

One other bike still sped after the tanker, closing in fast to the rear. Two sedans were charging alongside, moving inexorably up to the front cab windows where, Drake knew, they would probably open fire. Either that, or they would jump aboard and take over the wheel.

If that happened, they were lost, and so were Hayden and the others.

Drake feigned an attack, then dived sideways toward the far edge of the tanker. His body slid along the smooth surface, taking him way faster toward that deadly drop than he wanted. As he reached the safety rail, he grabbed the gun and twisted, aware that his legs were slipping over the edge.

Drake fired point black at his opponent, two bullets into his chest that killed him instantly.

But he couldn't stop his fall.

His legs fell over and then the whole bottom half of his body was swinging in the wind. His stomach slipped down and then his chest. At the last moment, he dropped the gun, saw it tumble away, and grabbed hold of the safety rail with the only part of his body left atop the tanker.

His hands.

Drake swung and struggled, battered by a gale, smashed into the side of the tanker more times than he could count. It took an entire minute to haul his body back to relative safety.

He was staring across at Mai. She fought hand to hand with her opponent on top of the tanker. Both had knives out and were fencing, striking, throwing their weapons between hands to affect surprise. It was a sight he'd seen before, and a fantastic sight. Mai at her best, bettering a strong opponent, but this time made even more dramatic by the fact that she stood atop a fast-moving petrol tanker.

Drake trusted her to deal with her enemy and crawled forward until he was over the cab. Then he looked down to the right. Both remaining sedans were closing in on the tanker's door, no doubt terrifying Mariko's parents even more.

Drake took careful aim, right where the drivers would be, and fired eight quick shots through the sedans' roofs. One veered into the other, then both slewed across the motorway, striking the one remaining bike. A sedan turned over, rolling sideways, crushing the bike and its rider in the process. The last sedan went headlong into the barrier, sending one man clear through the windshield.

Drake had finished them off. No more sedans followed, and no more bikes. They were free, at least for a little while.

He snapped a glance over at Mai. She'd feigned an injury, gone down on both knees. She rose up as her opponent charged, lifting him off his legs, spinning and hurling him right off the side of the truck. Drake winced as his head and face struck the road, leaving a red smear on the black tarmac.

Mai turned. Drake gave her a thumbs up. Mai communicated a message through the comms and the tanker slowed. Both Drake and Mai used the reprieve to climb back into the cabin.

"Did they see your faces?" Drake asked Mariko's mother, who'd been closest to the sedans as they came alongside.

"No," she said through Mai. "I kept my face averted. My head down."

"Good." That was one thing at least. He turned to Mai. "We've carved ourselves out a little time. We have to stash these two and get back to the compound ASAP."

"Right. Take this off ramp." Mai pointed. "The safe house is three minutes from here. Good escape routes."

Drake took a breath. The motorway was a mess behind them. He could still see a carnage of burning tarmac, flaming cars and wreckage. Sirens sprung up from everywhere. He took control of the tanker as they paused in traffic at the bottom of the off-ramp.

"Good job," he told Mariko's parents. "I hope we can soon reunite you with your daughter."

Mai caught his eye. "And us with Hayden, Mano and Molokai."

Drake nodded, thinking of Alicia's group too. *Where are they right now?* There was something on the radio about a fishing boat crashing into part of Tokyo's docks at the same time as Drake and Mai were causing motorway mayhem. But he couldn't imagine that would be Alicia. She was out chasing treasure not crashing ships into other ships.

Wasn't she?

Mai put a steady hand on his shoulder. "They'll be all right," she said. "All of them."

Drake wished he could be as confident. This enemy they were up against, the Tsugarai, were easily a match for them. Possibly better. And they outnumbered the Strike Force team about ten to one.

"Reinforcements would be nice," he said.

"Can we call out the other Strike Force teams?"

"If this was a sanctioned op, yes. But it isn't. Maybe we could persuade the hierarchy to help."

"The only person that could do that is locked in a Tsugarai compound."

"I know. Ironic, isn't it?"

"But now we can enlist Mariko's help," Mai said. She spent a few more minutes recording a second video with the girl's parents, asking for their daughter to come home, as Drake pulled up a mile away from the safe house.

"Time to move," he said. "I don't like to think what Hayden and the others are going through."

Mai nodded, her face grim, and got out of the cab.

CHAPTER THIRTY TWO

Drake made sure Mariko's parents were secure and had plenty of food and water for the next few days. He asked them not to go out or make any calls. He used Dai as a go-between with the police to help guard the safe house. Mai wasn't happy, but lack of time dictated they couldn't afford to wait around.

Soon, they were driving north again in one of the safe house's basic cars, heading to the Tsugarai compound, at first using main roads and then a roundabout, off-road route. It was early evening and if they drove at the right pace, they figured they could get back to Mariko this very night.

Weary, bruised, cut and aching, they took turns driving and sleeping. There would be no rest once they stopped.

As they neared the place where they would conceal the car, Drake gave Alicia a quick call, checking in. It had been an eventful few days and they spent the first five minutes swopping stories.

"That *was* you, at the dock?"

"Yeah, Luther can't drive for shit."

Drake laughed, eyeing Mai. "I think they're missing each other. Mai just jumped on top of a petrol tanker, grabbed a hose and started spraying it around."

Alicia choked. "She needs treatment for that."

Drake turned serious. "Good job finding the two treasures. Thoughts on the third?"

"We definitely do have thoughts. Most of them are crap though. We're being hunted in Tokyo right now. Trying to find somewhere safe. The Tsugarai have half the city looking out for us, but we're waiting for . . . our translator . . . to get back to us on the whereabouts of the third treasure."

"Good. Any clues about this fourth one?"

"Yeah, all bad."

"Right." Drake didn't want to push it any further. He could tell Alicia and the others were on edge, trying to keep a low profile. "Speak soon."

They signed off. Mai pulled into the same parking area they'd used before and camouflaged the car. Drake took their gear out, including the extra supplies they'd taken from the safe house.

"Same plan as before?" he said. "If it's not broke . . ."

Mai nodded. "Wait for full dark and then go get Mariko."

They rested and ate energy food, drank plenty of water. They dressed for the mission. Drake found himself recalling how well Mai and he worked together, how quickly they'd slotted back into the perfect two-person team. The only thing that had split them apart was circumstance. Should he have waited longer for Mai?

He couldn't stop his eyes tracking her now, as she changed behind the car. He saw the tops of her bare shoulders and her luxurious black hair.

Damn, a soldier's life was far from simple. And being alone for days with someone you used to love . . . that was a complication even Nikola Tesla couldn't unravel.

"It's not your good fortune to look at me anymore," Mai said.

Drake focused, realized he'd been caught watching. "Sorry," he said in a gruff voice.

Mai came around the car, fully dressed. "Hey, I'm kidding. The stuff we've been through . . . it's always yours. Always. We're just with other people, that's all."

Drake thought he understood what she was saying. They'd shared more than a lifetime of happiness, grief and battle. They'd shared so much more. The bond between them ran deeper than all attachments.

"You should know something," Mai said. "The change in Alicia? That's all down to you. It's down to her wanting to be fully accepted by you. You've helped her change herself for the better, Matt, and I hope you recognize that."

"She wanted to change."

"Of course, but everyone needs help. Even from an old Yorkshireman like you."

"And the world thinks we're tight." Drake smiled. "But we just give and give and—"

"Don't push it, my friend. She's still an active volcano."

Drake's smile widened because he saw he and Mai were still on the same wavelength. Alicia would always be a simmering cauldron of heat, emotion, reaction and confrontation.

"She'll always be that," he said. "And I wouldn't want her to change."

"Not any more," Mai agreed. "Because then she'd no longer be Alicia."

They moved out, following the same route toward the Tsugarai camp they'd taken the night before. A night that felt an age ago right now.

"At least she's not shagging her bosses anymore," Mai said with a smile.

"Pretty sure she did Hayden."

"No, it was a kiss. For fun."

"Well, she's her own boss right now," Drake reminded her.

"Oh, well then. Maybe I'm wrong."

The night turned pitch black as they neared the

compound. Drake crawled once more into the ditch, his eyes close to the grass, his nose full of its rich loamy scent. Nothing had changed in the compound. The spotlights still shone on the square and the flickering torches still illuminated streets and boundaries. The squat buildings were unguarded, appearing lonely in the stark light.

"Thanks," Drake said when they stopped for a rest. "For saying I helped Alicia. And for acknowledging our deeper connection. It means a lot to me."

"You enriched my life, Matt, and I hope I enriched yours. We wouldn't be the people we are today if we hadn't met each other."

Drake held her hand for a brief moment. Then he shrugged off the emotion for the final leg of their clandestine intrusion. They left the ditch and entered the Tsugarai compound, found the shadows beneath one of the low buildings, and waited for five minutes. Nothing occurred, not even the shuffling of a passing patrol.

Drake breathed shallowly, counting seconds. Both he and Mai were fully tooled-up, with spare ammo, flak jackets and comms devices. They were taking no chances where the Tsugarai and the safety of Hayden and the others was concerned.

They crept closer to Mariko's hut, found a hiding place and waited. Three hours later, the young woman emerged, as she'd promised to do. Mai waited until she knew the woman was alone, then gave her a low-key signal.

Mariko turned, saw them and hurried over. Together they huddled in the shadows at the back of the hut.

"You found them already? Are they safe?"

"They're fine," Mai said. "We brought you proof."

"You are Mai Kitano. I trust you," Mariko said.

Mai nodded her thanks but pulled out a cellphone

anyway. She wanted Mariko to see her parents, to give her that added incentive. She wanted Mariko to *feel*.

With the sound turned off she played the video. Mariko's face softened as soon as she saw her mother and father. Her eyes watered, but she wiped the wetness away. No doubt she'd been conditioned for years not to show emotion. Mai let the video play through and then put an arm on Mariko's shoulder.

"Will you help us?"

"I will be with my parents soon?"

"Yes, a new life."

"What do you want exactly?"

"To rescue our three friends."

"I know where they're being kept. You have a plan?"

"Wait, there's more." Drake knelt forward. "We want to end the Tsugarai too."

Mariko's large eyes widened so that they resembled saucers. "You meant that?"

"Take them down. Destroy them once and for all. Wipe them out."

"But where is your army?"

Drake coughed. "We're working on that. First, our friends. Tell us all you know, and we'll come back with a plan."

At that moment they heard whispering and the crunching of boots. Drake went absolutely still, blending with the deepest shadows until the two-man patrol passed them by.

"We must hurry," Mariko said. "I will be missed soon."

She proceeded to tell them where Hayden and the others were being kept, the number and routine of the guards watching them, and the general schedule of the camp. To Drake and Hayden, it sounded pretty standard. But they hadn't enlisted Mariko's help to tell them where prisoners were kept, they had recruited her as the distraction.

They explained the plan. Mariko took several deep breaths before acquiescing. It wouldn't be easy for the young woman.

"Is there anyone you care for here?" Mai asked her. "Anyone who might help you?"

"Trust is not a feeling the Tsugarai force upon us. It is fear. I have friends, but I do not know if they will break free of their chains."

Mai nodded. "I understand. Work alone but try to help them if you can. The Tsugarai are the monsters, not your friends."

Mariko nodded her understanding. Drake saw the deep, ingrained feelings Mai still harbored for the dreaded shinobi clan. Mariko insisted that she had to go and then the two of them were alone.

"Tomorrow night then." Drake cast a glance at the building where he knew Hayden and the others were being kept.

"It will be the end of the Tsugarai," Mai said.

"Or at the very least the rescue of our friends."

"I want that more than anything, my friend, but I have to see this demon die." She indicated the compound. "I thought I'd left them behind, but I've realized that's just not possible. How many have they murdered and abducted since I left? They need wiping off the face of the earth."

Drake didn't say any more, unwilling to reveal his mounting worry for Mai's state of mind where the Tsugarai were concerned. They couldn't do with any glitches with their friends' safety, especially with the caliber of the enemy they were up against.

"One more day," he said as they headed back the way they'd come. "Just hang on one more day."

CHAPTER THIRTY THREE

Alicia asked Dahl and Luther to take point, Dino and Kenzie to watch their backs, and walked in the middle of the group with Karin. Tokyo was a dark and dangerous place to be right now and they were at the very heart of it.

"What do you have?" Alicia asked Karin.

"News." The other woman tapped at her cellphone, the only piece of technology she'd been able to bring along after their boat crashed, except for their comms. "No Tsugarai even mentioned at the dock confrontation. No shinobi. No Zuki and whatever organization she runs. It's all an accident, apparently. Faulty guidance systems and such. There'll be telling us there's a bloody gas leak next."

Alicia examined dark windows on second and third floors as they passed. She studied shadows in the street, occasional faces. "Drake?"

"Well, as he said, they fucked up a motorway. There's spin on the chaos up there too. News reports that the cops found the tanker and took down an entire ring of fuel thieves," Karin shook her head. "Political spin on real people's real problems. The truth hidden in the shadows. It'll never change."

"Safe house?"

"Nothing near here for us," Karin said. "We're eight miles out."

"Bollocks."

Alicia relayed the news through the comms. They were stuck in central Tokyo, unable to use a taxi, hiding from every figure, hunted by the best clandestine killers on the planet.

"We smash our way to the safe house," Luther growled.

"Last resort," Alicia said. "We're making progress."

"If you call progress two miles an hour."

Alicia ignored the grumbling. "Anyone whose role model isn't the Hulk want to chime in?"

Dahl spoke up. "Steal a car," he said. "Next chance we get."

It sounded good to Alicia. "You hear that, Luther? Not everything's about mayhem."

"I don't agree."

"So how'd you get into Mai's pants? Smash and grab?"

Luther drew a sharp breath. She heard him over the night air. "Never I . . . I—"

"Relax, relax. I'm just busting your chops. I know Mai's a great judge of character."

"Oh yeah, and now she's with Drake."

Alicia went quiet, examining their surroundings with even more focus and a quiet anger. She trusted both Mai and Drake.

It was a fickle world. It was an unfair world. It didn't turn out how you wanted it to, and it never offered up the best choices. Alicia was a product of dishonor. She knew injustice occurred every hour of every day, sometimes by good people doing the wrong thing, often by bad people lining their pockets with silver. She couldn't help how she felt when she experienced it first-hand.

Kenzie interrupted her thoughts. "Umm, guys . . ."

It was an odd comment. Alicia feared the worst. She spun fast, gun already up in a firing stance. Karin turned a few seconds later. Alicia saw Kenzie standing, looking wary, and Dino pointing a handgun at the shadows that followed them.

Many shadows.

More than she could count. At least twenty. If they were all armed this was going to go down hard.

"Hostiles." She keyed her comms.

Everyone turned in the semi-darkness, trapped in a narrow alley with dumpsters on all sides, the star-strewn night above barely a slither, casting no light; able to stand only three abreast and carrying much less ammo than they were happy with.

Alicia waved her gun at the approaching figures. "Don't come any closer. We will shoot you."

She saw a moving pool of darkness come to a halt. She couldn't make out features, even discernible human shapes. No wonder Kenzie had warned them with little more than a grunt.

She, Kenzie and Karin stood facing them. A piece of darkness extracted itself from the unit and stepped forward, holding his hands out.

Alicia saw a tall, hooded figure. No wonder she couldn't make out any details. This man wore a tight-fitting tunic under a compact but flowing cloak. There was a sash in some dark color at his waist and a sword in a big scabbard at his side. As Alicia watched he folded back his hood.

"I am Tenmei," he said, "of the Shingen family. We are one of the shadow royal bloodlines. We," he said proudly, "are samurai."

Alicia fought to keep her jaw from dropping. "Fuck me, are you being serious?"

Tenmei took another two steps closer, again holding his arms out. "I have a story to tell you. A story of betrayal. Of samurai and shinobi becoming mortal enemies. Of distrust. And of Zuki, leader of the legendary Chiyome family, who wishes to kill us all."

"That sounds great," Alicia said with typical bluntness.

"But we're in kind of a hurry. We have friends to rescue and stuff to find. Oh, and we're on a clock."

"We know," Tenmei said. "We know all about you, Alicia Myles. We've been watching you for some time. Researching your team. You have found some of the greatest lost relics in our planet's history. You have our respect. You have saved the world. You have our gratitude. But now, you are out of your depth. You have our help."

"Help?" Alicia repeated.

"Look up."

With a sense of dread, Alicia and the others glance up. Arrayed along every rooftop were robed figures. They were on every balcony, every fire escape. Alicia whistled in admiration. "Samurai can do that too?"

"Doesn't change a thing," Luther grated. "We'll still take most of you mofos out."

Alicia winced. The samurai were standing at ease, offering no challenge. Tenmei himself came right up to her now so that she could see his features. His face was rough and lined, his blue eyes so hard they might cut through stone. This wasn't a man who'd known a great deal of peace.

"Stand down," Alicia told her team, taking the responsibility. She nodded at Tenmei. "I assume you have a safe place?"

"We will take you there."

Alicia stood with her team in an underground chamber. Black curtains formed the walls to three sides. The fourth looked on to a rectangular steaming pool where dozens of samurai warriors bathed, laughed and sang.

"They're all naked," Kenzie said.

"I noticed that," Alicia responded. "Do you think we should look away?"

"No, I'm good."

"Me too."

"Finally," Dahl spoke from their right. "We've found something you agree on. Naked men."

"Naked samurai," Alicia amended. "There's a distinction."

"Hey." Kenzie looked over at the Swede. "Are you gonna join them?"

"Are *you*?" Alicia asked.

"It's a viable option."

"Agreed."

Before Dahl could answer, a curtain to their right was drawn back. Alicia turned to see Tenmei, three elder men, and two women standing there. Tenmei beckoned them over. "My apologies for keeping you waiting."

"It's no problem at all." Alicia grinned. They were led into another underground chamber, this one a study in austerity. It had three walls and another curtain, held two dozen beanbags and several jugs of water. The samurai leaders took seats and waited for the Strike Force team to do the same.

Alicia straddled her beanbag, feeling a little off kilter. To be fair, it was comfortable.

"We owe you an explanation," Tenmei said. "A full explanation. As I mentioned, we are the Shingen family, one of the seven secret royal bloodlines of Japan, but not one of the First Three."

"The First Three?" Alicia repeated.

"Japan's Chiyome family, the Sulaiman sultans of Brunei and the Thai Chakri family are known as the First Three, simply because they carved out more lands, more wealth and more power during the early dynasties. We have been trying to draw level and perhaps overtake them for hundreds of years. Now, we are challenging every one of them."

"And why is that?" Dahl asked.

"It is partly due to recent land acquisitions and good investments. Partly due to wiping out three of our competitors' most lucrative arms and human smuggling rings. But mostly, it is because we know someone who knows the whereabouts of two of the fabled Four Sacred Treasures."

Alicia blinked. "Us, you mean?"

"Yes, you. Zuki, the leader of the Chiyome bloodline, has led her family down a darkening path. Not all her fault, to be fair. Her parents were murdered when she was young. But she is a privileged child, spoilt, drunk with power. Again, not all her fault. But the Chiyome family's failings has enabled all its challengers to rise. We are all close to defeating Zuki now."

"So where do we come in?" Kenzie asked.

"Very recently Zuki made two essential decisions. One will prove catastrophic for her. The other was a genius idea. Quite brilliantly, she realized the importance of finding the three treasures and how such a discovery would elevate her standing to the stratosphere. She would be forever untouchable, her family's savior and a legend for centuries to come."

"How?" Karin put in. "How would that work for a shadow queen?"

"A good question. The secret, true royal bloodlines have always influenced from a place where they cannot be seen. If it is known Zuki found the treasures, the other families will back her. The puppet government will love her, for she will allow them to take the glory and the people will love *them*. Wealth will flow. Her influence over *everyone and everything* will grow to new heights. She will keep the treasures hidden, under threat. She may be able to integrate the seven families or even destroy them."

"You mentioned she made a catastrophic mistake." Dahl shuffled on his beanbag, looking uncomfortable.

"Yes. She enlisted the help of pure dogs, the Tsugarai, the shinobi or ninjas, as the West calls them."

"We can understand that statement," Alicia said. "But why do you hate them?"

"Samurai and so-called ninjas are of a different class. Samurai are warrior class. Shinobi are outcasts, peasants. Samurai have always treated people fairly. Ninjas breed trouble, cause civil war and uprisings. Many innocents have died in the past. Millions. Shinobi are the lowest of the low, as proven by the fact that only one single clan remains. The Tsugarai. But they are a virus we have been unable to wipe out. And that means *all* the royal bloodlines, not just the samurai. Zuki's decision to hire them to find the treasures has galvanized everyone against her, especially the samurai. This time we will wipe them, and her, out for good."

"The samurai are going up against the ninjas?" Alicia breathed. "Whilst we're in town? Fuck me."

"Not just that. The other bloodlines—Thailand, Cambodia, Brunei, Bhutan and Malaysia—are also now seeking the Four Sacred Treasures. If there comes a showdown it will be a bloodbath."

"You keep saying *four* treasures," Dahl said. "But isn't that a myth?"

"You have found two of them. What do you think?"

"Wait, just wait." Alicia held a hand up. "I understand what you want out of this and why you're doing it. But why the hell do you want *us*? Do you really need our help?"

"Alicia," Tenmei said as if they were old colleagues. "The

Sacred Treasures of Japan have been lost for thousands of years. Nobody knew the Tsugarai passed haikus between leaders until you came along. The fakes have existed for decades, known to be fakes only by a handful of dignitaries and monks. You people *found* two of the four in only a few days, primarily to save your friends. You have no other agenda. We, the samurai, want to return the treasures to the people. To museums. To the world. We do not wish to gain profit or power from them. But we do want to end Zuki's cruel and ruthless reign and the sickening practices of the Tsugarai. You have the haikus. You are surely close to finding the third treasure and once you have that—the fabled fourth."

"And you're not gonna kill us because . . ."

"You are respected among samurai. We believe your team can accomplish something we never could."

Alicia couldn't help but turn to Kenzie and Dahl. "You hear that? I'm respected among samurai."

"I think he meant all of us," Dahl replied with a shake of his head.

"Do you? I didn't get that."

"You wouldn't," Kenzie said. "But all I'm wondering is when can I get my hands on a samurai sword."

"Is that a euphemism?"

"No! The samurai are the greatest sword-makers of all time."

"Interesting," Tenmei said. "And not strictly true. The samurai *employ* the greatest sword-makers of all time to make our swords. That is how the third treasure, the sword Kusanagi, came to its current state. Kusanagi means the Heavenly Sword of Gathering Clouds. It represents force and virtue, and resides in the Land of the Gods. In the fourteenth century the greatest swordsmith our world has ever known remade Kusanagi, setting the sword into an obsidian frame, a frame fashioned from the first meteorite ever to strike the earth. Haikus were transferred to the back of the frame, possibly because they were fading from the sword's steel. In any case, this swordmaker was named Masamune, and he is legendary. Even today, seven hundred years later, awards are frantically sought that have his name attached. It is said Masamune's swords were so perfect they could be laid in a river or a waterfall. All leaves that floated past would be split in two, but all fish could swim right up to it and then pass by unharmed. This proved his blade was the finest, for it didn't needlessly cut that which is innocent and underserving. Thus, Masamune's swords are holy, and represent the battle of good versus evil."

"We have somebody translating the haiku for the third and fourth treasures," Alicia told the gathering. "He should have an update by now."

"That is good." Tenmei bowed his head. "The samurai have been the military nobility and officer caste of Japan for thousands of years. In Japanese we are called bushi, you may recognize the name Bushido. We existed before the tenth century. We are warriors, just like you. Some say the translation of bushi is strictly: to serve. We wish to serve the Japanese people. We want to empower *them*."

Alicia looked to Karin. "Let's show them the treasures."

"Wait," Dahl said. "One more thing you didn't answer. You seem to be certain there are *four* treasures."

"We know very little, but our legends tell us that the fourth treasure is not of this earth. It is from the stars. You stated that there are *two* haikus with the treasures, not one as would be expected. One of those haikus on each treasure points the way to the fourth, which has some connection to the first meteorite. The fourth treasure is a myth, but if it exists, it is necessary for the very stabilization of our planet."

Alicia's mouth dropped open. "You're saying if it didn't exist our planet would just . . . fall apart."

"I know little more than that. But if it is real, I would like to safeguard it. We can't allow it to fall into the wrong hands and, especially, shinobi hands."

Alicia saw thousands of years of animosity behind Tenmei's statement. The fourth treasure would have to wait in any case. They'd cross that bridge when they reached it.

If they reached it.

"Read the haiku for the third treasure," Alicia asked Karin.

"Sure." Karin said and recited from memory. "The Heavenly Sword of the Gathering Clouds, In Takamagahara, The Shrine of Kami-ari-zuki."

"We understand the first two lines." Alicia saved Tenmei the trouble of explaining. "Basically, Kusanagi lies in the Land of the Gods. It's the last line that's baffling."

"I see. Kan-na-zuki means the Month of No Gods, from the Japanese calendar. I am unfamiliar with this twist on a well-known translation."

Alicia was relieved Tenmei hadn't simply come back with an easy explanation, something that made her feel unnecessary. She watched Tenmei converse with his elders and the women, but everyone ended up looking blank.

She raised a phone. "Can I call my contact?"

Tenmei gestured. "Our home is your home for now. You may do what you want—" he smiled "—except bathe with the warriors."

Alicia managed to make a noise of disappointment even as the call to Dai went through. "It's me," she said. "Where are you with the translations?"

To help reciprocate Tenmei's generosity Alicia put the call on speakerphone. "It took some doing," Dai said. "But we've solved the first haiku that reveals where Kusanagi was hidden. The second haiku however is still a riddle."

"We may need the third haiku to unravel that mystery," Alicia said. "So tell me, where is the sword?"

"The term 'the Shrine of Kami-ari-zuki' points us to an ancient Japanese village known as the Land of the Gods. In this place the term we know, Kan-na-zuki, meaning The Month of No Gods, is reordered to kami-ari-zuki, which actually means The Month of the Gods. The place is called Izumo, and, once a lunar year, legend says all gods in the Shinto religion, all eight million of them, come together there to discuss that year's happenings. The Shrine of Izumo is where they gather. Thirteen hundred years ago, Izumo was one of the most important cities in Japan, and its history is deeply tangled with myths and religious notables. Izumo is actually the Land of the Gods."

Alicia smiled at Tenmei. "Looks like we have a job to do."

"We will find the sword together."

Alicia nodded, then appraised her team. They all looked wary, rightfully so. Tenmei could talk a good deal but they wouldn't know his true colors until he showed them. Maybe he was telling the truth, maybe he wasn't. But Alicia had been counting the samurai clan's numbers—over eighty she'd seen so far—and that didn't include guards or bodyguards. The Shingen family were a force to be reckoned with.

A force that could potentially take out the Tsugarai.

But first things first, she thought. *Let's go get that bloody sword.*

CHAPTER THIRTY FOUR

Hayden looked over to Kinimaka and Molokai. Their wrists were raw, their nails torn, their fingers throbbing, but both men had fought relentlessly with their bonds so that, now, they could escape them with a flick of the wrist.

"Wait," she mouthed.

Footsteps passed outside their dark building. The guard patrol passed every twenty minutes. This was good. She nodded as the footsteps faded and a familiar silence fell.

Kinimaka and Molokai shed their bonds and bent over to release their ankles. It took some time. Then, both men tried to stand. Kinimaka wobbled, looking like he'd had a little too much of the special Hawaiian punch.

"You all right, Mano?" Hayden asked.

He fell to his knees. "Haven't used my legs in a few days," he said and crawled over to her. Hayden flexed her own tied limbs, trying to get the blood flowing. Molokai approached the door.

Kinimaka worked her bonds. Hayden rose from the position she'd been made to adopt for several days. Her limbs protested. Her head ached. Blood ran down her wrists. There was so much pain she found it hard to focus on a specific plan.

"Vehicles," Molokai said, seeing her struggle. "Failing that, we run out of here."

Hayden was aware that this was their only chance. So far, they'd been beaten, kicked and humiliated. Buckets of water had been poured over their heads after their mouths had been taped. Hayden had almost drowned twice. A handgun was pointed at Molokai's temple. When the

American refused to answer questions the trigger was pulled, falling on an empty chamber. Kinimaka had been dragged outside, tied to a waterwheel, and repeatedly had his head dipped underwater. They returned him hours later.

Hayden had been dragged away; her fellow captives told dreadful details about what would happen to her if they didn't talk. Of course, Kinimaka and Molokai could only reiterate the basic facts they'd already revealed. Four hours later Hayden was returned, unharmed.

It wasn't that they didn't hurt for each other on the inside. It was that all three of them knew that silence was the only thing keeping them alive. No matter what they endured, if it wasn't death, they could deal with it.

Last night, Kenshin the Tsugarai leader, came to them. "We are close to the three treasures," he said with a satisfied smile. "Once we have them, we will no longer need you. You live now only for the chance that we will need you, but tomorrow, I think you will die."

Hayden heard the truth of it in his voice. Kenshin had never lied to them. He'd explained their lot from the beginning. She'd kept hoping Drake or Dahl or somebody would find them and attempt a rescue, but as one dark day turned into another dark night that hope had all but vanished.

Now, free of bonds, she approached Molokai. "I'm ready."

With Kinimaka at her back, she followed Molokai into the cold night air. The ground was earthy; the breeze plucked at her with frozen fingers. The only sound was the distant hooting of an owl. Hayden thought of all the binds they'd been in and the adventures they'd shared. This moment felt very alone. Very final.

I wish the team were here.

She knew it was a desperate thought and forced it aside. Being taken prisoner did nothing for your confidence, it appeared. Being at the whim of terrible captors turned your mind fraught, your thoughts frantic.

She held on now, following Molokai around the building, into deeper shadow. Far to their left, was the compound's square, a floodlit area. Other buildings lay ahead, the shadows they cast offering concealment.

"Up the hill." Molokai pointed. "Three cars."

Hayden saw them and felt her heart lift. They started off in single file, racing from shadow to shadow to shadow, getting closer to the top of the hill, their bodies recovering with every free step they took, their resolve hardening, their drive returning. Soon, they were twenty feet from the parking area, hidden alongside a narrow building.

"Down," Molokai said.

They hit the dirt. A patrol passed not twenty feet to their right. Hayden watched them from her prone position, her nose in the grass, her eyes uplifted.

For shinobi, they're not very observant, she thought. But this was their element, their home for untold years. She assumed this was where they relaxed.

Molokai rose, a great hulk blocking her vision. Kinimaka was at his side, the two a pair of enormous craggy mountains. Molokai watched for five minutes and then crept toward the closest car. It was a white SUV, a Nissan of some sort. Hayden doubted it would be unlocked, but then she had no doubt whatsoever that Molokai could carjack anything on wheels.

Molokai went alone. Hayden watched, placing a hand on Kinimaka's shoulder. "It'll feel so good to be free again."

Mano nodded. Then Kenshin stepped out of the shadows just around the front of their building, training a 9mm

Ruger SR9C on her, one of the best handguns available. Hayden froze, staring in disbelief. From behind, came the sounds of more men. She turned to see twelve more ninjas behind them, brandishing swords and guns.

Kenshin gave her an evil leer. "I wanted you to taste freedom," he said, "before I kill you."

Hayden felt the acute loss, felt the pain. She watched as Molokai was attacked by six ninjas, knocked down, rolled over and secured once more. He kicked and fought and knocked two attackers out, but he was far too weak to bring any real skill to bear.

As were Hayden and Kinimaka. Hayden offered her hands to Kenshin for tying. Kinimaka could barely hold himself up.

The Tsugarai leader laughed. "Tie them to the cars," he said, "and take them for a drive."

The gathered shinobi were unable to hide their collective grins. Hayden found herself dragged over to the white SUV and thrown backward onto the hood, her arms and legs spread-eagled. Her wrists were roped to the vehicles wing mirrors, her legs secured over the front fender. When they were finished, she couldn't move. Her back was arched uncomfortably over the hood, and her limbs ached once more. Kinimaka and Molokai were tied in a similar manner across the front of two other vehicles.

They were hood ornaments. Hayden braced herself as several men climbed into her car and one started the engine. She screamed when the car set off at speed, its tires churning at the earth, its front end slewing to the left. It flew up the hill, took a sharp right and then headed down a sharp slope, picking up speed. Hayden was at the front, able to see the grass and the hillside coming very quickly, pelted by earth when the driver turned the wheels, taken around an impromptu rally stage at speed. Rocks struck her body. Grass and soil cascaded over her like a dirty stream. She was flung this way and that in her bonds, her skin flayed. When the driver braked, her weight was transferred to the bonds at her ankles, which cut in deep and rubbed her raw.

At times, she saw the other two cars. Kinimaka and Molokai struggled at the front of them. Twice her car came perilously close to the rear of one of the others, her skin and bone mere inches away from the other vehicle. If the car in front had braked, her legs would have been pulverized.

Thirty minutes later, the cars returned to the compound. Hayden was a mess, her body coated with dirt, her hair matted with soil, blood flowing from several wounds. The Tsugarai chopped at her bonds, cutting her free and allowing her to slither down the hood of the car to the ground. She found herself in a heap, body heaving, face planted in the dirt. From Kenshin's shouting and mirth she knew both Kinimaka and Molokai were lying similarly.

"This is good," Kenshin said after a while. "Let them eat dirt. Tomorrow we will chop them up for firewood and pigswill. Maybe we will drive the cars over them first. Slowly. Leave them right where they are."

Hayden couldn't move. She was wracked with pain, exhausted, and despairing. Tomorrow, they would die, and it wouldn't go easy. The Tsugarai were the best covert fighters in the world and this was their home.

They stood no chance of being saved.

CHAPTER THIRTY FIVE

Zuki stalked the length of her office, wondering what the hell could have gone wrong in so short a time. The Tsugarai hadn't broken Hayden Jaye and her colleagues, although they were trying something new tonight, before killing them. Two of the Three Sacred Treasures had been found, so clearly the Tsugarai had failed to capture the jewel and the mirror.

They were supposed to be the best. That's why she hired them. She had all the power, wealth and influence in the world at hand, but she'd hired *them*.

Zuki stopped at the far end of her office, dropped into a crouch then came up with a spin kick, delivering deadly force to the underside of a prisoner's chin, snapping the head back and breaking the neck.

She waved a hand to one of her slaves. "Bring the next one in and get rid of this."

He bowed. She felt betrayed. Nobody loved her enough to support her through this crisis. Since her parents died and left her in charge, she'd felt alone. Everyone, including her advisors, thought her a privileged brat, fit only for looking good as a figurehead; publicity fodder. Zuki despised them. She would remake this bloodline, this dynasty, and she would remake it in her own image.

The idea to find the Three Sacred Treasures had been hers and now, it appeared, all of the seven fucking secret royal bloodlines was hunting for them. *Every single one.* They could see the commercial value, the everlasting glory.

"But it was my idea!" She kicked out at the next prisoner,

203

who was clad so tightly in rope he couldn't move. Her foot drove into his stomach, breaking ribs and hopefully a spleen. He collapsed, coughing blood. She smiled down at him, enjoying his pain, waving her guards away.

"Leave him to die. Bring me another."

"There are no more," the guard said.

She glared. "What? We've gone through six already? Are there no more we suspect of treachery working in our household?"

"Not yet."

"Then go and find me some more."

The guard turned and left. Zuki wandered over to the window, wondering if Kenshin was still spying on her through his drones. It was midnight in her private palace, overlooking Tokyo, and she could see a million shimmering lights, the slopes of Mount Fuji, and a glittering harbor. But she could see no peace, no clear way forward. All her hopes and dreams rested on a knife edge.

The fourth treasure was now a viable possibility. The samurai family had intimated through secret channels that they knew the location of Kusanagi, the great sword, just to piss her off. The Tsugarai were disappointing her.

What did she have left?

A decent sized army, she thought. *And me.* She was a deadly fighter; she'd killed ninjas in all-out battle. She'd bested a revered samurai in sword combat. If there was something she knew she was good at—it was one-on-one murder.

Zuki had hired a hundred house guards and just as many mercenaries. The trouble was, she didn't know the whereabouts of Mai Kitano or the two relocated treasures. The spies she employed inside the other royal households weren't reporting back. Perhaps they'd been killed. Zuki cursed them for being so inept. They were useless. The man she'd kicked to the floor groaned so she stood on his mouth until he stopped.

Bloodlust filled her.

"I am a weapons master," she said aloud, her breath fogging the window-pane. "In the end, it will come down to battle and glory."

The phone rang. It was Kenshin, a fact that gave her an unaccustomed shiver, standing as she was before the window.

"What do you want?"

"A small update. I am sending you pictures."

Zuki looked down at her phone, clicking on each image as it came through. There were twelve in total, all showing their three captives tied to the front of cars, being driven at speed through mud and dirt, and then the aftermath. All three captives lying in the mud, close to being broken, close to death it seemed, unmoving.

"Have they talked?"

"They can't talk. In a few hours we will start interrogating them until they die."

"Then we may have a lead tomorrow?"

"If they know anything, we will learn what it is."

"And the others? The samurai? This team led by Alicia Myles? Where is Mai Kitano?"

"As you know, she surfaced in Tokyo yesterday. We were close to catching her but missed."

"Missed?" Zuki repeated. "You fucking failed me, Kenshin. All you fucking shinobi gutter rats have failed me."

Kenshin took almost half a minute to answer her. "You would do well not to insult a shinobi master and his clan. You would do well not to take sordid histories as gospel.

The shinobi are made from all classes. They are noble."

Zuki didn't accept that but didn't want to anger him either, having placed all her faith in these miserable peasants. "I am venting," she said. "I gather Kitano has gone to ground again."

"It seems so, but she will resurface when we start killing her friends tomorrow."

"Keep me informed." Zuki said.

"You should get some sleep," Kenshin said. "You look a little wasted. There might be battle soon."

Zuki stared into the heart of the city, where darkness nestled. That was where Kenshin's drone was watching her from. "I look forward to the bloodbath."

"I know. It will come."

"Have a drone record their deaths tomorrow and loop me in," Zuki said. "I want to see how they die."

"It will be done."

Zuki ended the call, then turned her back on the window and, with a click of a remote, turned the glass opaque. Her kingdom, her very dynasty, hung on the edge of a precipice right now.

Tomorrow's events would decide which way it teetered.

She walked over to her sword cabinet, which hung beside her weapons chest. She saw blood and honor and glory coming in the next few days. She would be ready to accept all of it.

CHAPTER THIRTY SIX

Through the night, Alicia, her teammates and the samurai flew to Izumo, the Land of the Gods. In a show of faith, they left the two Sacred Treasures they'd already found back at the samurai stronghold in Tokyo. They traveled now fully loaded with weaponry and tech, closing in on the third treasure.

Alicia was fascinated by the samurai garb. They wore black tunics and leggings made of a mix of leather and some rough fabric. Their clothing bore none of the colorful, regal splendor she associated with the samurai. It was simple, hard-wearing gear for hard fighting, not unlike the gear the Tsugarai wore. They also carried face masks and hoods, but hadn't put them on. Alicia didn't quite know how to start a conversation with a full-blooded samurai, so thought it best to stay quiet.

Dahl was seated next to her. "Never thought I'd see you intimidated."

"I'm not," Alicia said. "I'm imagining them without their clothes on."

Dahl shook his head. "Don't come back with that deflective Alicia crap. You never thought you'd find yourself running with a bunch of hard-ass samurai now, did you?"

"Actually, no. I quite like it."

Dahl leaned in and whispered, "Me too," before sitting back. Alicia nodded at Luther, Karin, Kenzie and Dino, making sure all was well before allowing her mind to switch off.

They would need the rest. They were going after the

third Sacred Treasure—the most famous one of all. Kusanagi, the sword, had been remade by Masamune, the expert swordmaker. It was the principal piece, the distinctive item that would stir the public's interest. And with all the other royal bloodlines now chasing it down they couldn't afford to fail.

They landed in the dead of night, disembarking and dispersing into waiting cars. They were a large entourage, speeding through the night.

They approached Izumo as dawn lightened the eastern sky.

The Izumo Taisha Grand Shrine had been built against a forest backdrop. Huge trees rose behind the long, low, wooden buildings like protective giants. The shrine appeared to be made up of several buildings with one, a great peaked, several-story structure, standing proud at the back. They approached across a gravel courtyard, their faces warmed by the rising sun.

Alicia and Dahl walked with Tenmei. "The previous clues told us pretty much where the treasures were hidden," she said. "This last one seems a little lacking."

"We think the fact that it mentions the sword by its legendary description, and not its name, is significant. It points us toward Masamune. Every sword he ever made bore a description and his name. For instance, the most famous blade, the Honjo Masamune. Then the Fudo Masamune. The Kotegiri Masamune."

"I've heard of the Honjo," Kenzie said, sidling up on the right. "I know swords, and that's the best. Forget your famous rubbish, Charlemagne's Joyeuse, the Viking's Legbiter and Sir William Wallace's blade. Even Kusanagi, the sword we're looking for which is the Japanese equivalent of Excalibur, pales in comparison. The Honjo is the world's greatest masterpiece."

Tenmei slowed and studied Kenzie as if noticing her for the first time. "You are a swordswoman?"

"Yes, it is my passion."

"You are right, of course. The Honjo is Masamune's finest. A terrible shame that it was lost at the end of World War II."

Kenzie inclined her head. "Tokugawa Lemasa gave it and fourteen other swords to a police station at Mejiro in December 1945. In January the Mejiro police gave these swords to a man identified as Sergeant Cody Bimore of the US Army. It was later learned that no records of a Sergeant Bimore exist. And the Honjo remains missing."

"Wait," Dahl said. "What does Masamune have to do with this shrine? Why do you think the description of the sword in the haiku is significant?"

"Because this grand shrine displays the Fudo Masamune and, we think, is an important nod toward Kusanagi which, as we know, he remade in the fourteenth century, adding the meteorite frame."

"There's a Masamune in here?" Kenzie looked surprised.

"Yes. It is not a widely known fact."

Alicia leaned close to Kenzie's ear. "I think he knows you're a relic smuggler."

"Used to be." Kenzie batted her away. "Not anymore."

"You're thinking if we find one Masamune, the other, the hidden Sacred Treasure, won't be far away?"

"It's a theory," Tenmei said. "Shall we test it?"

Alicia saw they had reached the main entrance of the grand shrine. It wasn't open at this early hour, but Tenmei had no problems persuading the few monks present to let them inside. Taking care, Alicia and her five teammates, Tenmei and eight samurai, walked into the shrine. They passed into a main hall which, according to Tenmei, used to be much larger in ancient times. He even pointed out the old pillars, no longer in use, that gave credence to this fact. The place was built in the old style and bore scissor-shaped finials at the front and back ends of the roof. The inside was built in four sections, the entrance offset. Alicia saw a lot of gold, glowing architecture, from walls to statues and even the floor.

Tenmei soon led them to the Masamune display, which stood almost irrelevantly to the right of a larger, full-wall exhibition of items. Tenmei bowed slightly when he set eyes on the Fudo Masamune, as did his colleagues.

Alicia stared at it. A short sword with a golden handle. Tenmei turned to her. "This samurai sword, or dagger, was crafted primarily for stabbing, but the edge is so sharp it can be useful for slashing too. If you look closely you will see it has been signed by the master himself."

Alicia peered at the dagger, which measured twenty-five centimeters long. She saw a carving of roots on the front outer edge, a dragon on the inner side and several other engravings she wasn't sure about. Kenzie pushed in alongside, giving the shining steel some wide eyes.

"Never thought I'd see anything like this."

Alicia backed away and took in the shrine, the emptiness, the open plan design. "Tenmei," she said. "Is this it?"

Tenmei nodded. "This is it," he repeated. "And the Fudo is the only sword."

Karin was walking through the open spaces. "You said this was the newest construction of several older shrines. Do you know how many?"

"At least four."

"And their build dates?"

Tenmei shook his head, but a word with an onlooking monk gave them an answer. "There is no record of when construction began. In 1200 though, the shrine was reduced in size. In 1744 it was reconstructed to its present size. It has been renovated at least four times."

"Ask them if we can see the oldest structure."

Tenmei looked puzzled.

"The Three Sacred Treasures have been lost for centuries, right? Only the Tsugarai knew their resting places. The Tsugarai clan originated in the year 1200."

Tenmei stared. "You think the Tsugarai rebuilt this shrine, making it smaller in the year 1200, to hide the great sword?"

"More than that," Karin said. "I'm thinking the Tsugarai clan were *formed* in 1200, for the sole purpose of hiding the sword. It was that important, along with the other treasures. I think the Tsugarai were the original protectors and that is how they came into being."

"Ninja?" Tenmei wondered aloud. "Shinobi? Created to hide the great treasures?"

"The newest form of assassins," Karin said. "It makes sense. Who would make better protectors?"

"They lost their way so very greatly," Tenmei growled. "They lost their honor, their purpose and their humanity."

"Agreed," Dahl said. "This theory of yours, Karin. It depends on us seeing the old structure?"

Tenmei got the hint and asked the question. The monk, an older fellow with deep wrinkles around both eyes and across his forehead, looked dubious at first. Tenmei asked again. He wouldn't threaten the old monk, Alicia knew, but he did sound persuasive.

"There is a place," Tenmei said, "but it is a much-revered passage and the ruins are very dangerous. They have collapsed in places. Nobody goes there anymore."

"Sounds perfect," Karin said. "A great place to hide a national treasure."

"Not for us," Luther growled. "Alicia, send the samurai in first."

Alicia grimaced as Tenmei shot Luther a displeased look. "Don't worry, he's not serious."

"American humor?" Tenmei asked.

"Well, more like dumbfuck humor, I guess."

They were led to the back of the shrine and out of a rear door. Outside and before them, the great gargantuan forest reared, thick tree cover to all sides. The morning was warm and quiet. Tenmei listened to the monk before speaking.

"He says the shrine extended into the trees hundreds of years ago. From this point. It will be next to impossible to find the ruins."

Alicia felt her stomach sink. "We can't give up now."

"We're not going to." Tenmei said. "I've just sent him to fetch the old plans."

Dahl shook his head in surprise. "They still have them?"

"We keep everything," Tenmei said. "That is why our culture is so far superior to yours."

Alicia stared as Tenmei was handed a sheaf of old papers. She caught Dahl's eye and gave him a hopeful look.

She just hoped the others had a few more days.

CHAPTER THIRTY SEVEN

Tenmei paced through the overgrown brush right up to the treeline, trying to map out the ancient shrine's footprint. It took all eight samurai about an hour to pinpoint the outer edges, giving Tenmei and Alicia's team something to look at. One of the issues was that the old shrine extended into the trees.

Alicia walked eight trunks deep before she came to what appeared to be the outer wall of the original structure. At least, according to Karin's calculations. There was nothing obvious, nothing physical.

Tenmei advised everyone to start digging, either with hands, spades or any makeshift tools they could find. Alicia fell to her knees and started pulling at the grass, finding the roots and feeling the ground with her hands, hoping to touch some old stone foundations or part of a long-forgotten floor. With fifteen of them working hard, an hour passed quickly.

They found two walls of the old temple, long overgrown and lost under the land. Samurai dug away the earth to better expose the ruins and give line of sight to others working further along.

Alicia, to her disgust, found nothing. Dino found a corner of something dark, hard and old, and Luther found the jagged remains of a wall. As the two-hour mark passed they had a pretty good idea of the ancient shrine's plan.

"Would they have had trees growing through the temple?" Karin asked. "How old are those trees?"

"Hang on, let me ask." Alicia turned to a gnarly trunk

before raising her hands. "How the hell would I know?"

"I was speaking my thoughts out loud. The Tsugarai came here nine hundred years ago. These trees are older than that. They could have made the argument that nobody wanted trees in a shrine, so they closed this part off." Karin was checking every tree as she spoke.

"Wait," Kenzie suddenly said.

Everyone looked up and stared at the dark-haired Israeli. Alicia glared. "What is it now?" she expressed her irritation at the woman she most disliked.

Kenzie either didn't hear her or chose to ignore her. "How long has the Fudo been here?"

Tenmei sighed, wiped his hands and sat in the grass. "I don't know. Masamune lived roughly around 1288-1328, so I guess over six hundred years?"

"And the Tsugarai were created in 1200, eighty years or so before his birth?"

"Yes, what are you getting at?"

"It's an old relic smuggling trick. You hide the greater prize beneath the lesser. Camouflage that which is more valuable under something of value, so nobody ever touches it. I mean, who would ever think of removing the Fudo to check if something else is underneath? Or close by?"

"Nobody," Tenmei said, scrambling up. "That is a good idea."

Everyone rose, brushed themselves off and stamped their boots before returning to the shrine. Alicia thought it ironic, considering what they were about to do, but went with the flow. Even Luther scraped his soles.

Inside, the atmosphere was tranquil. Low music played. A golden suffused light slanted through windows. Alicia saw that the place was empty.

She was relieved and said so. Dahl strode over to the

Fudo sword alongside Tenmei. "Would you rather I did it?" the Swede asked. "To save you a little grief."

Tenmei raised his eyebrows. "That is good of you."

Dahl considered the Fudo display. Alicia sidled up to his left shoulder. The dagger was displayed upright inside a wooden cabinet fixed to the wall. Dahl studied the cabinet, checking its measurements.

"I'd say its twelve or thirteen inches thick," he said. "Could easily fit two swords inside."

Alicia snorted. "Men," she said. "The cabinet's only nine inches. Believe me, I know."

"Doesn't change anything," Dahl said. "It's also over eighteen inches long, which is more than twice the length of the Fudo. I'm liking this theory more and more."

Kenzie grinned. Alicia watched Dahl reach out gingerly, grabbing hold of the wooden cabinet at both sides and lifting it off the wall. It resisted at first, age and two silver hooks holding it back, but the Swede only had to apply a little extra pressure to pull it free.

Then he knelt, Tenmei at his right. The other samurai assembled, crowding out Luther, Dino and Karin. Dahl turned the cabinet over.

"Anyone got a knife?" he asked.

Considering the company he was keeping it was a silly question, but as the samurai reached for their weapons Kenzie was already handing Dahl her own.

"Don't mistreat it, Torsten."

Alicia saw how she touched the Swede's hand, her fingers lingering, but was pleased to see Kenzie trying to be her old self again. The death of Dallas had knocked the wind right out of her sails, more so than any other member of the team. Dallas had been *her* friend, her protégé of sorts. Alicia knew a little of the void a friend's death left behind.

She made room for Kenzie, who knelt at Dahl's left. The Swede inserted the tip of the knife under a lip of wood and angled it, forcing the cabinet apart. It came slowly. He took his time, not wanting to break even the slightest part of something that belonged to Japan's incredible ancient culture.

Five minutes later, he had the back off.

He opened it. There was a collective gasp. There, fastened to the back of the same wooden panel to which the Fudo was held, was Kusanagi, the principal piece of the Three Sacred Treasures. It was a black sword, its blade set in the now familiar meteorite frame. Its old edges still gleamed in the light, sharp and deadly.

Alicia felt a rush of excitement. "With this sword we have all three treasures and the final haiku that points to the fourth. We have a means of saving our friends. We have leverage over Zuki."

"And we," Tenmei said, "have just elevated our bloodline."

It was a bold statement, but Alicia was elated and chose to ignore it. She saw the return of Drake and Hayden, Mai and the others. She saw that leading a team might even work out well in the end.

She saw an end to their battle with the Tsugarai.

Unaware that it had barely begun.

CHAPTER THIRTY EIGHT

Basking in the warm glow of sunshine after a cold night in the forest, Drake and Mai kept a close eye on the compound whilst prepping for the night ahead. Drake noticed the sudden flurry of activity.

"Mai," he said. "This is bad."

The Japanese woman scrambled for her field glasses. Together, they lay in the high grass on the edge of the forest, eyes trained toward the camp.

"We ran out of time," Mai breathed with anguish in her voice.

They saw eight Tsugarai warriors dragging three slumped, bedraggled shapes out of a building. The shapes had no discernible form; they were so covered in mud and dirt that their hands and faces were as black as their clothes and hair. They couldn't support themselves, though they did try to walk and push their captors away.

At first, Drake was uplifted to see Hayden, Kinimaka and Molokai still fighting, still active.

Then he saw where the warriors were leading his friends.

A clearing at the edge of the compound, dusted with a thin layer of fine gravel. It had a circular boundary marked in stone. At the center, five sturdy wooden posts had been driven into the ground and Mai pointed out three short objects lying on the ground right in front of the posts.

"That is an abomination," she whispered.

"What? I don't see anything but some posts."

"Look in front of the posts."

Drake refocused. "Looks like three scabbards, very short."

"They are going to offer our friends the chance to commit seppuku. If they refuse, they will be tied to the posts and hacked to death."

Drake fought down a surge of fear and revulsion. "Seppuku? Isn't that the samurai form of ritual suicide by disembowelment?"

"Yes. Also called Harikiri¸ it offers the samurai warrior a chance to die with honor. Of course, the Tsugarai shinobi hate the samurai, they are polar opposites. This is a perversion."

"Why would they want to dishonor the samurai right now?"

"I don't know. Seppuku is an elaborate ritual, performed in front of a crowd. It consists of plunging a short sword, a tanto, deeply into the stomach and then drawing it from left to right. To be clear, the act was abolished in 1873."

Drake couldn't believe his eyes. "They're gonna make Hayden, Mano and Molokai commit seppuku?"

"They can't *make* them. But they will kill them slowly afterward."

"Mai, we have to help them now."

"I know, but we can't. Those are genuine shinobi warriors, Matt. At night, staying hidden, we stand a chance. An attack right now means certain death."

Drake was already checking his weapons. He shrugged on body armor and then his backpack. "I won't watch my friends die."

Mai offered a hushed curse. "It might not come to that. We have Mariko inside. She might change things. And Hayden can't be underestimated. Plus, Alicia and the others are working for us somewhere."

"I'm not leaving it to that kind of chance. I'm getting closer, so I can act if needs be."

Without turning, he descended once more into the ditch and crawled toward the camp. Five minutes later he was halfway there and stopped. Mai was at his back. Drake took out the field glasses and focused in.

Hayden, Kinimaka and Molokai were standing alone, slumped, all three looking as if they were on the edge of passing out. They had been positioned behind the ceremonial swords. Tsugarai stood around the clearing, watching. One warrior stood behind each captive, their hands on the hilts of their swords.

Drake hurried, navigating the rest of the ditch in just a few minutes. When he reached the end, he sprawled headlong up its slope, unhooked his M17, and sighted in on the clearing. Mai crouched at his side, short-barreled machine pistol in one hand, wicked curved knife in the other. Her eyes were darker than the pits of hell.

"Tell me when we're charging."

Drake nodded. He was concentrating on what was happening in the clearing. Hayden, Kinimaka and Molokai had been forced to their knees. A single Tsugarai wearing the usual leather tunic and trousers, but with a red stripe that appeared to single him out as a leader, stood before them. He carried a curved, single-edged blade with a squared guard and long grip.

"Main dude's carrying a katana," he said. "Isn't that a samurai weapon too?"

"Yes, the new Tsugarai grand master is corrupting the samurai ritual as much as he can. But he will not do the killing."

Drake watched as Hayden looked downward at the short swords presented there. The Tsugarai leader was speaking, probably offering them the chance to commit seppuku.

Molokai and Kinimaka also looked down. Drake knew

what would be going through their heads. They knew they were dead. They hadn't seen any sign of rescue. Could they reach the short swords, grab them and attack the Tsugarai before all three of them were killed? Could they take some of their captors with them? Perhaps one of them might escape?

Drake sighted in on the three captors standing behind his friends, using Mai's guidance. First, he saw Hayden shake her head and then the others. But then he saw Molokai try to seize a blade but, with shocking swiftness, the Tsugarai leader brought the katana slicing down.

Its lethal edge stopped an inch from Molokai's right wrist, which was two inches above the short sword.

Drake winced, shocked at how fast the Tsugarai warrior had moved. Molokai drew back. Drake surveyed the circular clearing, counting forty Tsugarai, most of them men. He couldn't see Mariko.

"Ready?" he asked.

Three men dragged Hayden and the others to their feet and pulled them toward the wooden poles. Drake reasoned that it would be better to have his friends unchained when he acted so took careful aim.

"Three, two, one."

His first bullet blew Hayden's captor's head apart. His second killed Kinimaka's. His third caught Molokai's captor in the chest as he moved. By then Mai was up and running, but still with a hundred yards of open ground to cover. Drake shot at center mass, three bullets in quick succession fired into the Tsugarai as they grouped together. He covered Hayden, Kinimaka and Molokai too, shooting any warrior that stepped toward them.

Mai was halfway there. Drake emerged from cover, the rifle's sight pressed to his right eye, still shooting. He ran to

Mai's left, arcing around, flooring another two warriors with chest shots.

The Tsugarai leader had backed away. There were about fifteen men gathered around him. Mai used her machine pistol to whittle the enemy down even more. But they were charging her now, and the gap was down to just a few feet.

They raised swords. She fired a volley at them. As they came together, she stopped and rolled forward, slicing her knife in a wide arc, slashing two ribcages before she jumped to her feet. Then she fell to her knees and fired again, using her right hand. Her left wielded the knife to and fro, slicing it in sharp, lethal curves, ripping flesh and striking metal.

Drake ranged around her, sighting and killing individual foes. He counted fifteen still loosely gathered around Mai, far too many. The Tsugarai leader was advancing with his own bodyguard now, at least ten strong, and more warriors were running from buildings all around.

"With me!"

Drake backed off, heading in Hayden's direction. Mai broke away from her fight. They couldn't keep this up, but he had spare weapons he intended to pass to Hayden and the others. But the Tsugarai weren't as naïve as he hoped they were. Yes, they'd come to their own clearing carrying only swords, but those warriors joining the fight now from the compound were toting machine guns.

Drake reached Hayden, nodding grimly at her mud-and-blood-soiled face. "Forget to shower?"

The camaraderie gave her an added ounce of will. "Bring a gun?"

"Fucking right I did. In fact, I brought a dozen."

Drake saw the Tsugarai leader, with his guard of ten men, coming toward them, another group at their right. He handed out the guns, heart sinking as Kinimaka slumped to his knees even before he'd grabbed a weapon. But they steadied him. They stood together in a tight, ragged group, letting those that needed support lean on them.

"Surrender," the Tsugarai leader called. "We can talk."

"Fuck off, Kenshin," Hayden shouted back. "Your word is death."

Mai nodded in appreciation. "That describes the shinobi well."

Drake supported Kinimaka. Mai had Molokai resting on her left shoulder. Hayden was wilting but propped up by Kinimaka. All five of them held their guns steady, trained on their enemies.

"If you fight, you will die," Kenshin said.

"Stop talking like a bell end," Drake said. "And do your worst."

Kenshin frowned, unsure what that meant. He looked about ready to give the order to fire, but then a crafty expression crossed his face. "We can bargain for your lives," he said. "The filthy samurai have the Three Sacred Treasures. Or rather, your friends joined them and gave them the Three Sacred Treasures. We will exchange you, for them. That way, you will all live." His black eyes drifted over Mai, an evil glint in them. "Even you, the vilest creature that ever defiled our territory with your treachery. Even you, who murdered our grand master."

Drake watched as Mai held herself back with difficulty. Standing here, now, in this scenario, had to be one of the hardest things she'd ever done. He couldn't imagine how she'd feel if the Tsugarai captured them.

He considered Kenshin's words. If nothing else, it gave them time. But could they risk losing the Three Sacred Treasures? To be fair, the answer was "yes". Karin and probably Dahl would have photographed them, and losing the treasures today didn't mean they would be lost forever.

"Make the call," he said. "We'll wait."

"No. You will submit to chains first."

"Fuck off, dickhead. Do I look like a Fifty Shades kinda guy?"

Again, Kenshin hesitated. "Fifty Shades?"

"You don't get Netflix here? Well, the answer's no."

Kenshin raised an arm, as if preparing his men to fire. Drake was 99 percent sure it was a bluff. The man's earlier offer about using them to get the treasures rang true. Zuki had hired them to do exactly that. This was Kenshin fulfilling their contract.

And the Tsugarai cared about little else.

Then Mariko made her move.

Drake saw her coming. Kenshin did not. She came clad in black, from a distant doorway, sidling along the grass and then the gravel, right up behind the grand master. He knew nothing until her right arm encircled around his throat and her left poked a dagger at his ribs.

"Let them go."

Men whirled, moving to cover her, to strike, but Kenshin held up a hand. "You will not beat her to the blow," he said.

Drake felt sorrow for Mariko. Unfortunate circumstance had dictated they didn't need her in the end, but she hadn't known that. She was acting on initiative to prove her worth, to escape this torturous life.

Drake held a hand up. "Wait. She's with us and part of the deal."

"She is a traitor and will be executed without mercy."

"You touch her, and I'll remove your head." Mai stepped forward.

Mariko thrust the tip of the blade between Kenshin's ribs. The grand master gasped. Mariko looked ready to shove her sword up to the hilt. Kenshin must have sensed it for he suddenly cried out.

"Go then! Go to the traitor and her hateful friends. You leave behind the best part of you."

Mariko hesitated. She wanted to end this man's life right now. Drake called her name and shook his head.

Mai raised her own knife. "If you kill him now, they will kill you." She indicated the gathered warriors. "Save that justice for another day, when you might extract your revenge and survive."

Mariko glanced from Kenshin to Mai. Then she dashed away from Kenshin, passed through the Tsugarai ranks and ran to Mai's side. Drake kept his gun steady.

"So what are you gawping at? We don't have all day. Make the call."

CHAPTER THIRTY NINE

Alicia took the call, placing it on speakerphone when she realized the terrible seriousness of it.

"I am Zuki Chiyome. Get me Tenmei."

"I am here," the samurai leader said.

They were gathered inside the samurai HQ in Tokyo, seated around a low table, the phone resting in the middle. The perimeter of the room was lined with samurai.

"Good," Zuki said. "I have five captives, friends of those that found the treasures, whose shirttails you cling to. I offer a one-time deal. The treasures for the captives."

Alicia leaned forward, about to speak, but Tenmei held up a hand. She looked into eyes like ice.

"There will be no negotiation," Tenmei said. "We have everything we want and also the haikus to the fourth treasure. I won't negotiate with an obscenity that hires scum like the Tsugarai to do their dirty work."

Even Luther winced. "Steady, bro, steady."

But Tenmei showed no emotion, no sign that he was bluffing. Alicia saw exactly how this was going to go.

"Who is in charge there?" Zuki asked. "The fatuous samurai or the Special Forces team? I want to know."

"I am . . ." Alicia started to say, but Tenmei gestured at her. So furiously, that his men, ranged around the room, placed their hands on their swords and drew them three inches from their scabbards.

"Alicia Myles?" Zuki said. "Was that you? I have your friends. Five of them. If you don't give me the treasures by midnight, I will send them back to you a sliver at a time, for as long as you live. My Tsugarai friends are already arranging some suitable tortures. Among the captives is the somewhat infamous Mai Kitano. The Tsugarai will enjoy planning her slow, agonizing fate."

Alicia jumped to her feet, ignored the half-drawn swords, and grabbed the phone. "Don't you dare harm any of them."

"Or what? You'll come for me? I have an army of two hundred."

"We've faced worse odds."

"Maybe, but your friends will still be dead."

Alicia glared at Tenmei as she considered Zuki's words. The bitch was right. She took a moment to glance at Dahl and Luther, at Kenzie. "The treasures for our captives."

She spoke the words as a statement, not a question.

"Good. Midnight then." Zuki reeled off a set of coordinates.

"Wait. How do we know they're still alive?" Kenzie blurted out.

Zuki sighed and sent three phone images through. Alicia and the others saw Drake, Hayden and everyone else standing in a group, weapons trained, but they also saw a force of around eighty Tsugarai facing them.

"For now, there is stalemate," Zuki said. "I will order that your friends are fed and watered. But if the midnight deadline is not kept, I will order them destroyed like the cattle they are."

The connection was broken. Alicia held on to the phone, now choosing to meet Tenmei's eyes. Dahl rose at her side, and then the rest of her team, unarmed but ready to back her to the hilt. The six of them would be a formidable force in this room, even arrayed against twelve samurai.

Tenmei's glare could cut glass. "The Three Sacred Treasures are the Imperial Regalia of Japan. They have legendary status. Nothing is more important than returning them to their people. You will not barter them for mere human lives."

"The people don't know they're missing," Dahl said. "You've been duping them for decades. That's betrayal too, but suddenly you guys are feeling sanctimonious?"

"They will elevate Japan to a whole new level."

"No, they will elevate your bloodline, the Shingen family, to a whole new level. Probably the most influential family on the planet. That's what it will do."

"The fourth treasure must be found."

"We're working on that. We have photographs. We don't need the treasures."

Tenmei placed a hand on the hilt of his sword. His men took that as a sign to draw theirs. Alicia was left staring at a dozen wicked, glinting blades. "My word is final," Tenmei told them. "On pain of death, you will leave the treasures alone. You cannot have them. I will lend men if you wish to attempt to rescue friends before midnight, but that is all."

Alicia scowled. "We found those fucking treasures. We recovered them. That bitch is right—you did nothing but cling to our shirttails."

Tenmei's knuckles whitened around his sword. "We saved you in Tokyo, but I will not lose face with argument. My decision has been made."

And with that he, followed by his men, stalked out of the room. Alicia was left facing the rest of her team, face red, heart pounding as though she'd been in mortal combat.

"Fucking samurai," Kenzie said. "If we leave, I'm taking two of those katanas. One for me, one for that bastard's tires."

Alicia turned to Dahl. "What do you think?"

"He has the treasures. He owns this house. He offered to

help. It's not like we can leave and then sneak back in."

Alicia checked her watch. It was a little after 11 a.m. "All right," she said. "I agree, we can't. But I think I know someone else who can. I have a plan. Let's get the hell out of here."

Darkness was falling. Drake and the others had just two hours left to the deadline. Alicia stood in the deepest shadows, behind a row of dumpsters, staring across a quiet road at the samurai stronghold.

"Are you ready? Are you sure you can do this?"

A figure unfolded itself from the wall at her side. First, he nodded at her team and then he put a hand on her shoulder.

"What do you think? This is what I do. Am I the best thief in the world, or what?"

"Well, *best* is a bit of a broad description," Alicia said, "but you are pretty good, Yogi."

The Russian thief grinned at her use of his nickname. "If nothing else," he said. "That proves I'm back."

Alicia got serious. "Don't take chances. Those are bloody samurai in there. They'll chop you up for sushi without a second thought."

Yorgi moved away. It had been Alicia's idea to call the best thief they knew and ask him to steal the Three Sacred Treasures from the house of the samurai. The young man had been excited, chomping to get back into the life. The flight from Russia had taken five hours, sped up by Strike Force's international credentials. They had been prepping Yorgi and the building for the remaining time. Now, the minutes were ticking by faster than Alicia believed possible.

She saw Yorgi moving in the dark only because she knew

the route he was taking. He wore an all-black, tight-fitting catsuit and mask, gloves and special boots. He performed a buildering technique that made her wince, jumping from a wall to a window ledge and then a roof gable in just four leaps, each time trusting to balance, strength and skill.

She saw him crouched atop the tiled roof, a shadow against shadows.

"The trouble with that scene," Dahl said. "Is that he looks like a ninja."

"Yeah, and breaking into a samurai HQ." Luther shook his head. "I don't like it."

Yorgi crept like a cat across the roof tiles and then laid himself flat. Now, he was all but gone. Alicia saw the Russian remove several roof tiles before she let out a long breath.

"Now," she said. "We wait."

It was agonizing, and they had no way of knowing how Yorgi was doing. He'd left hospital several weeks ago just before they headed to Las Vegas to foil the Fabergé heist and had been resting ever since. Yorgi had assured them he was back to 90 if not 100 percent fitness. Alicia had been horribly reminded of his last mission—he'd headed to the frozen Russian wastes to recover the bodies of his siblings—and how it ended up. The new Blood King's men had tried to kill him one night, their murderous act stopped only by two brave SAS soldiers who lost their own lives in the process.

That was months ago. Yorgi was back and raring to go.

Alicia grabbed a bite to eat whilst she could and drank water. She checked the time. It was 23.20 hours. Only forty minutes until they had to meet Zuki's minions and hand over the treasures.

Forty minutes to decide Drake's fate. And the fates of all

their friends. Everything in the hands of a young Russian thief.

Still Yorgi didn't reappear. Alicia kept checking her phone, expecting a call from Tenmei, saying they'd caught him. But maybe there would be no call. Maybe Tenmei would just execute Yorgi and leave her friends to die. This was Alicia's plan. If it failed, she failed. She would die too.

23.30 passed.

Alicia touched Dahl's arm. "How long will it take to reach the coordinates Zuki gave us for the exchange?"

"Same as last time you asked. Twelve minutes."

"Damn, he's cutting it close."

23.45 passed.

Alicia tried to swallow but her mouth was too dry. They were out of time. It had all come to nothing. She didn't blame Yorgi, but he had been their last chance.

"Only one thing for it," Luther said. "We go to the handoff anyway and break bones until they give us something."

"If we left now, we could be at the Tsugarai compound by 3 a.m.," Karin said. "Surely they won't do anything before dawn."

Alicia chewed her top lip, considering that. It was, slightly, the better plan. Nothing was certain and she imagined that the Tsugarai would want full daylight before assaulting a crack Special Forces team, even if there were only five of them. They wouldn't want to throw their own lives away. She nodded her agreement and the team moved out toward their car.

"Hey," Yorgi said from a patch of darkness to their right. "You aren't quitting on me, are you?"

Alicia's heart leapt. "Did you get the treasures?"

Yorgi held up a black rucksack. "All three."

Alicia leapt at him, pulling him into a tight hug. "Well done, you little Russian bastard. Well done, I could kiss you."

Yorgi pulled away, holding out the bag. They were running now, racing for the car and the meeting place.

"Is that what happens now you're in charge? You kiss everyone who makes you happy?" The thief looked genuinely frightened.

"Yeah," Alicia said. "And you should see what I do when they really thrill me."

CHAPTER FORTY

Drake's legs felt like lumps of lead, but he refused to show any weakness. His companions stood around him, each one resting on the other, their eyes tired, their faces drawn, but not once letting their gun arms waver.

Midday had passed into afternoon. The sun beat down relentlessly. A refreshing shower came around 2 p.m., and a little after that Kenshin sent two men over with a bundle of food and water. The men made a show of drinking from every bottle and sampling every tray of food before walking away to prove it wasn't poisoned.

Drake ignored it for thirty minutes.

Kenshin walked over, shaking his head. "You will need it," he said. "Negotiations have been made for midnight tonight. You will be released if the treasures are handed over, but you will be making your own way out of here."

After that Drake and Mai fell on the sustenance, handing it out to Hayden, Kinimaka and Molokai, making them eat the majority of it. Drake and Mai had provisions in their backpacks, which they ate sitting warily on the ground.

"You three have any serious injuries?" Drake asked.

"Nothing rest won't heal," Hayden said. "But I'm guessing we're still some way off that."

"Very true," Mai hissed. "Every one of the Tsugarai will die first."

There wasn't a lot of talk after that. Hayden, Kinimaka and Molokai used spare water to wash their hands and faces, and scraped mud off their clothes. They tore clean T-shirts that Drake provided into strips to bind their flayed skin. The food gave them strength. The hours passed.

As night fell once more, Kenshin returned to them.

"The exchange is in three hours. If it happens you are free to go. If it doesn't, I will order my men to attack and bind you. We will then spend many months breaking you all down. I'm sure you know which way I want this to go."

"This Zuki must be paying you pigs in fine swill," Mai spat.

"We have a contract with a woman of royal blood, the leader of one of the most powerful families in the world. For now, we work for her, but if that changes anytime—" Kenshin shrugged "—we might pay her a visit."

"So, you're afraid of her?" Mai wouldn't let it go, cutting at Kenshin as if she were wielding a sword at his flesh and bone.

"The shinobi have a long memory, as you know. We can capitulate now to eradicate another day. Vengeance is a pleasure that matures with time. And you, Mai Kitano, you hear me now. We will never rest until we kill you. Your blood, your family and your friends will never be safe. And you will never see us coming."

Mai shot to her feet. Drake leapt up, restraining her. He got in between her and Kenshin. "No," he said, hanging on to her shoulders. "They don't know. *They don't know.*"

Finally, Mai's eyes focused. "What?"

"They don't know we're going to destroy them."

Mai fought her inner urges. Drake saw lightning, fire and fury in her expression. But finally, with help, she turned away from Kenshin, leaving him fuming at her back.

"You answer me, Kitano. Coward. Traitor. Clan-slayer. You answer me."

Mai whipped around, slipped Drake's grip, and shoved him back. She stalked forward until she was standing in front of Kenshin, nose to nose.

"The atrocities you perpetrate will be answered for. The

233

children you buy and force-train will turn on you. There is no clan when there is no peace. A brotherhood is not ruled by fear. A home is not a prison. You, Kenshin, you will pay hardest when I exterminate you all."

Mai turned away, coming back to Drake and sitting with her back to Kenshin. Drake squatted down next to her.

"I hope Alicia sorts that bloody treasure exchange out now."

Hayden smiled faintly. Kinimaka gave Mai a brotherly pat on the arm. Molokai scanned the camp. "How long?"

The hours passed with excruciating sluggishness but at midnight Kenshin approached them once more and said they were free to go. Disbelieving, Drake and Mai formed a rear guard as Hayden, Kinimaka and Molokai walked toward the far forest. It was a tense ten minutes at first. Drake waited for bullets to fly, or perhaps crossbows, but nothing happened. The half-moon created some light and Mai gave two of her flashlights to Kinimaka and Molokai.

They approached the edge of the forest.

Drake led them to the covered car, checking before throwing off its camo and opening the door. He turned the ignition as Hayden and the others settled in the back seat. Still, they carried their weapons high, ready for any kind of surprise attack.

Drake reversed out of the forest hide and headed for the main road without using headlights.

Mai studied the darkness, expecting movement, expecting an attack. She handed out more food to those in the back, the last of their rations.

Ten minutes later they were on the main road.

Drake finally did something he'd been dying to do all day. Kenshin had forbidden the use of phones. They'd been forced to capitulate. But now he called Alicia.

"Hello?" she sounded breathy, expectant.

"Hey love, it's me."

"Yes!" Drake imagined Alicia leaping into the air before she came back on the line. "Are you all okay?"

"We're good. Banged up, but good. We're heading home."

"We're waiting."

"Is this thing over?"

"Shit, no. There are seven secret royal Japanese families about to do battle in search of the fourth, fabled Sacred Treasure. There are shinobi, pissed-off samurai, mercenaries and Special Forces involved. Does that sound over to you?"

Drake widened his eyes at Mai. "No. And we have another small addendum to that. We've vowed to destroy the Tsugarai."

"Oh, well, we'll just add that to the list then."

"Wait," Hayden said from the back, leaning forward. "What you said doesn't sound plausible. You were with the samurai, right? Zuki and now the Tsugarai have the treasures, and thus the haikus that leads to the fourth treasure. But how do the other families know?"

"Because I just sent the knowledge public," Alicia growled back. "Because the samurai are hypocrites and really fucked me off. Because Zuki is a royal brat that plays with innocent lives every goddamn day. And because the Tsugarai are just a big bunch of wankers. That's why, and how."

Drake whistled. "That's gonna hot things up a bit," he said. "I'd get to work on that final haiku if I were you. We'll be with you in two hours."

"Look forward to it," Alicia said, her voice softening.

"Me too," Mai added.

And then Yorgi spoke up. "And me!"

Drake laughed and shook his head. It really was shaping up to be the oddest end to a mission he'd ever been involved with. He ended the call and turned to those in the back seat.

"I'd get some rest," he said. "Sleep if you can. We're not even close to the end of this yet."

CHAPTER FORTY ONE

In Tokyo, the Strike Force team were reunited.

With little time to waste and think, they rented an expansive room at the Keio Plaza, ostensibly to allow Hayden, Kinimaka and Molokai use of its two showers, but also to allow everyone the chance to sit in comfort for a few hours, the chance to relax, and the use of some superfast Wi-Fi.

"Where's the bloody mini bar?" Alicia was the first to grab two miniature bottles of whiskey.

Dahl jumped on the telephone, ordering up everything on the menu. Karin settled herself at a table in front of the panoramic window overlooking north-eastern Tokyo. Drake was happy to shrug out of his body armor and clothes and just sit there in his T-shirt and boxer shorts whilst he waited for the shower.

"Ey up," he said as Alicia brought him a miniature Jim Beam. "Is that it?"

"More on the way." She clinked his plastic bottle with hers, unscrewed the top and drank it down in one. Drake did the same.

"Where's my kiss then, love?"

Alicia gave him the eye. "It can wait until you've showered. And besides, you're wearing boxers. I wouldn't want to embarrass you in front of our friends."

Drake looked blank for a moment before shaking his head as it finally sank in. "You stayed out of trouble the last few days?"

"Of course not. You?"

"Don't be daft."

"That's good then. And Mai?"

"She definitely didn't stay out of trouble." Drake knew Alicia, that she trusted both him and Mai completely, but also that she couldn't help herself. Her upbringing instilled very little trust in her, and army life had taught her there were few friends she could rely on in this world. Those friends were here in this room.

Yorgi came over. Alicia explained how he'd returned with a heroic bang, stealing the Three Sacred Treasures from under the noses of the samurai.

"Of course, you're gonna be number one on their hit list now," she told Yorgi. "But that's a good thing. Embrace it."

"Why is it good?"

"You're kidding me? Screw FBI wanted lists, Interpol Most Wanted and all that crap. You're the top dog on the fucking *samurai* hit list. Well done, man!" She gave him a high five.

Yorgi shook his head. Karin, working hard at the table, shouted that she was ready to lead them through everything she'd managed to collate so far.

"About bloody time," Hayden grumbled, stepping out of the bathroom after her shower, a towel wrapped around her body and another brushing vigorously at her hair. Drake jumped up to use it. Ten minutes later he was back in the front room, feeling refreshed and wrapped up in yet another large luxurious towel.

It was an odd looking crew then, that sat down in that sumptuous suite, half wrapped in fresh towels, half wearing old T-shirts and shorts, all trying to grab a little rest, food, drink and togetherness before heading out to what they knew could well be the battle of their lives.

Karin waited for everyone's attention before speaking.

"The third Sacred Treasure, the sword Kusanagi, was set into the same ancient meteorite frame as all the others. Hidden in plain sight in Izumo, the Land of the Gods, behind a valuable sword made by Masamune, it was there for centuries. On its reverse, engraved into the meteorite, was but a single haiku. This is it:

"Beyond the Stone Ruins of Akya,
"The Source and Axis of the Emerald River,
"Through Bora Pass,
"To Mythical Kojiki."

"What the hell does that mean?" Molokai grumbled. "Are we supposed to make any sense of it?"

"You don't know the half," Karin said. "That's the last of three verses. Do you want to hear them all?"

"Do I have to, or can you just tell me where the fourth treasure is?"

Karin shrugged. "I don't know. We have to work this out. I have Dai and his translator and several historians working on it, but rest assured the samurai, the Tsugarai, and all the other royal families will be working on this right now."

Molokai held up a hand in surrender. "Run it by me."

Drake smiled slightly at the big man's laconic attitude. It was good to see him getting involved. Karin took a deep breath and read out the full haiku that supposedly pointed them to the fourth fabled treasure.

"Through stars I fell,
"The Chalice in the Shield,
"The Treasure of Orion.
"Old Rock stabilizes Planet,
"Old Rhythms maintained,
"For Healing, For Wishing, For Purification,
"We Saturate Space.
"Beyond the Stone Ruins of Akya,

"The Source and Axis of the Emerald River,
"Through Bora Pass,
"To Mythical Kojiki."

Molokai blinked several times. Alicia wondered aloud if it was a new Miley Cyrus song and suggested calling her agent. Mai spoke up first.

"Three different haikus," she said, "written in distinctive styles, suggests three different meanings. For instance, the first haiku appears to hint at what the treasure might be. The second, what it does. The third, where it is."

Karin pursed her lips and nodded. "That's good."

"I know my haikus," Mai said.

"Get Dai on the phone," Alicia said. "He's been working this for days."

Mai fixed her with a frown. "He's what?"

Alicia grimaced. "Shit, sorry. I know you said not to get him involved but we couldn't have gotten this far without him."

Mai continued to glare.

"Look, we can fight it out later. For now, call Dai."

But Mai didn't back down. "When this is done," she said. "I'm going to teach you respect. I asked you not to involve my family. That's only three people on the planet. Grace, Chika and Dai. You had everyone else to choose from. If anything happens . . ."

Alicia took it on board, the weight settling on her shoulders. Karin took out a cellphone and called Dai. "Any luck?"

"I have eight people around the world working on this. The best researchers and intellectuals in their fields. One of Japan's best academics, who's famous for working on the oldest texts. I have a genius professor. I even have a feisty historian from the gnarly relic hunter crew that recently found Atlantis."

"Fantastic," Drake said. "What did they find out?"

"Loosely put together? We've obviously had more time to study the first two haikus. The first describes the coming to earth of a great treasure. Literally, it crashed down from the stars. It originated from the constellation Orion."

"The treasure of Orion," Drake breathed. "Understood. Are you talking about a meteorite here?"

"Exactly. The treasure is a product of the first meteorite ever to impact our earth, many millions of years ago, which explains why the Three Sacred Treasures were later mounted in a frame of that meteorite. This brings us to the second haiku. The treasure was formed when the meteorite impacted our earth. These impacts create moldavites, black or green glass rocks. The treasure, when formed by this first event of its kind, gained significant properties, as explained by the second haiku. It is highly magnetized. It can heal, due to the minerals in its makeup. It is said, due to its vibrational nature, that it resonates at high frequencies, that merely being in its presence can bring calm and purity to the human mind. But it's actually much more than that."

Drake looked askance at Mai and then at Dahl. "*More?*"

Kenzie spoke up too, "Does it have a name?"

"Yes, well, of course. It is a very well-known treasure, especially here in Japan. It is called the Chintamani Stone, an eastern equivalent of the Philosopher's Stone. Most likely the base for that purely western legend."

"Bloody hell," Alicia said. "You're kidding?"

"I wish I was. There is no greater treasure. Even Lucie Boom, the relic hunter's historian, agrees with me. Bigger than Atlantis, the Chintamani Stone keeps the world safe."

Drake frowned at that last comment. "Safe? How?"

"Imagine how young the earth was when the meteorite hit and the new stone, new mineral, possibly new element was formed. I mentioned it was highly magnetized, more so than anything else on the planet. Legends say that its magnetic properties are crucial for sustaining our planet's natural rhythms," Dai breathed. "It saturates space."

"It keeps everything in balance, I get it," Karin said.

"And it grants wishes," Alicia put in.

"That's taking the legend to the extreme," Dai said. "Some stones do vibrate at some level, and they have natural healing and calming minerals in their makeup. That's a good foundation for any legend to grow out of. A million years ago a sick boy stares at a stone, sees quartz or some other crystallized ore and grins, forgetting his illness for a while. The legend grows."

"Right." Luther stood up and paced. "Let's move this along. Do we have a location for the Chintamani Stone?"

"We're halfway there. The final haiku uses ancient descriptions for places that no longer exist. At least, they don't exist in the same way. The stone ruins of Akya are long gone. The Bora Pass exists in the Southern Alps, though the name has been attributed to more than one mountain pass in that area through the years."

Drake sat up. "The what? The Alps are a long way from here, pal."

"The Japanese Alps," Mai gave him an exasperated look, "bisect the island of Honshu. They encompass many mountain ranges and include Mount Fuji. You can't really miss them, Drake."

"All right," he said. "So what about the rest of the haiku? The Emerald River? The Kojiki?"

"Those are the parts we're still working on. But it's safe for you to start heading for the Southern Alps. We'll update you in flight."

The team stirred. Drake attempted to digest everything

he'd been told. If the Chintamani Stone had anything like the renown of the Philosopher's Stone, if it *was* in fact the basis for that western legend, then these royal families would be throwing all their resources at it. The stakes were as high as they would ever get.

"Dai," he said. "You fancy sending us some help?"

"Don't worry," Dai said. "I'm sending the marines."

DAVID LEADBEATER

CHAPTER FORTY TWO

The trek to the mountains was fraught with danger. First, they took a plane to Shizuoka which, Mai told them, was the home of the first Tokugawa shogun. Shizuoka city was a concrete mess of office blocks and high rises, all shining gray and white in the sun, much like many cities around the world. The Strike Force team didn't stay long. They jumped in rented SUVs and headed straight for the Akaishi mountains; in particular, a green central peak called Mount Notori. The scenery was lush, the views stunning.

Drake, Mai, Hayden and Alicia saw little of it. Though Hayden, Kinimaka and Molokai were still recovering from their ordeal they were improving fast, taking in the right fluids and the right foods, and resting whenever they could. Hayden was already trying to wrest control of the team back from Alicia, which was proving difficult.

"I'm liaising with the police," the Englishwoman said. "Finally. They're trying to keep track of the seven secret families and the Tsugarai. Of course, it's a losing battle."

"I'll contact the marines," Hayden said. "Get an ETA."

"Already sorted," Alicia said. "They're meeting us at the base of Notori at midday."

"Right." Hayden looked at Drake and then Dahl. "What the hell did you do to Alicia?"

"Oh, don't worry," Drake said warily. "She's still herself."

Dahl nodded, sat shoulder to shoulder with Kenzie. The two had been close for the entire mission, Drake had noticed, but made a point of never spending any private time together. He wondered if that was for the team's sake,

244

for show, or for *their* sake. It was early for Dahl to look beyond his wife, and Kenzie was still grieving for Dallas.

Maybe confronting the Tsugarai would help her with that.

The road wound up into the Japanese Alps. The car bounced across rutted roads and slowed for sharp switchbacks. Alicia and Hayden kept in touch with the authorities, hoping to hear how their enemies were faring, maybe get a location for them, but came up with nothing. Oddly, it seemed as if all seven royal families had dropped off the radar.

Odd? Drake thought. *Not a chance. They're all coming here.*

The trunk of their car was full of firepower. Guns, ammo and grenades rolled and clanked about as the car weaved through the hills and rising mountains. The day outside was sunlit and crisp, with no wind.

When their cars came to the foot of Mount Notori, Luther parked the first vehicle, Dino the second. The teams climbed out, the only sound being the loud ticking of cooling engines. It was vast up here, fresh and silent.

"Hey," Karin said. "I have Dai calling."

"And look." Drake pointed at a bunch of soldiers melting out of the nearby landscape. "Marines."

Dahl walked over to them, accompanied by Dino, Molokai and Luther, making first introductions. Karin put Dai on speakerphone for the rest.

"Below and beyond Mount Notori is the Migokusawa Valley, through which flows the Noro River. Due to its lush surrounds and the fact that it flows through mountainous verdant valleys and peaks rather than sheer rock crags and peaks, it has often been called the Emerald River of the Akaishi. Its source is said to lie beyond the Bora Pass,

245

somewhere remote. The terrain will become more rugged and less well-trodden as you reach the Bora Pass, but it is beyond that where you will find mythical Kojiki."

"And what's a bloody Kojiki?" Drake asked.

"Basically, the oldest surviving account of Japanese myths and legends. It reaffirms that the legendary Chintamani Stone is the subject of the haiku."

"We're heading for the Noro," Karin turned and told the Japanese marines. "You okay with that?"

They nodded and made ready. Drake joined his colleagues at the trunk of their car, shrugging on gear and grabbing weapons. Nobody skimped on the ammo. All manner of arms were chosen, from throwing knives to machine pistols. When they were ready, Hayden turned to look at the closest mountain, compass in hand.

"Let's move out."

The slopes were thick with vegetation, making the hike more arduous. It was a tough slog, made more dangerous by intermittent bouts of rain. Drake put his head down as the sudden downpours continued into the afternoon, brief but soaking. Kinimaka slipped twice, once caught by Molokai, once falling head over heels for several rotations before a soft, grassy hillock brought him to rest. Luckily, this time, he was unhurt.

They went higher and then descended into a valley. They crossed the river at its base before rising again, threading their way through thick stands of trees. The conversation was muted, the rest stops infrequent. They passed tumbling cascades, just tiny streams further up the valley. They crossed rickety bridges made of two nailed-together logs, sometimes over hundred-foot drops. Alicia complained, but it didn't make the journey any easier.

"Ever hear of riding a chopper?" she asked no one in particular as 2 p.m. passed.

Drake regarded her. "Is that the start of a one of your crude jokes?"

"No! I mean a bloody helicopter. We could take it to the source."

"But we don't know where the source is," Hayden said. "On foot is the only way to be sure we don't miss something."

"I'll tell you what I'm missing. Riding on a bloody chopper."

"Same old Alicia." Mai shook her head.

Drake couldn't hide his grin. The team continued, marines ahead and behind, watching the trail and their environs. Their presence allowed the Strike Force team chance to relax, to recuperate despite the demanding trek.

Large boulders littered the path through the trees. Dead, fallen trunks barred their way, forcing them to find a way around. There was no trail, no path. This was unknown land, where few sought to make headway. The landscape was sodden, the earth soft and loamy. At length, they came to a bumpy ridge that seemed to ride the crest of the Alps, green, rocky slopes descending to both sides. They walked along the ridge, taking great care. Drake felt so high up he imagined he was walking along the spine of the world. Mists shrouded the valleys to both sides, swirling and errant, affording fine views one minute before smothering them the next.

As the spine of the mountains came to an end, a steep descent into a wide valley opened up. With extreme caution they descended to the base where the marines announced the Noro River flowed.

It gave them all a boost. As Drake walked its banks he looked ahead, seeing how the abundant vegetation reflected upon the swirling waters, giving this particular tributary its name. The Noro branched off in lesser streams ahead, each one passing around a high, distant mountain. An hour later they were following the river into the mountains, rising toward its source.

"Bora Pass," Karin said, pointing at the sky.

Drake looked up, shielding his eyes. The pass was a small crevice between mountains at this distance. As they approached it grew wider, although not immensely. They sat down as a team at the head of the pass, resting on boulders and breaking out rations.

"Not far now," one of the marines told them in rough English. "This Bora Pass is two miles long."

Drake nodded his thanks. "This Bora Pass?"

"Many unnamed passes," the marine waved at the mountains. "Many with same name through the years."

It was a good fact to know. The Noro River was a trickle at this point.

Hayden held a hand up. "I want to thank you all for saving us from the Tsugarai. There were times I expected you, times I cursed you, times I gave up on you. I'm not proud of that. But you came through, and without you I'd be dead. Or dying horribly. So . . ." She held up a bottle of water and drank a toast.

"You'd have done the same for us," Drake said.

"I quite enjoyed being in charge," Alicia said.

"And you did a great job." Dahl raised his own bottle. "Apart from crashing into Tokyo Harbor."

"And stealing from the samurai," Luther said.

"And wrecking at least two ancient shrines," Kenzie said.

"Never said I was perfect," Alicia muttered and drank with them.

Soon, they were up on their feet and traversing the Bora Pass. It was rock strewn, making the going treacherous, threatening a broken ankle or leg with every step. The team took it steady, walking as far up the mountain slope as they were able before continuing ahead.

"Don't know why they call this a pass," Karin moaned, " 'cause it's pretty much impassable."

But they reached the far end at last, where the Noro River appeared to trickle out into a large round basin of rock. Dahl looked up at the surrounding slopes. "I would not like to be here in heavy rainfall," he said.

That spurred them on. Beyond the end of the Bora Pass, they stopped on the edge of yet another valley with spines of rock marching left and right across the rim. Drake turned slowly, taking it all in. The Noro, what was called the Emerald River, had ended a few hundred yards at their back, although it had several tributaries that branched off a few miles back.

"Now what?" he said.

"I feared this," Karin said. "The haiku is very vague about our final destination, isn't it?"

"It's a big land." Dahl stared at distant valleys, left and right, and at the huge peaks ahead. The Swede was panting because the air was thin. Hayden, Kinimaka and Molokai were sitting down, still drained, catching their breaths.

"We are clear," one of the Japanese marines said, coming up to them after his men made a quick sweep of the area. "No . . . visitors."

That meant they weren't being followed or watched. Drake took in the grand vista, the enticing scenery, the majesty of the mountains. It was incredibly humbling, a place that demanded respect, but it was also too vast to be of any use to him in this moment.

"Let's go back to the haiku," Mai said. "In my experience a haiku relates exactly what it needs to. *Beyond the Stone*

Ruins of Akya, the Source and Axis of the Emerald River, through Bora Pass, to Mythical Kojiki."

Luther came up to her. "We covered all that."

Mai nodded. "We're right here," she said. "And still, I think we're missing something."

"The source is at our back," Hayden said. "The Bora Pass ends here. It should be right in front of us."

Drake saw only a steep descent ahead, the same high peak to their right that had been there since they started in on the Bora, and a graduating rocky landscape to the left. "No doorways," he said. "No signposts."

"Axis," Dahl said. "We've kind of forgotten that word because we were focusing on the source. I wondered why it was needed at all. It's the only word we haven't covered."

"An axis is an imaginary line about which a body rotates, as in *the earth's axis.*" Karin said. "So, in context, we'd be looking for a body around which the Emerald River rotates, or *flows.*"

"We passed tributaries back there," Drake said. "Three or four, traveling varying degrees of east."

They looked to the east.

Drake whistled. "Which means the axis of the Emerald River is that massive mountain to the right."

"And we're at the end of our pass," Hayden said. "The entrance should be along here." She started out along the rocky spine that dissected the valley and the mountain. It was a narrow ledge, only three feet wide, but it was traversable in single file.

Twenty minutes later, Hayden came to a rockfall. The collapsed boulders were old, pitted and bore mold, but it was clear on closer inspection that a small cave lay behind them. On first examination the cave was shallow, merely an indent in the mountain, but when Karin crowded in she swept the ground with her feet. Slowly, and then more quickly, she kicked rubble and moss aside, lifted rocks and threw them outside. Drake and Dahl soon helped and, within ten minutes, they had cleared the floor of the cave.

Engraved there, was the depiction of a large stone.

"It's a mani stone," Karin said. "I thought I saw the faint outline of something under the rubble. A mani stone is a magical jewel, which manifests anything one desires. It is a metaphor for the teachings and virtues of Buddha but, in this case, I think it is much more."

"Symbolically," Dahl said, "we go through the stone."

Karin nodded, moving away. "We go through the stone."

They strapped a small explosive to the floor, barely enough to cause a blast, but they hoped that, if the engraving was hiding something, the rock wouldn't be too thick. A few minutes later the marines detonated the explosive and waited for the dust to settle.

Drake and Dahl were the first in. "We've found something," the Swede shouted back as the Yorkshireman whistled and fought off an attack of the shivers.

"That is one bloody deep hole, pal. What the hell do we do if it's bottomless?"

Dahl shrugged, looking down. "Maybe there's a hole the other side."

Drake turned to the marines. "Break out the rope and tackle, boys."

CHAPTER FORTY THREE

Mai grabbed the rope, a maelstrom of emotion churning at her stomach. Her earliest memories were of fighting the Tsugarai, objecting as they dragged her away from her parents, rebelling as they sought to train her, mold her into their image. She hated everything they stood for, everything they did, and especially the men that had the audacity to call themselves *grand masters.*

She would face the Tsugarai one more time and she would destroy them all . . . or die. There was no other option. The showdown of her life was close.

But that thought raised myriad other poignant issues. The Strike Force team was with her. What if one of them got hurt? Newly whipped up feelings for Drake threatened to shred her attention. Luther had been fantastic ever since she returned, not changed a bit. The fact that he trusted her so implicitly made everything harder.

The rope was over a hundred feet long, actually two ropes tied into one. It was anchored into one of the cave's walls and fell away into darkness. The shaft was two men wide, not a lot of room for a soldier and his pack. Four were already climbing down: Dahl, Luther and two marines. She would be next.

Watching far below, she saw the signal: a flashlight clicked on and off three times. Mai started her descent of the rope, the feeling that she was sinking into a dark and volatile hell not lost on her. There were times back at the Tsugarai compound when she'd thought they would all die—she'd switched between not caring to furious anger at losing out on her revenge, to sorrow that she'd never see Grace and Chika again. Now, all she wanted was to end this mission and end the Tsugarai.

Her boots struck rock. She saw light ahead. Drake and Luther leant against a rock wall. A marine gave the signal for the next person to descend.

"You done a recce?" she asked.

Drake's expression had a look of awe. "Yeah, it kind of takes your breath away, love."

Dahl gave her a warning glance. Mai took out her own flashlight and followed a narrow tunnel ahead. It curved one way and then the other before ending abruptly at a wide ledge.

Mai stepped out onto the ledge, gasping.

What she saw beggared belief. A wide path stretched away from her with unfathomable drops to both sides. It was, literally, the only way forward, and measured six feet from edge to edge. Above, the cave became a cavern, its roof disappearing into unknown heights, making a vast ill-lit space. Everything she saw was illuminated by high-powered flashlights, but *that* light, strong as it was, was swallowed by an immense, overarching darkness—a testament to the enormous size of this cavern.

Ahead, the path stretched for perhaps a hundred feet. Mai gasped once more as she saw, dim in the distance, but illuminated by *other* flashlights and glowsticks, more paths reaching across the deep cavern to her left and right. There was at least one more path at each point of the axis, which meant at least two more entrances.

More tributaries of the Emerald River.

But it was the very center of the cavern that took her breath away. A pillar of stone rose up from the immeasurable depths of the cavern. Its surface was about sixteen feet higher than the paths, a perfect square; sixty feet by sixty feet at least. Close to the western side of the square stood a small castle, its battlements raised another twenty feet above the surface.

She heard footfalls behind but couldn't tear her gaze away. A few seconds later Drake spoke in her ear. "I haven't seen anything like this since the tombs of the gods."

She nodded. "I don't know what to say, what to think."

"The good thing is," Drake said in that open, endearing way of his, "that there's only one way to go. Even Alicia couldn't cock that up."

Mai laughed and the spell of the cavern broke. She was ready to move forward, her friends at her side.

She was ready to end this.

Drake waited for the whole team to climb down the shaft and get their first eyeful of the incredible sight that awaited them. During that time, he tried to discern more of the cavern's features as his eyes grew accustomed to the predominant dark, and more flashlights helped to illuminate the cavern from the east and west ledges.

"The stone pillar is the axis," Hayden said. "It has four paths connected to it, one at each side. North, east, west and south. The path across from us may be hidden, but you can just make out the faint radiance of flashlights across there. I see all our opponents."

Drake could see them too.

To his right, running along the eastern path were the Tsugarai, recognizable in their leather clothing, along with a number of mercenaries and what looked like a house guard, clad in red robes. Mai's guess was that they were Zuki and her men, allied with the Tsugarai.

To the left, filling the western path, he saw battling men, all dressed differently. That had to be some of the other houses clashing as they came. They fought all along the path, men falling into the abyss and screaming, swords clashing, gunfire echoing around the cavern. Drake saw no sign of the samurai.

"They're closer than we are." Mai indicated the Tsugarai. "Shall we move?"

It wasn't a request. Drake fell in behind her as she sprinted off, a Glock handgun in one hand, a Heckler and Koch MP5 in the other. Once out on the six-foot wide path, a gust of wind struck him, serving only to highlight the lethal darkness to left and right. Fighting on this path would be sheer hell.

We were lucky in the end. We found a path nobody else did.

He slowed, checking his backup. They were all behind him, his team and the Japanese marines. Just one look at their faces told him they were ready for this. His left foot slipped slightly, ancient dust kicking up and scattering off the path. Drake stilled his thudding heart and ran on.

The Tsugarai had stopped at the end of their path and were looking up toward the top of the pillar of stone, sixteen feet above their heads. Mai was approaching the same point on their path. Drake saw three shallow steps ending at a vertical surface. There was no way up the sheer pillar of stone.

Mai spun. "Grappling hooks."

Drake waited whilst the tools were brought up by the marines, which involved some careful shuffling around the path. A glance to the left showed him four different clans fighting on the western path.

And then, on the eastern path, he saw another clan

attacking the Tsugarai from the rear, clearly new arrivals. Zuki's mercenaries knelt and opened fire, bullets ripping through men and women, and sending them spinning into their colleagues, smashing people off the ledge.

Drake checked their own rear. It was clear.

A marine threw a grappling hook over the top of the stone pillar, then pulled it back until its strong steel claws gripped something solid up there. Next, he tested his weight. He was about to start up when Mai pushed him aside and started to climb.

Three more grappling hooks were thrown. They climbed four abreast, Dahl dangerously beyond the edge of the path, climbing above the void. Mai reached the top first, shook her head, then leaned down.

"This just gets better and better," she said. "Once you reach the top, don't dare put a foot wrong."

CHAPTER FORTY FOUR

Drake took Mai's advice, stepping lightly over the edge and onto the stone pillar's surface. There was a lip running along all four sides of the large pillar, which was what the hooks had caught on. The rest of the floor was made up of countless square tiles, gray in color and coated with dust. They ran all the way around and right up to the small castle structure at the eastern side.

"Stow your hooks," Luther told the marines. "We'll need them for the castle."

Drake stood alongside Dahl and Kenzie, staring at the tiles. "They're not here for ornamentation," he said. "I sense a trap."

Karin was on her knees, leaning out over the lip they stood on, examining one of the tiles. "This one is plain. The next has an engraving. The third has a different engraving. And the fourth is plain. There's some kind of pattern."

"What happens if you get it wrong?" Dino asked, crouched down with her.

"Let's not find out." Karin studied all the tiles she could see. She was looking for a pattern. Drake stared too, but, to him, ornate stone tiles all looked pretty much the same.

From their left came the sound of battle. Drake ducked down as three men came over the top of the pillar's western side, two dressed in blue robes, one dressed in white. The latter made it first, jumping onto the ledge and drawing his sword. The blue-robed men fired up at him. Bullets destroyed his chest and sent him staggering out across the tiles.

Drake watched, wincing, but nothing happened. The man fell with a groan, bleeding out. Two more blue-robed figures then appeared and walked out onto the tiles, falling into kneeling positions and turning as two green-clad enemies came over the pillar's edge and attacked them.

The first green-clad warrior ran, gun firing on auto, but with a loud cracking sound and a sharp whoosh of air, a ten-foot-long log with a sharpened spike shot up through the floor, straight through his chest, bursting out the other side. At the same time, one of the blue-robed men staggered away and hit the wrong tile. Another sharpened pole speared up through the floor, smashed through his lower belly, then traveled through his body and out of the top of his skull.

Drake's mouth fell open. "Fuck me fucking sideways."

Alicia sat down on the ledge. "No way am I risking that, guys. No way at all. It makes my ass clench just seeing it." She shuddered.

To the right, coming up from the eastern path, Drake spotted the Tsugarai. Gunfire still rattled around the cavern, but their men were advancing. They'd probably left Zuki's mercs to deal with their enemies.

Then he saw movement opposite too, from the path he hadn't been able to see. Figures were moving over there, climbing up onto the stone pillar.

"Set a load of flashlights up," Kinimaka told the marines. "We have to be able to see everything up here."

Expecting darkness, the entire team had packed as many high-powered sources of illumination as they could and arrayed them around the lip of the pillar. Light illuminated everything, making the scene that much clearer.

And even more threatening.

The Tsugarai ninjas were at Drake's right, staring at the

tiles. The samurai came up onto the pillar straight ahead. And the green-robed clan appeared to have won the battle to his left. They climbed over the pillar's lip, studying the tiles and the men that had died.

Karin still leaned perilously far out over the tiles, studying them so close her nose practically brushed the dust. Drake cringed for her safety and opened his mouth to call her back.

"I've got it," she said, leaning back. "I think. One of the engravings, repeated many times, depicts a mani stone. Remember those? Magic jewels related to the Chintamani Stone. They must be the safe tiles."

She looked back at them. Drake and the others shifted nervously.

"Umm, who's gonna test that one?" Kinimaka asked.

Mai groaned and threw her Glock at the nearest tile that bore the mani symbol. Nothing happened. She rose fast and jumped on to it, making the others gasp and reflexively reach out for her.

Nothing happened.

It looked good, but Drake had one more idea. He reached for a spare coil of rope and threw that onto one of the tiles that didn't bear the mani symbol. A deadly pole shot up, smashing through the tile and piercing thin air.

"Theory proved," Dahl said. "Let's move."

One by one, they moved out onto the tiled surface, Drake, still uneasy, felt like a chess piece being moved against his will. The mood lightened a little when Alicia waved welcomingly at the samurai and their leader, Tenmei, and shouted: "Good to see you again, boys. Did you miss me? Anyway, here's a tip: Use the plain squares!"

The Strike Force team and the marines spread out, using the tiles to advance toward the castle. It turned out most of the tiles bore the mani symbol, so they ended up leaving a glowstick on top of the safe tiles. It wouldn't help their enemies, for they hadn't figured out how to cross the first six rows of tiles yet.

The trouble was, the western clan had an advantage, being closer to the castle. But they too weren't moving, still trying to solve the problem.

Drake and his team approached the castle.

It turned out that every tile, six deep around the castle, was engraved with the mani stone. Mai indicated that quietly through the comms. The group closed in, still wary. It was right then though, that their enemies decided to take their focus off solving the tile puzzle and remembered they had guns.

One opened fire and then another. Drake threw himself headlong beside Kenzie, their bodies coming together, her sword digging into his leg.

"Ow."

"Stop whining."

They crawled forward, exposed. Drake rolled onto his back and fired back, sighting down his stomach. Bullets crisscrossed the cavern from all directions. Kinimaka and Dino took shots to the chest, which felled them, but had them groaning loudly since their body armor had saved them.

A bullet flashed past Drake's nose, just a few feet above his head.

"We can't stay here," Luther cried out. "Move!"

But where could they go? They returned fire until the Tsugarai and samurai leaders yelled at their own men to stop. In the resounding silence that followed, Drake heard the order to proceed across the tiles.

They'd figured it out.

"Shit, they're coming," Kinimaka said.

Drake rose to a sitting position, stunned by the epic scale of what he could see. The shinobi had drawn swords and were advancing from the east. The samurai were drawing theirs and coming from the north. Zuki was following her shinobi friends, a sword twirling in each hand. Drake saw Tenmei of the samurai and Kenshin of the Tsugarai leading their clans into battle. The green-robed clan had been decimated by gunfire, but still half a dozen figures remained. Already close to the castle, they were leaping onto the safe tiles.

Drake rose, exchanging an empty mag for a full one. "Is everyone ready?"

His team drew deep breaths and prepared for the battle of their lives.

CHAPTER FORTY FIVE

Drake joined the rest of his team and the marines as they lined up along a row of safe tiles beneath the eighteen-feet-high castle walls. Their enemies were running at full pace, knowing the gap had to be closed quickly. Drake saw three men choose unwise footing. Two were impaled, their flesh and bone shredding and flying off into the faces of their brethren. The third somehow managed an incredible feat, dodging the pole and continuing unfazed. Drake was reminded of the caliber of opponent they faced.

"Kill as many as you can," he said. "We can't let them get close."

Thy unleashed their weapons, but mercenaries and reinforcements fired back from around the pillar's lip. A marine was killed instantly. Alicia was struck in the shoulder, saved by her body armor but holding her left arm in agony. Drake felt the impact of a passing bullet; it just skimmed his chest and made him stagger. Dahl stumbled back as another slug caught him in the stomach.

But Tsugarai fell too, sprawling across the tiles, triggering more traps. Sharpened poles speared up to left and right. Mercenaries were killed or wounded and fell off the platform, tumbling into the black abyss. Samurai collapsed dead and injured, their swords clattering away. As the two forces came closer, Kenzie drew her sword and Mai took out a long, curved knife.

Drake switched to a handgun. Their enemies were just feet away. He emptied round after round into them, indiscriminately, firing at everything. A wall of running bodies struck from the east, smashed into the line his team had made, shattering it. Drake fell back; Kinimaka staggered away to his left. Hayden and Dino were felled. Mai, Dahl, Alicia and Luther had braced well for the coming together. They made their enemies falter, flinging them aside, forcing them backward. Bullets flew and swords flashed.

Drake whirled, looking up. His vision was a kaleidoscope of bodies and blades, a flurry of chaos. A sword slashed down at him. He couldn't stop it in the crush. It smashed into his shoulder, hitting the Kevlar, and glanced away. Drake shot the wielder in the stomach and lunged to his feet.

A ninja was in his face. Drake planted an elbow into the man's nose, seeing him reel away. There was no skill this close, only brute force and luck. He whirled to escape another thrust and, fleetingly, saw the green-robed clan assaulting the walls of the castle.

In the chaos, they were going for the treasure.

Drake struck out, fired twice and spun away. Lines of battling men and women stretched to left and right. He saw Alicia throw a samurai, spine first into the ground; Kinimaka land atop another with his full weight; Hayden empty her mag at three onrushing mercs. He saw Luther and Dahl fighting together, back to back, almost at the edge of the zone where the safe tiles ended. Then Dahl stepped out of the zone, his foot coming own onto a plain tile.

Drake screamed a warning but couldn't help his friend. Dahl was a warrior though, he would know his extremities and positioning at all times. He would know where he was in relation to his enemies. So, the moment he stepped on to the deadly tile he pulled away. Fortune made the pole surge up in front of one of his enemies who ran point black into it and knocked himself out. Dahl was left with a grazed outer shin.

Drake saw Karin, Dino and Yorgi struggling, fighting together in a knot. They were beset by almost a dozen samurai. Drake yelled out and made his way over to them, ignoring the clan trying to breach the castle walls. As he barreled his way through the crowd, he noticed Molokai was with him.

"I'm at twenty," the big robed man said.

Drake hadn't been counting. "Twenty one," he said.

Molokai smashed a stiffened arm into the neck of a struggling mercenary, flinging him to the ground. "Evens," he said.

Drake jumped in to help Yorgi.

Mai ignored the samurai charging from her left and attacked what she viewed as the worst enemy in the room. The Tsugarai closed fast, slashing with their blades. Mai shot them mercilessly with one hand and parried their swords with the other, opening throats where she could. It gave her no solace killing these men and women, they were trained pawns. It only saddened her, but they were deadly, and they had been brainwashed. If she didn't kill them, they would kill her.

To her mind, there was but one target.

Kenshin stood in the third row of ninjas, shouting out orders. Mai hacked and shot her way close to him. He saw her coming and sent more men to face her. Mai faltered, but then found she had help.

Kenzie was at her side and carrying a blood-slicked, shining katana.

"Now we're talking," Mai said.

Together, they fought. Progress was slow and difficult. Ninjas didn't go down easily. It was a stroke of luck that brought Mai within reach of Kenshin. She saw Zuki, the leader of the greatest secret royal bloodline and instigator of Hayden's kidnapping, of the Tsugarai's involvement, of countless deaths that had occurred since she decided to find the Sacred Treasures. For a moment, she swung at Zuki, but the woman had great skills and deflected her attack.

Mai stumbled to her left and found herself face to face with Kenshin.

It was fate, everything she wanted. She shoved her gun into her waistband and attacked with the dagger, slicing at her opponent's face. Kenshin dodged and then struck back, thrusting with his sword. It missed her ribs by inches.

Mai raised an elbow, stepped in, swiveled, and brought it down hard into Kenshin's neck. The man's eyes bulged. Mai spun ever faster, drawing on her training, lifting up a foot and slamming it into his chest.

Arms waving, Kenshin stumbled back.

Mai dealt with another Tsugarai that stepped up, pushed his lifeless body away and confronted Kenshin.

"This is my revenge," she growled and leapt at him.

With no other choice, Alicia ignored her pain and jumped into the fray. A bullet hurt, no matter how good the armor, but samurai were in her face. She ducked and dodged their sword swings, their harsh thrusts, firing her weapon into their chests and faces. Several wore armor too. They fell away, clutching their chests, but then rolled and tried to stand. She saw two impaled, the whoosh of both poles so close to her right ear she felt the wind of their uprising. She kicked and fought, and cleared a path through the samurai.

Faces filled her vision. Hard, severe faces. She staggered under numerous blows, took sword strikes to the chest and stomach, barely dodged a slash to the face. Her body armor saved her life countless times. Her blood ran hot both in her veins and down her forehead. A katana had slashed her, separating two flaps of skin. Alicia fell away for a moment, vision obscured, wiping her face and eyes.

Boots landed to her right. She knew before she looked up who it was.

Tenmei.

The samurai leader stared down at her with his sword raised. "This is for your dishonor," he said.

Alicia lunged to the left, lucky to find room. She rolled against the castle walls before she stopped, then rose to her feet, trying to stem the flow of blood from her forehead. Tenmei leapt at her, sword raised.

Alicia dodged, the sword struck stone. Its blade was then swept crosswise at her. She ducked, feeling the deadly steel cleave off a portion of her hair. When she looked up all she saw was blood and blonde locks floating before her eyes.

"Now you will die," Tenmei said.

Kenzie backed Mai, fighting in her element, thrusting the incredible katana left and right, forced to use all her skills against the powerful shinobi fighters arrayed against her. She felled several, but others bypassed her, running headlong into the battle. She saw another Japanese marine fall under the stroke of a sword. She saw Alicia pursued and bloody. But then her vision was filled with steel as she met one more attack.

Kenzie parried the blade, let it slide off to her right and then came under the other man's outstretched arm. She buried her katana through his armpit until it burst out the other side, then withdrew, watching him fall. Another figure came in from the left, but this man was a mercenary and aimed a pistol at the spot between her eyes.

"Fucking ninjas," he said. "Do my head in."

He fired, but Kenzie had long since left his line of sight. She slid left, using her right hand to pull a throwing knife from her waistband which she then threw with a flick of her wrist. The knife lodged into the merc's windpipe before he could pull the trigger. Kenzie whirled and threw a second knife into the chest of another enemy and moved on.

Bullets tore through the crush. She couldn't believe people were still firing, but then Zuki's mercenaries didn't have any other means of attack. And Zuki wouldn't care about casualties so long as she got the fourth treasure.

With that thought, Kenzie came face to face with Zuki. The royal queen appeared to be a competent fighter, with a short sword in each hand, both coated with samurai blood. When she saw Kenzie, her eyes blazed.

"One of the Strike Force? Good, you will feel my steel."

Zuki rushed in, swords swirling in the air. Kenzie tracked their flight with both eyes, raising her katana to deflect them. Zuki booted her in the chest. Kenzie took it without flinching and stood her ground.

Zuki went low but then came straight up, hoping to thrust a blade through Kenzie's throat, but Kenzie expected the feint and pulled away to the left.

Zuki was slightly unbalanced.

Kenzie swept her blade down, taking skin from Zuki's shoulder, seeing blood leap into the air. Zuki didn't retreat, just whirled and swept both blades in a low arc, narrowly missing Kenzie's right wrist.

Both women circled each other, deadly predators with fire in their eyes, waiting for the chance to attack.

*

Drake pulled away from the battle for a moment to take stock. Mercs were lined up along the pillar's edge, taking pot shots, several laughing and smirking as they sent bullets into the backs of unknowing enemies. Drake and Dino opened fire on them, knowing that slugs striking their Kevlar would send them stumbling off the stone pillar and into the great abyss yawning below. Those mercs that survived scrambled around the floor, one jumping face first into a surging spiked pole.

Drake spun to meet the attack of a green-robed fighter. The man swung at him with a curved sword. Dino didn't stand on ceremony, just shot the man in the stomach and then the head. Karin staggered toward them, fighting hard.

"Let them wipe each other out." Drake said. "That's what most of them are here for."

It was a great, swelling, violent struggle. The samurai charged the shinobi, swords flashing, screaming their wrath. The shinobi rose to meet them, and there, in the great cavern under the mountain, atop the raised stone pillar, the battle of the ages was resurrected. Men came together, peasants and royalty, and there wasn't a way to tell them apart nor an inch to pick between them.

Drake watched the samurai surge into the Tsugarai ninjas. Men collapsed and blades flashed in the artificial light. Skills were displayed and well met. No more bullets flew. The honor of both sides was on display and at stake here.

Drake looked to the right. The green-robed clan, only four strong, had thrown grappling hooks over the castle's eighteen-foot-high battlements and were climbing. Drake had a decision to make.

He dropped to one knee and picked the highest man off with a shot to the ribs. He plunged off the wall, falling onto the next man, taking him clean off. Drake then shot the third.

The fourth jumped down and ran at Drake, screaming, sword raised.

Karin shot him through the face.

She was alongside him with Yorgi. The Russian shook his head.

"I've been back one day only," he said. "I've robbed a samurai stronghold and been in the middle of a battle between secret royal families, ninjas and samurai," he said. "It is typical SPEAR team."

"Didn't you know?" Drake said. "We're the Strike Force now." He fired three shots at advancing mercs who'd crept around the pillar's lip, sending them to their deaths.

Karin aimed and shot a samurai who had Dahl around the throat. The Swede recovered fast and charged at two more.

Drake braced himself as a knot of embattled samurai and shinobi burst out of the main pack and swayed their way. He counted at least twenty men and women. Swords and daggers flashed. Robes were torn and bloodied. Faces were the same. Drake pushed back as the knot crashed into him, diverting it slightly, but several men broke away and lunged at him, swords raised.

He was lucky they were staggering, unbalanced. They fell at him rather than attacked. Their swords flashed. He backpedalled and fired, hitting three with four bullets. Karin and Dino fired from the sides and Yorgi used a Glock to take out one more.

Still, over a dozen men came at Drake.

He ducked and barreled into them, taking three off their

feet. He rolled, coming up to one side. He shot the closest man to him. Two blades glanced off his chest. Another split his nose at the tip, making his eyes water.

He was on his knees, looking up. Two samurai and two shinobi stood above him. One brought his sword down, the other three collapsed in agony as their chests exploded with bullets. Blood spattered Drake.

The lone sword came down at his skull. Dino was already scrambling to help, flying in feet first, one arm raised to grab the sword-wielder's wrist, the other aiming his Walther handgun at the man's stomach.

He fired the pistol and reached for the wrist at the same time.

Drake threw himself gracelessly to the side, hoping to evade certain death.

The sword chopped through flesh and bone as the man died, Dino's bullet striking his heart and killing him. But the damage had already been done.

Drake whirled to see Dino's hand severed at the wrist. Blood pumped from the wound, spattering the floor and Drake's boots. Dino fell in agony, holding the stump, screaming. Drake swiveled on the floor, unable to help his friend as the rest of the knot of fighters clambered over him.

It was hell. A desperate deadly melee where nobody was safe. All around him, Drake heard the crying and grunting of warriors and the yells of his outnumbered team.

CHAPTER FORTY SIX

Mai clashed swords with Kenshin, the hateful Tsugarai leader glaring at her impassively. "I should have gutted you," he said. "Like the traitorous rat that you are."

Mai didn't waste her breath on him. She thrust the knife left and right, feinting in all directions. Kenshin parried and struck back, backpedalling toward the pillar's edge. Once there he sidestepped, rolling under her strike so that Mai stood with her back to the deep abyss.

"Weak," he said.

She used her feet, kicking, spinning and kicking again, each blow smashing into Kenshin's armor. She caught a glimpse of her team battling near the castle walls. She stopped her right boot less than an inch above a plain tile. She hopped from one good tile to the next.

Kenshin baited her, drawing her in before pushing her away. She saw a chance, fell back toward the edge of the pillar, and dropped to one knee. Kenshin attacked, blood flying from many wounds as he darted in.

Mai waited.

Kenshin pulled up short, realizing he'd been about to step on the tile right in front of Mai to finish her. That tile that would have ended his life.

"Not good enough," he said, and leapt over it, feet in the air, knife raised high and slashing toward her face as his body descended.

Mai dropped her knife and stepped off the pillar's ledge, falling off the edge. As she fell, Kenshin's leap took him through the space she'd vacated and above her head.

He fell into the black pit, screaming.

Mai's fingers caught the lip of the pillar and held. After a long moment she hauled herself back up.

Their leader was gone, but the shinobi fought on.

Alicia blew and spat blood from her face. There was so much it flew into Tenmei's eyes, blinding him. The samurai leader stepped back, clearing his vision. Alicia brought her gun up. The samurai was fast though, flicking at her wrist with his sword, striking the gun and sending it clattering away.

"Now," Tenmei said, "we will see how good you are."

Alicia wasn't good, not with a sword. But she was fantastic using her own brute force. Still blinded by blood flowing from her head wound, she jumped at Tenmei, inside the swing of his weapon, striking him with both knees at once.

She hit him in the chest, driving him back. Tenmei backpedalled so fast he flew off his feet, landing on his tailbone. Alicia stayed in his face, following him all the way, less than an inch between them. The samurai's sword was still active, but her proximity and visceral attack occupied all his attention. She smashed her right knee up into his groin, drove an elbow into his throat. As her right knee came down, she jumped again, rising with the left, again point blank into his groin. Her other elbow swung into his right eye, sending shards of agony to his brain.

Shattered, screaming with pain, Tenmei lost his grip on his sword. As he fell backward Alicia whirled, scooped it up, raised it, then buried it through the front of his neck, striking so hard the tip burst through the man's spine and dug into the ground.

Leaving him propped up like that, she ran to grab her gun.

Kenzie circled Zuki, sword poised. It was the first time they'd looked each other dead in the eyes. Kenzie saw an implacable foe; a woman raised in battle and faced with adversity every day of her life. Zuki was a survivor, a fighter. In a different life they might have been friends.

Today, they were worlds apart.

Zuki was fighting for her legacy, her family's survival. She was a woman at the very top of the royal food chain, a force behind the world's governments, and she was here playing a direct part in maintaining that role.

Kenzie admired her a little for that. She admired her for her skills with a sword. But that was where the respect ended. Zuki was a cold-blooded killer, a psychopath, a privileged brat with morals as low as the sewer.

Zuki sidestepped and attacked, a double slash of her sword from overhead. Kenzie dodged both and thrust at the woman's abdomen. Zuki leapt back. Kenzie's sword sliced the leather of her opponent's tunic. Zuki attacked again, left, right, left, ending up with a thrust to the throat. Kenzie let it come, dodging at the last moment before stepping in close, dropping her shoulder and lifting the other woman physically off the ground.

Zuki looked shocked, gasping.

Kenzie let her drop and then kicked her between the legs. She jumped onto the woman's sternum, then rolled off. She paused on one knee next to Zuki's gasping frame.

"Learning to fight is all well and good," she hissed. "But learning to fight with spiteful boys and girls is better."

She jabbed at Zuki's eyes, closing one. Zuki's left hand

scrabbled for the hilt of her sword, closing around it. The blade came up fast, incredibly fast, cleaving the air in front of Kenzie's face before she could pull away.

She fell backward, shocked. She'd never experienced such speed. Zuki rose to her knees, glaring at her from under hanging locks of black hair, bruised and bloodied.

"I've been fighting since my parents were killed," she muttered. "I've fought every manner of beast. I've killed for sport and in self-defense. You will not beat me so easily."

Kenzie jumped up and struck at the same time as her opponent. Their blades clashed in the air, shedding sparks that flickered away into the abyss. They struck at each other again and again, evenly matched, drawing blood for blood and standing their ground.

They were in the eye of the storm, at the heart of the battle and, around them, the fight raged.

Drake picked off samurai and mercenaries. He stood shoulder to shoulder with Dahl and Luther as eight men charged at them. Together they prevailed, using bullets against swords but taking immense punishment in their victory. Luther was on his knees. Dahl was holding skin together where it had been slashed below his shoulder armor.

Behind them, Karin and Yorgi treated Dino.

Karin had removed the padded jacket that covered her body armor and now pressed it hard against Dino's streaming stump. As she stemmed the flow of blood, Yorgi ripped his shirt apart and balled it up, ready to act as a bandage. Together they took Karin's jacket away, padded the stump and then wrapped it tightly, applying a tight tourniquet above the wrist. It was a battlefield dressing, but it would have to do. Karin fed Dino a handful of painkillers before propping him up against the castle walls and then stepping in front of his body.

Here, she would protect him or die.

Yorgi stood with her, now holding two Glocks; the second taken from a dead enemy. Drake, glancing back, caught Karin's eye and got a grim nod in return. Dino was as good as he was going to get until they got out of the cavern.

Slowly, the Strike Force team backed away from the main battle until they came up against the castle walls. It was a tactic fed to them by Karin via comms, a way of disengaging and allowing the enemy to slaughter themselves. Ahead, a swirling mass of samurai and shinobi fought tooth and nail, struggling for every inch of ground. Drake saw a red, flashing chaos of robes and swords, of bodies and blood. Men fell to their knees, run through. Heads tumbled through the air, severed. Arms and hands slapped grotesquely to the ground.

With Luther at the far left and Molokai at the far right, with Drake, Hayden and Alicia in the middle of the remaining Japanese marines, the Strike Force team raised their weapons as if they were a firing squad. They sighted in on the warriors, noting that Mai and Kenzie were fighting off to their right, and opened fire.

Bullets decimated the warriors. Drake didn't like it one bit but knew that if the boot was on the other foot, his opponents wouldn't hesitate to kill him and all his friends. Samurai and shinobi fell dying, their ranks decimated. Some reached for guns as they fell but another volley of bullets finished them.

Drake was confronted by a small knot of surviving samurai, a handful of Tsugarai and half a dozen mercenaries. He saw Zuki and Kenzie locked in an epic battle at the far side, both exhausted beyond their limits, practically facing each other on their knees, but refusing to back down.

Dahl and Luther sighted in on the Japanese warriors, but Drake's voice stopped them. "They are soldiers like us," he said. "Give them the chance to live."

The samurai stared back grimly, unmoving, understanding what Drake meant, and clinging to their honor. But the Tsugarai had been taught otherwise by successive grand masters: Kill and escape at all costs.

Mai knew from experience what they would do. She'd found a machine pistol earlier and now turned it on to full auto as the Tsugarai reached for weapons. Her bullets decimated them, sending them pirouetting to their deaths. Drake winced as the samurai cheered.

When there were no Tsugarai left standing, Mai dropped her gun. She walked over to the strewn bodies, looking down. Luther followed her, staying at her side. Drake raised his gun once more, sighting on the surviving mercenaries.

As one, they raised their hands and dropped their guns. First one and then the others started running, heading back toward the eastern path to escape the cavern. Alicia raised her gun suggestively, but Hayden shook her head.

"Not in cold blood."

"No," Alicia said in agreement. "We're not the same as them."

Drake waved at Karin, Yorgi and Molokai to stay with Dino. He checked himself for wounds and then stared at his colleagues.

"We all in one piece?"

There were nods and sighs of relief from everyone except Dahl. The big Swede was approaching the battle between

Kenzie and Zuki. Both women were raw and bloody, their clothing tattered, shredded so that their body armor and lower arms were bare. Kenzie's hair was crimson. She knelt in a pool of blood, not all of it hers. Zuki was yelling as she struck again and again with her sword, each blow narrowly missing Kenzie, or parried by the other's sword.

Dahl walked right up behind Zuki, clenched his fist, and hammered it down onto the top of her skull as if trying to drive her through the floor. Her body slumped, her sword fell from her grip, but she was strong. She didn't collapse. Dahl had to smash her again to send her into oblivion.

Then he walked over to Kenzie, bent down and lifted her. Molokai and Kinimaka were already at his side, securing the unconscious Zuki. Dahl picked his way back to the castle, Kenzie in his arms.

"I'll tend her wounds," he said. "You guys go get that treasure."

Drake looked up at the battlements rising eighteen feet high. He'd almost forgotten the reason they were here. The fabled Chintamani Stone waited on the other side of those walls, carved from the first meteorite, born of the stars, an extra-terrestrial object, supposedly integral to their own planet's natural alignment.

"All right," he said. "Who's with me?"

CHAPTER FORTY SEVEN

Drake used the grappling hook once more to climb the wall. His joints ached. His head ached. Even his bones ached. Twelve marines had survived the battle and helped secure their hooks over the top of the castle's battlements.

Drake reached the top first and poked his head over, but the view was simple. Below lay a square courtyard, surrounded on four sides by the battlements. At the courtyard's center stood an altar, maybe four feet high, wider at the bottom than the top.

On top of the altar sat the Chintamani Stone.

Drake rested for a while, hanging, with his chin resting on the stone crenellation, Alicia, at his side, said, "What do you think?"

"No tiles. No ledges. No abyss. I think we're clear."

Alicia motioned. "After you then."

"Not a chance."

"Together?"

"Sure. So long as you go first."

Drake climbed over the top onto a narrow ledge and saw a set of stairs to the right leading from the battlements to the courtyard's floor. Luther was closest. He gave the American a big thumbs up and started along a ledge. Luther jumped onto the stairs and headed down. Molokai was next, followed by Drake and Alicia.

"We think this is safe?" Luther stared at the ground.

"Considering the importance of the Chintamani Stone," Drake said. "I doubt they would risk destroying it."

"Every trap so far has been aimed at eradicating the

unworthy," Hayden said. "Those that don't know their history, and especially the stone's history. I agree with Drake. There are no more traps."

Luther nodded and proceeded with care across the courtyard. Drake joined him. Soon, they were standing in front of the four-foot-high altar, staring down at the Chintamani Stone.

"The fourth Sacred Treasure," Hayden breathed. "The fabled prize. Is this really the Philosopher's Stone?"

"I could test the theory," Alicia suggested. "Wish for the death of all sand spiders maybe?"

"I'd prefer you wished for a Cobra," Drake said. "Of the AC variety."

"Well, maybe I wish that—"

"Stop," Hayden interjected. "It's not for us to decide. It's for the Japanese authorities. It's time we passed this over to them."

Drake studied the fourth Sacred Treasure. The Chintamani Stone was a ten-sided jewel, shining brilliantly in the light of their flashlights. It was both emerald green and sapphire blue, and it sent tiny shafts of light refracting in myriad directions. It was the size of a small rock, so that it might fit in the hand of a large man. Drake was reminded that this stone was formed when the first meteorite struck the earth billions of years ago. It was genuinely immaculate.

Perfect.

"The word Chintamani translates as 'wishing stone,'" Hayden told them, unable to tear her gaze away. "It vibrates on a frequency said to saturate space, keeping our planet's natural rhythm in check. It has been said that the Chintamani Stone, the Philosopher's Stone and the Holy Grail are one and the same thing."

Drake didn't know what to say so he stayed quiet.

Another few moments passed before Luther reached out and plucked it from its stone perch.

Everyone stayed still, waiting . . . wondering . . .

Nothing happened. The ancients who had hidden this treasure, it seemed, did not want it lost or destroyed.

One more mystery layered upon it.

Slowly, carrying their wounded, the Strike Force team and Japanese marines made their way out of the vast cavern, crossing the narrow path and finding the tall shaft. It took some considerable time to get everyone up, especially Dino.

By the time they made it outside, darkness had fallen.

"I believe it was you that mentioned choppers," Karin said to Alicia. "Well, now that we know our location, what are you waiting for?"

Alicia sat down with her back to the mountain, heaved a great sigh of relief, and gestured for a radio.

"I hope it's comfy," she said. "I gotta say, I'm sick of this hiking lark."

CHAPTER FORTY EIGHT

Three days later the Strike Force team were seated in Tokyo International Airport, their normal gear arrayed in duffel bags all around them, lounging back as they stared out of a panoramic window at taxiing jets and speedy airport vehicles.

Drake had both feet on a duffel, his head back, and a baseball cap tilted over his eyes. It felt incredible to rest, to kick back. Since the Tsugarai attacked them in Hawaii this was their first real portion of downtime.

"Zuki has been arrested," Hayden reported after ending her most recent call. "They're incarcerating her inside a very special cell, where she will be interrogated for the rest of her life. That's some come down from a royal high."

"Glad to hear it," Mai said. "She risked countless lives to save her family's bloodline, their place in the world."

"Well, she should be able to point the finger at dozens of organizations and executives, spies and traitors," Hayden said. "I wouldn't want to be her for the next few months."

Kenzie winced as she shifted, her body bandaged and plastered in a dozen places. "I'll give her one thing, she was good with a sword."

"Was she?" Mai raised an eyebrow. "Or . . ."

Alicia caught on. "The Sprite's right. Maybe you're just full of shit, Kenz."

Kenzie closed her eyes, taking it on the chin. They had all seen the fight between Kenzie and Zuki. They had seen the skill it took both women to hold their own, to continue fighting even on their knees, wracked with exhaustion.

"When I get better," Kenzie breathed. "Let's organize a three-way."

Drake tilted his baseball cap up, showing interest. Alicia slapped him on the thigh. He sat up then, surveying the little group of friends. Molokai sprawled with Luther and Mai. Dahl reclined alongside Kenzie. Hayden and Kinimaka were together too. Karin and Dino had no choice but to stay in Tokyo so that Dino could receive urgent, essential medical attention. Everyone else lazed around in varying stages of repose, awaiting their economy flight back to the States. They could have waited for military transport, but this was faster.

Yesterday, the Japanese Special Forces had raided the Tsugarai compound, finding only a dozen people at home. These had been rounded up for questioning and potential rehabilitation. Mariko had been identified and brought to the safe house to reunite with her parents, a long-awaited, poignant and emotional reunion. Mai and Drake had watched the entire operation unfold from a command center. Both had wanted to be present but were not considered fit enough to join in. They were both still healing.

"What next?" Alicia said. "Back to Hawaii?"

Even Kinimaka shook his head. "Not for a while, eh?"

Luther nodded. "Good call."

Drake understood. It would be a traumatic return if they ever went back. They still had Dallas's funeral to attend. Having no known relatives, the man was due to be flown back to the United States on a separate flight.

"Back to Strike Force Headquarters," Hayden said. "Where we'll await the next mission."

"Any news on you know who?" Alicia asked.

"The Blood King? No. The Devil? No. They're off plotting somewhere."

"Let's hope they're plotting to kill each other." Dahl raised a half-drunk bottle of water in toast, making Yorgi chortle.

Drake smiled and listened. It had been a tough mission, one of the hardest he could recall. They had been up against some of the most dangerous men and women in the world. And yet, here they were. Battered but still alive. For Dino, the future was unsure, but the team was still together, still positive, and still fighting.

As for him, the alone-time with Mai had raised several unanswered questions. He'd never say anything to her, and would never mention it to Alicia, but the simple fact that he'd wondered if he should have waited longer for Mai proved his insecurity. Of course, Alicia held all his attention now and rightly so—she was the most dynamic, forthright person he knew and she tried admirably every day to stay a better person. He loved her. He couldn't see himself with anyone else.

He moved, groaning slightly. Around him the airport bustled, individuals and families bound for mostly happy destinations, their lives and their futures set firmly in their heads, no dark and deadly thoughts surrounding them, the worst of their fears allayed by the unknown, selfless men and women who fought hard for a civilian's right to live their lives democratically every day.

"You see this," he said, indicating the steady, comfortable bustle. "This is because of us. These people live without fear, without having to look over their shoulders, because of us and thousands of other operatives around the world. Feel good, guys. Feel better. We help maintain this freedom from strife."

And so, the Strike Force team sat unobtrusively amid the airport hubbub, just ten faces among a never-ending sea of faces, barely noticed by the men, women and children walking by them, seen only as a group of friends sat waiting for a flight.

And nobody passing knew they walked among heroes.

THE END

Thank you for purchasing and reading *Four Sacred Treasures* (Matt Drake 22). I really enjoyed writing this book and hope you liked it. Next up, should be both Drake 23 and Relic Hunters 3, releasing comparatively close to each other towards the end of the year!

If you enjoyed this book, please leave a review.

Other Books by David Leadbeater:

The Matt Drake Series
A constantly evolving, action-packed romp based in the
escapist action-adventure genre:

The Bones of Odin (Matt Drake #1)
The Blood King Conspiracy (Matt Drake #2)
The Gates of Hell (Matt Drake 3)
The Tomb of the Gods (Matt Drake #4)
Brothers in Arms (Matt Drake #5)
The Swords of Babylon (Matt Drake #6)
Blood Vengeance (Matt Drake #7)
Last Man Standing (Matt Drake #8)
The Plagues of Pandora (Matt Drake #9)
The Lost Kingdom (Matt Drake #10)
The Ghost Ships of Arizona (Matt Drake #11)
The Last Bazaar (Matt Drake #12)
The Edge of Armageddon (Matt Drake #13)
The Treasures of Saint Germain (Matt Drake #14)
Inca Kings (Matt Drake #15)
The Four Corners of the Earth (Matt Drake #16)
The Seven Seals of Egypt (Matt Drake #17)
Weapons of the Gods (Matt Drake #18)
The Blood King Legacy (Matt Drake #19)
Devil's Island (Matt Drake #20)
The Fabergé Heist (Matt Drake #21)

The Alicia Myles Series
Aztec Gold (Alicia Myles #1)
Crusader's Gold (Alicia Myles #2)
Caribbean Gold (Alicia Myles #3)
Chasing Gold (Alecia Myles #4)

The Torsten Dahl Thriller Series
Stand Your Ground (Dahl Thriller #1)

The Relic Hunters Series
The Relic Hunters (Relic Hunters #1)
The Atlantis Cipher (Relic Hunters #2)
The Amber Secret (Relic Hunters #3)

The Rogue Series
Rogue (Book One)

The Disavowed Series:
The Razor's Edge (Disavowed #1)
In Harm's Way (Disavowed #2)
Threat Level: Red (Disavowed #3)

The Chosen Few Series
Chosen (The Chosen Trilogy #1)
Guardians (The Chosen Tribology #2)

Short Stories
Walking with Ghosts (A short story)
A Whispering of Ghosts (A short story)

All genuine comments are very welcome at:

davidleadbeater2011@hotmail.co.uk

Twitter: @dleadbeater2011

Visit David's website for the latest news and information:
davidleadbeater.com